Eclipse

Eclipse

A novel by

JOHN BANVILLE

ALFRED A. KNOPF   NEW YORK

2001

THIS IS A BORZOI BOOK
PUBLISHED BY ALFRED A. KNOPF

Copyright © 2000 by John Banville

All rights reserved under International and Pan-American
Copyright Conventions. Published in the United States by Alfred A.
Knopf, a division of Random House, Inc., New York.
Distributed by Random House, Inc., New York.

www.aaknopf.com

Originally published in Great Britain by Picador, an imprint of
Macmillan Publishers Ltd., London, in 2000.

Knopf, Borzoi Books, and the colophon are registered trademarks
of Random House, Inc.

Library of Congress Cataloging-in-Publication Data
Banville, John.
Eclipse : a novel / by John Banville. — 1st American ed.
p.   cm.
ISBN 0-375-41129-1
1. Actors—Fiction.   I. Title.
PR6052.A57 E25 2001
823'.914—dc21   00-062014

Manufactured in the United States of America
First American Edition

In Memoriam
Laurence Roche

I

At first it was a form. Or not even that. A weight, an extra weight; a ballast. I felt it that first day out in the fields. It was as if someone had fallen silently into step beside me, or inside me, rather, someone who was else, another, and yet familiar. I was accustomed to putting on personae but this, this was different. I stopped, struck, stricken by that infernal cold I have come to know so well, that paradisal cold. Then a slight thickening in the air, a momentary occlusion of the light, as if something had plummeted past the sun, a winged boy, perhaps, or falling angel. It was April: bird and bush, silver glint of coming rain, vast sky, the glacial clouds in monumental progress. See me there, the haunted one, in my fiftieth year, assailed suddenly, in the midst of the world. I was frightened, as well I might be. I imagined such sorrows; such exaltations.

I turned and looked back at the house and saw what I took to be my wife standing at the window of what was once my mother's room. The figure was motionless, gazing steadily in my direction but not directly at me. What did she see? What was it she was seeing? I felt diminished briefly, an incidental in that gaze, dealt, as it were, a glancing blow or blown a derisive kiss. Day reflecting on the glass made the image in the window shimmer and slip; was it she or just a shadow, woman-shaped? I set off over the uneven ground, retracing my steps, with this other, my invader, walking steadily inside me, like a knight in his armour. The going was treacherous. The grass clutched at my ankles and there were holes in the clay, under the grass, made by the hoofs of immemorial cattle when this edge of town was still open country, that would trip me up, perhaps break one of the myriad delicate bones it is said are in the foot. A gush of panic rose in me like gorge. How, I asked myself, how could I stay here? How could I have thought I could stay here, all alone? Well, too late now; I would have to go through with it. This is what I told myself, I murmured it aloud: *I shall have to go through with it, now.* Then I smelled the faint salt reek of the sea and shivered.

I enquired of Lydia what it was she had been looking at.

"What?" she said. "When?"

I gestured. "From the window, upstairs; you were looking out at me."

She gave me that dulled gaze she had lately developed, drawing her chin down and in, as if she were slowly swallowing something. She said she had not been upstairs. We stood in silence for a moment then.

"Aren't you cold?" I said. "I'm cold."

"You're always cold."

"I dreamed last night I was a child and here again."

"Of course; you never left here, that's the truth."

A fine feel for the pentameter, my Lydia has.

The house itself it was that drew me back, sent out its secret summoners to bid me come . . . *home,* I was going to say. On the road one winter twilight an animal appeared in front of the car, cowering and yet fearless-seeming, sharp teeth bared and eyes flashing in the glare of the headlamps. I had stopped on instinct before I registered the thing, and sat aghast now smelling mephitic fumes of tyre smoke and listening to my own blood hammering in my ears. The animal made a movement as if to flee, then stopped still again. Such fierceness in that stare, the electric eyes an unreal neon-red. What was it? Weasel? Ferret? Too big for these, yet not big enough for fox or dog. Just some wild unknown thing. Then at a low run, seemingly legless, silently, it was gone. My heart was pounding yet. The woods leaned inward on either side of me, blackly brown against the last faint radiance of the dying day. For miles I had been travelling in a kind of sleep and now I thought I was lost. I wanted to turn the car around and drive back the way I had come, but something would not let me go. Something. I switched off the headlights and struggled out and stood befuddled on the road, the damp half-darkness folding me about, making me its own. From this low hill the twilit land ahead fell away into shadow and mist. An unseen bird above me in the branches gave a cautious croak, a wafer of ice in the wet verge snapped glassily under my heel. When I sighed, an ectoplasmic flaw of breath stood in front of me briefly like a second face. I walked forward to the brow of the hill and saw the town then, its few little glimmering lights, and, beyond, the fainter glimmer of the sea, and I knew where unknowingly I had come to. I went back and got behind the wheel again and drove to the top of the hill and there I switched off the engine and the lights and let the car roll down the long incline in bumping silence, dreamily, and stopped in the square, before the house standing in its darkness, deserted, its windows all unlit. All, all unlit.

Now as we stood together at one of these same windows I tried to tell my wife about the dream. I had asked her to come down with me, to look over the old place, I had said, hearing the wheedling note in my voice, to see, I said, if she thought it could be made habitable again, if a man might inhabit it, alone. She had laughed. "Is this how you think you'll cure whatever it is that's supposed to be wrong with you," she said, "by running back here like this, like a child who has had a fright and wants its mama?" She said my mother would be laughing in her grave. I doubted it. Even in life she was never a great one for mirth, my mother. *Laughing will end crying,* that was one of her sayings. As I described my dream Lydia listened impatiently, watching the tumultuous April sky above the fields, huddled into herself against the dank air of the house, the wings of her nose whitening as she suppressed a yawn. In the dream it was an Easter morning, and I a child standing on the doorstep looking out at the recently rained on, sun-dazzled square. Birds flitted, whistling, a breeze swooped and the already blossoming cherry trees shivered in vernal anticipation. I could feel the cool of outdoors on my face, could smell from within the house the smells of the feast-day morning: fusty bedclothes, tea smoke, the charry embers of last night's fire, and something redolent of my mother, some scent or soap, a woody tang. All this in the dream, and so clear. And there were Easter presents, as I stood in the doorway they were a palpable glow of happiness behind me in the depths of the house: eggs that my dream-mother had emptied and then filled somehow with chocolate—that was another smell, the fuggy smell of melted chocolate—and a yellow plastic chicken.

"A what?" Lydia said with a snort of almost-laughter. "A chicken?"

Yes, I said stoutly, a plastic chicken standing on spindly legs and when you pressed down on its back it laid a plastic egg. I could see it, in the dream, could see the moulded wattle and blunt beak and hear the click as the spring was released inside the bird and the yellow egg joggled down the channel and plopped on the table, wobbling. The wings flapped, too, with a clatter, when the egg was coming out. The egg was made of two hollow halves glued together slightly out of true, I could feel with my dreaming fingertips the twin sharp ridges at either side. Lydia was regarding me with an ironical smile, scornful, not unfond.

"And how does it get back in?" she asked.

"What?" Lately I had been finding it hard to understand the simplest things people said to me, as if what they were speaking in were a form of language I did not recognise; I would know the words but could not assemble them into sense.

"How do you get the egg back into the chicken," she said, "for it to come out again? In this dream."

"I don't know. It just . . . pushes back in, I suppose."

Now she did laugh, sharply.

"Well, what would Doctor Freud say."

I sighed angrily. "Not everything is . . ." Sigh. "Not everything . . ." I gave it up. Still she held me fixed in fond disparaging regard.

"Oh, yes," she said. "Sometimes a chicken is only a chicken—except when it's a hen."

Now we were both angry. She could not understand why I wanted to come back here. She said it was morbid. She said I should have sold the place years ago, when my mother died. I stood in sullen silence, offering no defence; I had none to offer. How could I hope to explain to her the summons I had received out on the road that winter eve, when I could not explain it to myself? She waited, still watching me, then shrugged and turned back to the window. She is a big-shouldered, handsome woman. Through her thick dark hair a broad plume of silver flows up from the left temple, a startling silver flame. She favours shawls and scarves, rings, bangles, bits of things that glitter and clink; I imagine her a desert princess, striding amidst a sea of sand. She is as tall as I am, even though it seems to me I can remember a time when I had a good hand's span on her. Perhaps I have shrunk, it would not surprise me. Misery is a certain shriveller.

"It's something to do with the future," I said. "In the dream." If only I could communicate to her the quick, keen sense of being here, the dense all-roundness of the dream, and everything in it so piercingly familiar, and I being I and also not. Frowning, I nodded, dull as a dog. "Yes," I said, "I'm standing in the doorway, in the sun, on an Easter Sunday morning, and somehow it is the future."

"What doorway?"

"What?" I shrugged, sloping a shoulder. "Here, of course," I said, nodding, baffled, certain. "Yes, the front door here."

She lifted her brows at me, leaning backwards a little her large-boned head, her hands stuck deep in the pockets of her big coat.

"It sounds more like the past, to me," she said, losing interest, what little there had been.

The past, or the future, yes, I might have said—but whose?

Cleave is the name, Alexander Cleave, called Alex. Yes, that Alex Cleave. You will remember my face, perhaps, the famous eyes whose flash of fire could penetrate to the very back row of the stalls. At fifty I am, if I say so myself, handsome still, albeit in a pinched and blurry sort of way. Think of your ideal Hamlet and you have me: the blond straight hair—somewhat grizzled now—the transparent, pale-blue eyes, the Nordic cheekbones, and that out-thrust jaw, sensitive, and yet hinting at depths of refined brutality. I mention the matter only because I am wondering to what extent my histrionic looks might explain the indulgence, the tenderness, the unfailing and largely undeserved loving kindness, shown me by the many—well, not *many*, not what even the most loyal Leporello would call *many*—women who have been drawn into the orbit of my life over the years. They have cared for me, they have sustained me; however precipitate my behaviour may be at times, they are always there to break my fall. What do they see in me? What is there in me to be seen? Maybe it is only the surface that they see. When I was young I was often dismissed as a matinée idol. This was unfair. True, I could, as I say, be the flaxen-haired hero when occasion called for it, but I played best the sombre, inward types, the ones who seem not part of the cast but to have been brought in from the street to lend plausibility to the plot. Menace was a specialty of mine, I was good at doing menace. If a poisoner was needed, or a brocaded revenger, I was your man. Even in the sunniest roles, the ass in a boater or the cocktail-quaffing wit, I projected a troubled, threatening something that silenced even the hatted old dears in the front row and made them clutch their bags of toffees tighter. I could play big, too; people when they glimpsed me at the stage door were always startled to find me, in what they call real life, not the shambling shaggy heavyweight they were expecting, but a trim lithe person with the wary walk of a dancer. I had mugged it up, you see, I had studied big men and understood that what defines them is not brawn or strength or force, but an essential vulnerability. Little chaps are all push and self-possession, whereas the large ones, if they look at all presentable, give off an appealing sense of confusion, of being at a loss, of anguish, even. They are less bruiser than bruised. No one moves more daintily than the giant, though it is always he who comes crashing down the beanstalk or has his eye put out with a burning brand. All this I learned, and learned to play. It was one of the secrets of my success, onstage and off, that I could put on size. And stillness, a quality of absolute stillness even in the midst of mayhem, that was another of my tricks. This is what the critics were groping for when they talked of my uncanny Iago or my coiled Richard Crookback. The biding beast is always more seductive than the one that springs.

I do not fail to note the use of the past tense throughout the above.

Ah, the stage, the stage; I shall miss it, I know. Those old saws about the camaraderie of theatre folk are, I have to report, all true. Children of the night, we keep each other company against the encroaching dark, playing at being grown-ups. I do not find my fellow man particularly lovable, only I must be part of a cast. We actors like to complain of the lean times, the stints in provincial rep., the ramshackle fit-ups and rained-out seaside tours, but it was the very seediness of that gimcrack world that I secretly loved. When I look back over my career, which seems to be ended now, what I recall most fondly is the cramped cosiness of some dingy hall in the middle of nowhere shut fast against the loamy darkness of an autumn night and smelling of fag smoke and wet overcoats; in our box of light we players strut and declaim, laughing and weeping, while out in the furry gloom before us that vague, many-eyed mass hangs on our every bellowed word, gasps at our every overblown gesture. In this neck of the woods, when we were children, we used to say of show-offs in the school playground that they were *only shaping;* it is something I never got out of the habit of; I made a living from shaping; indeed, I made a life. It is not reality, I know, but for me it was the next best thing—at times, the *only* thing, more real than the real. When I fled that peopled world I had no one except myself to keep me from coming to grief. And it was to grief that I came.

Acting was inevitable. From earliest days life for me was a perpetual state of being watched. Even when alone I carried myself with covert circumspection, keeping up a front, putting on a performance. This is the actor's hubris, to imagine the world possessed of a single, avid eye fixed solely and always on him. And he, of course, acting, thinks himself the only real one, the most substantial shadow in a world of shades. I have a particular memory—though memory is not the word, what I am thinking of is too vivid to be a real memory—of standing in the lane that goes down beside the house one late spring morning when I was a boy. The day is damp and fresh as a peeled stick. A broad, unreally clear light lies over everything, even in the highest trees I can pick out individual leaves. A cobweb laden with dew sparkles in a bush. Down the lane comes hobbling an old woman, bent almost double, her gait a repeated pained slow swing around the pivot of a damaged hip. I watch her approach. She is harmless, poor Peg, I have seen her often about the town. At each lurching step she shoots up sideways at me a sharp, speculative glance. She wears a shawl and an old straw hat and a pair of rubber boots cut off jaggedly at the ankles. She carries a basket on her arm. When she draws level with me she pauses and looks up at me eagerly with a lopsided leer, her tongue showing, and mumbles something that I cannot make out. She shows the basket, with mushrooms she has picked in the fields, which perhaps she is offering to sell to me. Her eyes are a faded, almost transparent blue, like my own, now. She waits for me to speak, panting a little, and when I say nothing, offer nothing, she sighs and shakes her old head and hobbles painfully on again, keeping to the grassy verge. What was it in the moment that so affected me? Was it the lambent air, that wide light, the sense of spring's exhilarations all around me? Was it the old beggar-woman, the impenetrable thereness of her? Something surged in me, an objectless exultancy. Myriad voices struggled within me for expression. I seemed to myself a multitude. I would utter them, that would be my task, to be them, the voiceless ones! Thus was the actor born. Four decades later he died in the middle of the last act and staggered off the stage in sweaty ignominy just when the action was coming to its climax.

The house. It is tall and narrow, and stands on a corner of the little square across from the high white wall of the convent of the Sisters of Mercy. In fact, our square is not a square at all, but converges and funnels off at the far end into a road that climbs a hill leading out into the country. I date a fascination with spec-ulative thought, uncommon in my profession—the thinking man's thespian, that is another thing the critics used to call me, with a detectable smirk—from the moment in childhood when it occurred to me to wonder how a triangular space could have come to be called a square. Next door had a madwoman in the attic. Really, this is true. Often of a morning when I was setting off for school she would pop her golliwog's head out at the mansard window and call down to me, shrieking gibberish. Her hair was very black and her face was very white. She was twenty, or thirty, some age like that, and played with dolls. What ailed her no one seemed to know for sure, or would not say; there was talk of incest. Her father was a coarse, puce-faced person with a big round head set necklessly on his shoulders like a stone ball. I see him in gaiters but surely that is just fancy. Mind you, pelt shoon and hempen trews would not be out of place, for those days are so far off from me now they have become a kind of antiquity.

See how I parry and duck, like an outclassed boxer? I begin to speak of the ancestral home and within a sentence or two I have moved next door. That is me all over.

The incident with the animal on the road in the wintry gloaming was definitive, though what it was that was being defined I could not tell. I saw where I was, and I thought of the house, and knew that I must live there again, if only for a little while. So came the April day when I drove with Lydia down those familiar roads and found the keys, left under a stone beside the doorstep by an unknown hand. Such seeming absence of human agency was proper also; it was as if . . .

"As if what?" my wife said.

I turned from her with a shrug.

"I don't know."

Once I had made my arrangements—a contract brusquely broken, a summer tour abandoned—it took no time at all, one Sunday afternoon, to move my things down here, the few necessities of what I insist on thinking will be no more than a brief respite from life, an interval between acts. I loaded my bags and books into the boot and the back seat of the car, not speaking, while Lydia looked on with folded arms, smiling angrily. I shuffled from house to car and back again without pausing, afraid that if I stopped once I would not start up again, would dissolve into a puddle of irresolution on the pavement. It was summer by now, one of those vague hazy days of early June that seem made half of weather and half of memory. A soft breeze stirred the lilac bush by the front door. Across the road a pair of poplars were excitedly discussing something dreadful, their foliage tinkling. Lydia had accused me of being a sentimentalist. "All this is just some kind of ridiculous nostalgia," she said, and laughed unsteadily. She stopped me in the hallway, planted herself and the barrier of her folded arms in front of me and would not let me pass. I stood breathing, burdened with baggage, staring morosely at the floor by her feet, saying nothing. I pictured myself hauling off and hitting her. This is the kind of thing that comes into my head nowadays. It is strange, for I was never a brawler: the word was always weapon enough. It is true that when we were younger and our relations more tempestuous Lydia and I would sometimes resort to fisticuffs to settle a difference, but that was less from anger than other things—how erotic is the sight of a woman winding up her fist to deliver a punch!—for all that one or other of us might come out of the fray with a ringing ear or a chipped tooth. These new thoughts of violence are alarming. Is it not right that I should have put myself out of harm's way? The harm *of* others, that is; the harm *to* others.

"Be honest," Lydia said. "Are you leaving us?"

Us.

"Listen, my dear—"

"Don't call me *my dear*," she cried. "Don't you dare speak to me like that." I was, I realised, bored. Boredom is the brother of misery, that is something I have been discovering. I gazed away from her, into the soft, unresting air. There were moments even then when the very light seemed thronged with figures. She waited; still I would not speak. "Oh, go, then," she said, and turned away in disgust.

But when I was in the car and about to drive off she came out of the house with her coat and her keys and got in wordlessly beside me. Soon we were bowling along through the countryside's slovenly and uncaring loveliness. We passed by a circus, going in our direction, one of the old-fashioned kind, rarely to be seen any more, with garishly painted horse-drawn caravans, driven by gypsy types with neckerchiefs and earrings. A circus, now, this was surely a good sign, I thought, and began to feel quite gay. The trees were puffs of green, the sky was blue. I recalled a page from my daughter's homework book I had kept since she was a child, hidden at the back of a drawer in my desk, along with a clutch of yellowed first-night programmes and one or two clandestine love letters. *The Bud is in flower,* she had written, in the big, wide-eyed hand of a five-year-old. *Mud is brown. I feel as fit as a Flea. things can go wrong.* A spasm of sweetish sadness made my mind droop; I thought perhaps Lydia was right, perhaps I am a sentimentalist. I brooded on words. Sentimentality: unearned emotion. Nostalgia: longing for what never was. I remarked aloud the smoothness of the road. "When I was young this journey took three hours, nearly." Lydia threw up her eyes and sighed. Yes, the past, again. I was thinking of my Easter-morning dream. I still felt invaded, as I had that day out in the fields: invaded, occupied, big with whatever it was that has entered me. It is still here; I feel I am pregnant; it is a very peculiar sensation. Before, what I contained was the blastomere of myself, the coiled hot core of all I was and might be. Now, that essential self has been pushed to the side with savage insouciance, and I am as a house walked up and down in by an irresistibly proprietorial stranger. I am all inwardness, gazing out in ever intensifying perplexity upon a world in which nothing is exactly plausible, nothing is exactly what it is. And the thing itself, my little stranger, what of it? To have no past, no foreseeable future, only the steady pulse of a changeless present—how would that feel? There's being for you. I imagine it in there, filling me to the skin, anticipating and matching my every movement, diligently mimicking the tiniest details of what I am and do. Why am I not writhing in disgust, to feel thus horribly inhabited? Why not revulsion, instead of this sweet, melancholy sense of longing and lost promise?

The house too had been invaded, someone had got in and had been living here, some tramp or fugitive. There were crusts of bread on the kitchen table and used tea bags in the sink, obscene, squashed brown things. A fire had been lit in the parlour, in the grate were the charred remains of books the intruder had pulled from the shelves and used for fuel. Some titles and parts of titles were still legible. I leaned down and tried to make them out, intent as a scryer: *The Revenant, My Mother's House*—apt, that one—something called *Heart's Needle*, and, most badly burned, *The Necessary* . . . with a final word obscured by a scorch mark that I thought might have been *Angel*. Not your run-of-the-mill book-burner, evidently. I sat back on my heels and sighed, then rose and picked my way from room to room, frowning at the grime, the faded furnishings, the sun-bleached curtains; how could I stay here? Lydia called to me. I went and found her standing in the lime-smelling lavatory under the stairs, a wrist on her hip, in the pose of Donatello's *David*, pointing disgustedly into the bowl, where a gigantic turd was wedged. "Aren't people lovely," she said.

We cleaned up as best we could, gathered the rubbish, opened windows, flung bucketfuls of water down the lavatory pan. I had not dared to venture upstairs yet.

"I heard from Cass," Lydia said without looking at me, wringing the neck of a bulging plastic bag.

I felt the usual constriction in my chest. Cass is my daughter. She has been living abroad.

"Oh, yes?" I said, cautiously.

"She says she will be coming home."

"The harpies gather, eh?" I had intended it lightly, but Lydia's brow grew red. *"Harpazein,"* I said hastily, "to seize. Greek, that is." Playing the fussy old professor, remote but kindly; when in difficulty, act.

"Of course, she'll take your side," she said.

I followed her into the parlour. Large dark masses of furniture stood sullenly at attention in the dimness of the gaunt room like almost living things. Lydia walked to the window, lighting a cigarette. On her delicate pale long feet she wore a pair of crimson velvet slippers suggestive of Araby. I marvel to think there was a time when I would have fallen on my face before her in the sand and covered those Arabian feet with kisses, caresses, adoring helpless tears.

"I didn't know that there were sides," I said, too innocently.

She gave a full cold laugh.

"Oh, no," she said, "you know nothing." She turned, her head swathed in a swirl of ash-blue cigarette smoke, the garden's menacing greenery crowding in the window behind her, and, between the green, a patch of the sky's delicate summer azure. In this light the shock of silver in her hair was stark, undulate, ashine. Once in one of our fights she called me a black-hearted bastard and I experienced a warm little thrill, as at a pretty piece of flattery—that is the kind of black-hearted bastard that I am. Now she gazed at me for a moment in silence, slowly shaking her head. "No," she said again, with a bitter, weary sigh, "you know nothing."

The moment came, which I had been both impatient for and dreading, when there was nothing left for her to do but leave. We loitered on the pavement outside the front door in the milky light of late afternoon, together yet already apart. The day was without human sound, as if everyone else in the world had gone away *(how can I stay here?)*. Then a motor car came fizzing across the square and passed us by, the driver glaring at us briefly, in angry surprise, so it seemed. The silence returned. I lifted a hand and touched the air by Lydia's shoulder.

"Yes, all right," she said, "I'll go."

Her eyes turned glossy and she ducked into the car and slammed the door. The tyres skidded as she drove away. The last I saw of her she was leaning forward over the wheel with a knuckle stuck into an eye. I turned back to the house. Cass, I was thinking. Cass, now.

Things to do, things to do. Store the kitchen supplies, set out my books, my framed photographs, my lucky rabbit's paw. Too soon it was all done. There was no avoiding upstairs any longer. Grimly I mounted the steps as if I were climbing into the past itself, the years pressing down on me, like a heavier atmosphere. Here is the room looking out on the square that used to be mine. Alex's room. Dust, and a mildew smell, and droppings on an inside sill where birds had got in through a broken windowpane. Strange, how places, once so intimate, can go neutral under the dust-fall of time. First there is the soft detonation of recognition, and for a moment the object throbs in the sudden awareness of being unique—that chair, that awful picture—then all composes itself into the drear familiar, the parts of a world. Everything in the room seemed turned away from me in sullen resistance, averting itself from my unwelcome return. I lingered a moment, feeling nothing except a heavy hollowness, as if I had been holding my breath—as perhaps I had—then I turned and went down a flight, to the first floor, and entered the big back bedroom there. It was light still. I stood at the tall window, where that other day I had seen my not-wife not-standing, and looked out at what she had not-seen: the garden straggling off into nondescript fields, then a huddle of trees, and beyond that, where the world tilted, an upland meadow with motionless miniature cattle, and in the farthest distance a fringe of mountains, matt blue and flat against the sky where the sun was causing a livid commotion behind a heaping of clouds. Having used up the outside, I turned to the in: high ceiling, the sagging bed with brass knobs, a night table with wormholes, a solitary, resentful-looking bentwood chair. The floral-patterned linoleum—three shades of dried blood—had a worn patch alongside the bed, where my mother used to pace, unsubduably, night after long night, trying to die. I felt nothing. Was I here at all? I seemed to be fading in face of these signs, the hollow in the mattress, the wear in the lino; a watcher outside the window would hardly see me now, a shadow only.

There were traces here too of an intruder; someone had been sleeping in my mother's bed. Outrage flared briefly, then faded; why should not some Goldilocks lay down her weary head where my poor mother would never again lay hers?

I loved to prowl the house like this when I was young. Afternoons were my favourite time, there was a special quality to afternoons indoors, a wistfulness, a sense of dreamy distance, of boundless air all around, that was at once tranquil and unsettling. There were hidden portents everywhere. Something would catch my attention, anything, a cobweb, a damp patch on a wall, a scrap of old newspaper lining a drawer, a discarded paperback, and I would stop and stand gazing at it for a long time, motionless, lost, unthinking. My mother kept lodgers, clerks and secretaries, schoolteachers, travelling salesmen. They fascinated me, their furtive and somehow anguished, rented lives. Inhabiting a place that could not be home, they were like actors compelled to play themselves. When one of them moved out I would slip into the vacated room and breathe its hushed, attentive air, turning things over, poking into corners, searching through drawers and mysteriously airless cupboards, diligent as a sleuth hunting for clues. And what incriminating leavings I came up with—a set of horribly grinning false teeth, a pair of underpants caked and brittle with blood, a baffling contraption like the bellows of a bagpipes made of red rubber and bristling with tubes and nozzles, and, best of all, pushed to the back of a wardrobe's highest shelf, a sealed jar of yellowish liquid in which a preserved frog was suspended, its slash of mouth blackly open, its translucent toes splayed and touching delicately the clouded glass walls of its tomb . . .

Anaglypta! That was the name of that old-fashioned wallpaper stuff, stiff with layers of yellowed white paint, with which every other wall in the house is covered to the height of the dado. I wonder if it is manufactured any more. Anaglypta. All afternoon I had been searching for the word and now I had found it. Why glyp not glyph? This, I told myself, this is the way I shall be condemned to pass my days, turning over words, stray lines, fragments of memory, to see what might be lurking underneath them, as if they were so many flat stones, while I steadily faded.

Eight o'clock. The curtain would be going up and I not there. Another absence. I would be missed. When an actor walks out of a performance no understudy can entirely fill his place. He leaves the shadow of something behind him, an aspect of the character that only he could have conjured, his singular creation, independent of mere lines. The rest of the cast feel it, the audience feels it too. The stand-in is always a stand-in: for him there is always another, prior presence, standing in him. *Who if not I, then, is Amphitryon?*

I heard a noise from downstairs and a shock of fright passed through me, making my shoulder blades quiver and my head feel momentarily hot. I have always been a timid soul, for all the blackness of my heart. I went out creakingly on to the landing and stood amid the standing shadows and listened, clutching the banister rail, registering the clammy texture of old varnish and the oddly unresistant hardness of the wood. The noise came faintly again up through the stairwell, an intermittent, brittle scratching. I recalled the strange animal on the road that night. Then a surge of indignation and impatience made me frown and shake my head. "Oh, this is all completely...!" I began to say, and stopped; the silence took my words and tittered over them. Down there, someone uttered a low, guttural oath, and I went still again. I waited— *scratch scratch*—then stepped backwards cautiously into the bedroom doorway, squared my shoulders, took a breath, and marched out on to the landing once more, but differently this time—for whose benefit did I think I was putting on this dumb show?— slamming the door behind me, all bluff business now, a man at home in his world. "Hello?" I called out grandly, actorily, though my voice had a crack in it. "Hello, who is there?" This brought a startled silence, with a suggestion of laughter. Then the voice again, calling upwards:

"Ah, it's only me."

Quirke.

He was in the parlour, on his hunkers in front of the grate, with a blackened bit of stick in his hand. He had been poking among the remains of the charred books. He turned up his head, an amiable eyebrow cocked, and watched me as I entered.

"Some tinker must have got in here," he said without rancour. "Or was it you was burning the books?" This amused him. He shook his head and made a clicking noise in his cheek. "You can't leave a thing untended."

Stalled at the foot of the stairs I nodded, for want of better. Quirke's sardonical composure is both annoying and unchallengeable. He is the superannuated office boy a solicitor in the town appointed years ago at my request to look after the house. That is, I requested a caretaker: I did not bargain on it being Quirke. He tossed the stick into the fireplace and rose to his feet with surprising agility, brushing his hands. I had already noticed those

unlikely hands: pale, hairless, plump in the palm, with long, ta-
pering fingers, the hands of a Pre-Raphaelite maiden. The rest
of him is shaped like a sea elephant. He is large, soft-skinned,
sandy-haired, in his middle forties, with the ageless aspect of a
wastrel son.

"There was someone living here, some intruder," I said, with a
heavy emphasis of reproof, wasted on him, as I could see by his
unruffled look. "He left more than burned books." I mentioned,
with a qualm of disgust, the thing Lydia had found in the lavatory.
Quirke was only the more amused.

"A squatter is right," he said, and grinned.

He was quite at his ease, standing on the hearth rug—another
furrow there, kin to the one beside the bed upstairs—and looking
about him with an expression of arch scepticism, as if the things in
the room had been arranged to deceive him and he was not
deceived. His protuberant pale eyes reminded me of a virulent
kind of boiled sweet much fancied when I was a boy. There was a
raw patch on his chin where the morning razor had scraped too
closely. From the pocket of his balding corduroy jacket he brought
out a bottle in a brown-paper bag. "Warm the house," he said,
with a lopsided leer, showing the whiskey.

We sat at the oilcloth-covered table in the kitchen and drank while
the day died. Quirke was not to be got rid of. He squirmed his big
backside down on a kitchen chair and lit up a cigarette and planted
his elbows on the table, regarding me the while with an air of high
expectancy, his boiled eyes roaming speculatively over my face
and frame like those of a rock climber searching for a handhold on
a not very serious but tricky piece of cliff. He told of the history of
the house before my family's time—he had gone into it, he said, it
was a hobby of his, he had the documents, the searches and affi-
davits and deeds, all done out in sepia copperplate, beribboned,

stamped, impressed with seals. I meanwhile was recalling the first time I had found myself weeping in the cinema, soundlessly, unstoppably. It was the ache in my constricted throat that I registered first, then the salt tears that were seeping in at the corners of my mouth. It was deep winter, the middle of a sleety afternoon. I had ducked out of a matinée performance—young Sniveling my understudy's impossible dream come true—and sloped off on my own to the pictures, feeling foolish and elated. Then when the film started there were these inexplicable tears, hiccups, stifled wails, as I sat shuddering with fists clenched in my lap, the hot drops plopping off my chin and wetting my shirt-front. I was baffled, and mortified, too, of course, afraid the afternoon's other shadowy voyeurs around me would notice my shameful collapse, yet there was something glorious too in such abandon, such childish transgression. When the picture ended and I skulked out red-eyed into the cold and the early dark I felt emptied, invigorated, rinsed. It became a shameful habit then, twice, three times a week I would do it, in different picture-houses, the dingier the better, with still no notion of what I was weeping for, what loss I might be mourning. Somewhere inside me there must be a secret well of grief from which these springs were pouring. Sprawled there in the phantasmally peopled darkness I would sob myself dry, while some extravaganza of violence and impossible passions played itself out on the vast screen tilted above me. Then came the night when I dried onstage—cold sweat, mute helpless fish-mouths, the works—and I knew I must get away.

"So what are you up to?" Quirke said. "Down here, I mean."

Last of evening in the window, dishwater light and the overgrown grass in the garden all grey. I wanted to say, I have lived amid surfaces too long, skated too well upon them; I require the shock of the icy water now, the icy deeps. Yet wasn't ice my trouble, that it had penetrated me, to the very marrow? *A man thronged up with cold* . . . Fire, rather; fire was what was needed . . .

With a start I came back to myself, from myself. Quirke was nodding: someone must have said something of moment—Lord, I wondered, was it me? Often lately I would be startled to hear people replying to things I had thought I had only spoken in my head. I wanted to jump up now and tell Quirke to leave, to leave and leave me alone, to my own devices, my own voices.

"That's the trouble, all right," he was saying, nodding slowly, solemnly, like that black saint on the collection box who nodded when as a little boy you put a penny in. Mnemosyne, mother of sorrows!

"What is?" I said.

"What?"

"The trouble—what is the trouble?"

"What?"

A kind of quacking. We gaped at each other helplessly.

"I'm sorry," I said then, lifting a hand wearily to shade my eyes. "I have forgotten what we were talking about."

But Quirke's attention too had wandered, and he sat motionlessly at gaze with one shoulder hunched and his virginal hands with fingers palely linked resting on the table before him. I stood up at an angle and everything in the world slid abruptly to one side and I realised I was drunk. I said that I must go to bed. Quirke looked up at me in hurt amazement. He too must be drunk, but evidently he was not ready to go home. He made no stir, and let his wounded gaze drift to the window.

"Not dark yet," he said, "look. And still when it does get dark the nights seem like they'll never end. This is a terrible time of the year, if you're not a sleeper."

I would speak no more, but stood with steepled fingers pressed on the table, softly snorting, head ahang. Quirke heaved a sigh that turned into an involuntary sorrowful little chirrup at the end and hauled himself to his feet at last and yanked open the door to the hall, making the tongued lever of the latch joggle in its worn hole, *quirquirquirke*. He staggered going out into the passageway, lurched hugely sideways and struck his shoulder on the door jamb, swore, chuckled, liquidly coughed. "Good luck, then," he said, bowing under the low lintel and giving a stiff-armed salute behind him. Wordlessly we walked in single file through the dark house. When I opened the front door the smells of the summer night came into the hall, of tar and lupins, and something mushroomy, of sun-warmed pavements gone cold now, of salt sea-mist, and a myriad of other, nameless things. Quirke's bicycle, a high, black, old-fashioned affair, was tethered to a lamppost. He tarried a moment, looking blearily about him. The deserted square at dusk, with its low, humped roofs and windows sullenly aglow, has a slightly sinister, alien air, a touch almost of Transylvania. "Good luck," Quirke said again, loudly, and uttered a phrase of mournful laughter, as at some painful joke. The saddle of his bicycle was furred with dew. Indifferent to damp discomfort he mounted up and pedalled away unsteadily, as I turned back and shut the door, maundering chaotically in my disordered heart.

As I drifted toward sleep, my whiskeyed breath staling the air, I seemed to feel another rise up out of me into the room and hang there on the dark like smoke, like thought, like memory. A night breeze stirred the hem of the dusty lace curtain at the window. There was a glimmer even yet in the far sky. I fell into a dream. There was a room, cool, marble tiled, as in a Roman villa, with a view through unglazed windows of a stepped ochre hill and a line of sentinel trees. Scant furnishings: a couch with ornately scrolled ends and a low table nearby bearing unguents in porphyry pots and coloured glass phials, and in a far corner a tall urn in which a single lily leaned. On the couch, of which I was permitted only a three-quarters view, a woman was lying back, young, ample, impossibly pale skinned, her naked arms lifted and hiding her face in abandonment and shame. Beside her sat a turbaned negress, naked also, a mountainous figure with polished melony thighs and big hard gleaming breasts and broad pink palms. The middle finger and thumb of her right hand were plunged to the knuckle and ball in the two holes of the woman's wantonly offered lap. I noted the angry-pink frilling of the vagina, dainty as the volutes of a cat's ear, and the taut oiled tea-coloured cincture of the anus. The slave turned her head and looked at me over her shoulder with a broad, jaunty grin and for my benefit joggled her mistress's gaping flesh, and the woman shuddered and made a mewling sound. In succubus sleep my face formed a rictus, and as the little seizure took me I arched my back and pressed the back of my head into the pillow and then went still and lay like that for a long moment, like a dead dictator lying in state sunk to his ears in the plush.

I opened my eyes and did not know where I was. The window was in the wrong place, the wardrobe too. Then I remembered, and the old, mysterious foreboding seized on me again. There was neither darkness nor light, but a dim grainy glow that seemed to have no source, unless the source were the room itself, the very walls. I felt the patter and skip of my labouring heart. The sticky wetness on my thigh was growing cold already. I thought I should get up and go to the lavatory and wipe myself, I even saw myself rise and fumble for the light switch—was I still dreaming, half asleep?—yet I lay on, swaddled in flocculent warmth. Languorously my fancy found its way back to the woman in the dream and traced again the outline of her white limbs and touched her secret places, but without agitation now, curious only, mildly wondering at the unreally white flesh, the fantastical lewdness. Musing thus in drowsy torpor I turned my head on the pillow and it was then I saw the figure in the room, standing motionless a little way from the side of the bed. I took it for a woman, or womanish old man, or even a child, of indeterminate gender. Shrouded and still it stood facing in my direction, like one of those guardians of the sickroom long ago, the dim attendants of childhood fevers. The head was covered and I could make out no features. The hands were clasped at the breastbone in what seemed an attitude of beseeching, or of anguished prayer, or some other extreme of passionate striving. I was frightened, of course—cold sweat stood on my forehead, hairs prickled at the nape of my neck—but what I registered most strongly was a sense of being the object of intense concentration, a kind of needful scrutiny. I tried to speak but could not, not because I was struck dumb with fear but because the mechanism of my voice could not be made to work in the other-world between dream and waking in which I was suspended. Still the figure did not stir, nor give any sign, only stood in that pose of ambiguous extremity, waiting, it might be, for some desired response from me. I thought: *The Necessary* . . . and as I did, in that momentary blink of the mind, the figure faded. I was not aware of its going. There seemed no transition between its state of being seen and its invisibility, as if it had not departed but only changed its form, or refined itself into a frequency beyond the reach of my coarse senses. At once relieved and regretful at its going I closed my eyes, and when I unwillingly opened them again, no more than a moment later, so it seemed, a streaming blade of sunlight had already made a deep slash through the parting in the curtains.

This is how I wake now, sidling warily out of sleep as though I had spent the night in hiding. That falling shaft of gold at the window was blinding. In the corners of the room brownish shadows thronged. I have a deep dislike of mornings, their muffled, musty texture, like that of a bed too long slept in. Latterly there are dawns when I wake up wishing it were night again and the day done with. I have come to think of my life as altogether like a morning's interminable passing; whatever the hour, it is always as if I have just risen and am trying to clear my head and get a grip on things. I sighed, and kicked back the covers and squirmed my limbs on the lumpy mattress. The day would be hot. Last night, in my drunkenness, I had thought to sleep in my mother's bed—yes, there is the Herr Doktor again, with his beard and his cigar—but must have changed my mind, for here I was in my old room. How often I had lain here as a boy on summer mornings just like this one, afloat in a gauze of expectation, convinced of great events being just about to happen, of a bud inside me waiting to burst into the marvellously intricate blossom of what would be my life when at last it really began. Such plans I had! Or no, not plans, they were too vague and large and distant to be called plans. Hopes, then? Not that, either. Dreams, I suppose. Fantasies. Delusions.

With a grunt and a heave I got myself up from the bed and stood scratching. I suspect I am coming more and more to look like my father, especially as he was at the end, with that same peering, apprehensive stance. It is a parent's posthumous revenge, the legacy of increasing resemblance. I padded to the window and opened the tattered curtains, wincing in the light. It was early still. The square was deserted. Not a soul, not even a bird. A tall sharp wedge of sunlight leaned against the white wall of the convent, motionless and menacing. One Maytime here when I was a boy I built a shrine to the Virgin Mary. What inspired me to this uncommon enterprise? Some visionary moment must have been granted me, some glimpse of matutinal blue, or radiance in a limitless sky at noon, or lily-scented exaltation, at Evening Devotions, in the midst of the Rosary, as the Glorious Mysteries were given out. I was a solemn child, prone to bouts of religious fervour, and that May, which is the month of Mary—and also, curiously, of both Lucifer and the wolf; who decides these matters, I wonder?—I had determined I would make her a shrine, or grotto, as such things were called, at that time, in this part of the world, and probably are still so called. I chose a spot in the lane beside the house where a little brown stream squirmed along under a hawthorn hedge. I was not sure if stones were free, and gathered them with circumspection from the fields and vacant lots roundabout, prizing in particular the flinty white ones. From hedgerows I plucked primroses, and when I saw how quickly the blossoms died I dug the plants out roots and all and sowed them on my bit of bank, among the stones, first filling the holes with water and watching with satisfaction the muddy bubbles rise and fatly plop as the tufted sods sank and settled and I trod them home with the heel of my wellington boot. The statue of the Virgin must have come from the house, or perhaps I persuaded my mother to buy one specially: I fancy I can recall her grumbling a the expense. She viewed this venture of mine with grudging regard, distrustful of such a show of piety, for despite her own veneration of the Virgin she liked a boy to be a boy, she said, and not a namby-pamby. When the work was finished I sat contentedly for a long time by myself looking at the shrine and feeling proud, and virtuous in a cloying sort of way. I heard old Nockter the apple-seller with his horse and cart calling his wares in a far street, and mad Maude up in her attic crooning to her dollies. Later still, as the sun declined and shadows lengthened, my father came out of the house in shirt-sleeves and braces and looked at the grotto and at me and at the grotto again, and sucked his teeth, and smiled a little and said nothing, remote and sceptical, as always. When it rained the Virgin's face seemed tear-stained. One day a gang of older boys passing by on their bikes saw the shrine and dismounted and grabbed the statue and tossed it from one to another, laughing, until one of them fumbled it and it fell on the road and shattered. I retrieved a fragment of blue mantle and kept it, awed by the exposed whiteness of the plaster; such purity was almost indecent, and whenever afterwards I heard the priests recall that the Blessed Virgin had been born without stain of sin I experienced a troubled, dark excitement.

She must be of Minoan origin, the Virgin; even her colours, cobalt and lime-white, suggest the Isles of Greece. Mary as Pasiphaë, serpent in hand and her conical bare breasts on show, there is a thought to frighten the priests.

I have remained a devotee of the goddess, and she in turn has been attentive to me, in the various forms in which she has been manifest in my life. First of course there was my mother. She tried to but could not understand me, her changeling. She was a querulous, distracted person, given to worries and vague agitations, always labouring under unspecified grievances, always waiting, it seemed, tight-lipped and patiently sorrowing, for a general apology from the world. She was afraid of everything, of being late and of being too early, of draughts and of stuffiness, of germs and crowds and accidents and neighbours, of being knocked down in the street by a stranger and robbed. When my father died she took to widowhood as if it were the natural state for which her life with him had been merely a long and heartsore preparation. They had not been happy; happiness had not been part of life's guarded

promise to them. They did not quarrel, I think they were not intimate enough for that. My mother was voluble, at times to the point
of hysteria, while my father kept silence, and so they struck a violent equilibrium. After he died, or finished fading—his physical
demise was only the official end of a slow dissolution, like the full
stop the doctor stabbed into his death certificate that day, leaving a
shiny blot—she in her turn began gradually to fall silent. Her
voice itself turned thin and papery, with a whining cadence, like
that of one left standing in the dust of the road, watching the car-
riage wheels roll away, with a sentence half finished and no one
left to finish it for. All her dealings with me then became a kind of
ceaseless pleading, by turns piteous and angry. What she wanted
was for me to explain myself to her, to account for what I was, and
why I differed so from her. It was as if she believed she could
through me somehow solve the riddle of her own life and of the
things that had happened to her, and of the so many more things
that had not. But I could not help her, I was not the one to take her
and lead her back along that shadowed pathway past the shut gates
guarding all the unspent riches of what she might have been. The
end for her was bafflement and furious refusal, as she clung to the
posts of the last gate, the one that had finally opened for her, bracing her feet against the threshold, until the gateman came and
prised her fingers loose and brought her onward finally, into the
dark place. No, I could not help her. I did not even weep at the
graveside; I think I was thinking of something else. There is in
me, deep down, as there must be in everyone—at least, I hope
there is, for I would not wish to be alone in this—a part that does
not care for anything other than itself. I could lose everything
and everyone and that pilot light would still be burning at my
centre, that steady flame that nothing will quench, until the final
quenching.

I clearly recall the day I first became truly aware of myself, I
mean of myself as something that everything else was not. As a

boy I liked best those dead intervals of the year when one season had ended and the next had not yet begun, and all was grey and hushed and still, and out of the stillness and the hush something would seem to approach me, some small, soft, tentative thing, and offer itself to my attention. This day of which I speak I was walking along the main street of the town. It was November, or March, not cold, but neutral. From a lowering sky fine rain was falling, so fine as to be hardly felt. It was morning, and the housewives were out, with their shopping bags and headscarves. A questing dog trotted busily past me looking neither to right nor left, following a straight line drawn invisibly on the pavement. There was a smell of smoke and butcher's meat, and a brackish smell of the sea, and, as always in the town in those days, the faint sweet stench of pigswill. The open doorway of a hardware shop breathed brownly at me as I went past. Taking in all this, I experienced something to which the only name I could give was happiness, although it was not happiness, it was more and less than happiness. What had occurred? What in that commonplace scene before me, the ordinary sights and sounds and smells of the town, had made this unexpected thing, whatever it was, burgeon suddenly inside me like the possibility of an answer to all the nameless yearnings of my life? Everything was the same now as it had been before, the housewives, that busy dog, the same, and yet in some way transfigured. Along with the happiness went a feeling of anxiety. It was as if I were carrying some frail vessel that it was my task to protect, like the boy in the story told to us in religious class who carried the Host through the licentious streets of ancient Rome hidden inside his tunic; in my case, however, it seemed I was myself the precious vessel. Yes, that was it, it was *I* that was happening here. I did not know exactly what this meant, but surely, I told myself, surely it must mean something. And so I went on, in happy puzzlement, under the small rain, bearing the mystery of myself in my heart.

Eclipse

Was it that same phial of precious ichor, still inside me, that spilled in the cinema that afternoon, and that I carry in me yet, and that yet will overflow at the slightest movement, the slightest mis-beat of my heart?

I passed the years of my youth practising for the stage. I would prowl the back roads of the town, always alone, playing out solitary dramas of struggle and triumph in which I spoke all the parts, even of the vanquished and the slain. I would be anyone but myself. Thus it continued year on year, the intense, unending rehearsal. But what was it I was rehearsing for? When I searched inside myself I found nothing finished, only a permanent potential, a waiting to go on. At the site of what was supposed to be my self was only a vacancy, an ecstatic hollow. And things rushed into this vacuum where the self should be. Women, for instance. They fell into me, thinking to fill me with all they had to give. It was not simply that I was an actor and therefore supposedly lacking an essential part of personality; I was a challenge to them, to their urge to create, to make life. I am afraid they did not succeed, with me.

Lydia had seemed the one capable of concentrating sufficient attention on me to make me shine out into the world with a flickering intensity such that even I might believe I was real. When I first encountered her she lived in a hotel. I mean, her family home was a hotel. That summer, more than half my lifetime ago now, I would see her almost every day as she came and went through the revolving glass doors of the Halcyon, got up in outlandish confections of cheesecloth and velvet and beads. She wore her black hair very straight, in the soulful style of the day, the bold silver streak in it less pronounced than it would be in later years but still striking. She became an object of keen speculation for me. I had a room in a rotting tenement in one of those cobbled canyons off the river, where at dawn the drays let loose from the brewery gates woke me with the thunder of apocalyptic hoofs, and the nights were permeated with the sickly sweet smell of roasting malt. Loitering along the embankment I watched for Lydia by the hour, in the gritty airlessness of the summer city. She was an exotic, a daughter of the desert. She walked with a sort of sulky swing, rolling her shoulders a little, always with her head down, as if she were meticulously retracing her steps to somewhere or something momentous. When she pushed through the hotel door the revolving glass panels threw off a splintered multiple image of her before she disappeared into the peopled dimness of the lobby. I made up lives for her. She was foreign, of course, the runaway daughter of an aristocratic family of fabulous pedigree; she was a rich man's former mistress, in hiding from his agents here in this backwater; certainly, she must have something in her past, I was convinced of it, some loss, some secret burden, some crime, even. When by chance I was introduced to her at an opening night—she was a great one for the theatre, in those days, and seemed to go to every production that was put on, with undiscriminating enthusiasm—I experienced an inevitable jolt of disappointment, as of something subsiding with a crunch under my diaphragm. Just another girl, after all.

"I've seen you," she said, "hanging about on the quays." She was always disconcertingly direct.

But that Levantine tinge to her looks, the hothouse pallor and stark black brows and faintly shadowed upper lip, remained a powerful attraction. The Hotel Halcyon took on for me the air of an oasis; before I entered there I imagined behind that revolving door a secret world of greenery and plashing water and sultry murmurings; I could almost taste the sherbet, smell the sandalwood. Lydia had a magnificence about her that was all the more enticing for her seeming unawareness of it. I admired her fullness, the sense she gave of filling whatever she wore, no matter how ample or flowing. Even her name bespoke for me a physical opulence. She was my big sleek slightly helpless princess. I loved to watch her as she walked to meet me, with that heavy-hipped slouch and that distracted, always vaguely dissatisfied smile. I basked in her; she seemed the very source and origin of the word uxorious; I decided at once, without having to think about it, that I would marry her.

I should say in fact that my tender-eyed wife's real, or given, name is Leah; in the hubbub of the crush bar that night when I was introduced to her I misheard it as Lydia, and when I repeated it later she liked it, and we kept it between us as a love-name, and eventually it became established, even among the more easygoing members of her family. It occurs to me to wonder now if this surrender and substitution of names worked a deeper change in her than one of mere nomenclature. She had relinquished a part of herself, so surely she took something on, as well. From Leah to Lydia is no small journey. When I was starting out in the theatre I toyed with the possibility of taking a stage name, but there was already so little of me that was real, I felt I could not afford to sacrifice the imperial label my mother—I am sure my father had no say in the matter—pinned on me so that I might be at least a noise in the world, though at once everyone, including my mother, went to work shortening my name to Alex. In my first parts I billed myself as Alexander, but it did not stick. I wonder what it takes to be proof against abbreviation.

I looked up the name Leah in a dictionary, which told me that in Hebrew it means cow. Dear me. No wonder she was willing to relinquish it.

Over all my recollections of that period of my life there lingers a faint warm bloom of embarrassment. I was not entirely what I pretended to be. It is an actor's failing. I did not tell lies about myself, exactly, but I did permit certain prominences to show through the deliberate fuzziness of my origins that were, frankly, larger than life. The fact is, I would happily have exchanged everything I had made myself into for a modicum of inherited grace, something not of my own invention, and which I had done nothing to deserve—class, breeding, money, even a run-down riverside hotel and a drop of the blood of Abraham in my veins. I was an unknown, as we say of fledgelings in our trade: in my case, truly an unknown, even to myself.

I think I took to the stage to give myself a cast of characters to inhabit who would be bigger, grander, of more weight and moment than I could ever hope to be. I studied—oh, how I studied for the part, I mean the role of being others, while at the same time striving to achieve my authentic self. I devoted hours to my exercises, far beyond the demands of even the most demanding among my coaches. The stage is a great academy; I mastered all manner of useless accomplishments: I can dance, I can fence, I can, should circumstance demand it, swing down from the rafters on a rope with a cutlass in my teeth. When I was younger I used to do a frightening fall, straight over, crash! like a pole-axed ox. For a year I took elocution lessons, at five bob a time, from a genteel old thing in black velvet and musty lace—"By *a negg*, Mr. Cleave, do you perhaps mean *an egg*?"—who at intervals in our weekly half-hours together would excuse herself and turn aside demurely to steal a swig from a naggin-bottle she kept hidden in her reticule. I did a course in ballet, stuck at it throughout a whole winter, sweating away doggedly at the barre, stared at by lumpen schoolgirls and doe-eyed ephebes of doubtful intent. I devoured improving texts. I read Stanislavski, and Bradley on tragedy and Kleist on the puppet theatre, and even double-barrelled old buffers like Granville-Barker and Beerbohm Tree on the art of acting. I sought out the most obscure treatises. I still have somewhere on my shelves Perrucci's *Dell'arte rappresentativa, premeditata ed all'improvviso*—I used to roll that title around my tongue like a line from Petrarch—on seventeenth-century Venetian comedy, which I would carry about with studied aplomb, and some pages of which I even read, laboriously, with the aid of a primer. I was after nothing less than a total transformation, a making-over of all I was into a miraculous, bright new being. But it was impossible. What I desired only a god could manage—a god, or a marionette. I learned to act, that was all, which really means I learned to act convincingly the part of an actor seeming not to act. It brought me no nearer to that exalted metamorphosis I had so hoped to achieve. The self-made man has no solid ground to stand on. He who pulls himself up by his bootstraps is in a permanent state of somersault, and in his ear always is the world's laughter as, look! there he goes again, arse over tip. I had come from nowhere, and now at last, through Lydia, I had arrived at the centre of what seemed to be somewhere. I was compelled to invent, of course, to elaborate on myself, for how could I expect to be accepted for what I merely was in the exotic new accommodation she was offering me?

We were married in a register office, a scandalous thing, in those days; it made me feel quite the iconoclast. My mother stayed away, not so much out of disapproval of the miscegenous match I was making—though disapprove she assuredly did—as from a fear of what to her was the dauntingly exotic world I was entering. The wedding breakfast was held at the Halcyon. It was a hot day and the stink from the river gave to the celebrations a bilious cast of the bazaar. Lydia's many black-haired, big-bottomed brothers, hearty and curiously childlike young men, clapped me on the back and made harmlessly lewd jokes. They kept walking away from me; that is how I remember them that day, walking away from me, all with the family's heavy-hipped gait that in them was a waddle, laughing back over their shoulders with a sort of amiable scepticism. My brand-new father-in-law, a watchful widower with the incongruously noble brow of a philosopher king, patrolled the occasion, wearing more the aspect of the hotel's detective than its proprietor. He had not liked the look of me from the start.

Have I described the Halcyon? I was fond of that old place. It is gone now, of course. The sons got rid of it when their father died, and then there was a fire, and the building was razed and the site sold on. It seems extraordinary, that something so solid could be so thoroughly erased. The interior as I remember it was generally brown, not the brown of mellowed wood but of old varnish, many-layered and slightly gummy to the touch, like toffee. A flabby smell of overcooked food stood in the corridors night and day. The bathrooms had enormous throne-like lavatories with wooden seats, and baths that seemed made for rendering murdered brides in; when the taps were turned on a tremendous knocking would run back along the pipes and make the very walls tremble all the way up to the attics. It was in a vacant room up there under the roof, one stifling Sabbath afternoon in summer, on a high broad bed troublingly reminiscent of an altar, that Lydia and I first made illicit love. It was like clasping in my arms a big marvellous flustered bird that cooed and cawed and thrashed wild wings and shuddered at the end and sank down beneath me helplessly with faint woeful-sounding cries.

That submissiveness of the boudoir was deceptive. Despite her scattered air, despite her father-fixation and her awe of the stage, despite all those bangles and beads and fluttering silks— there were days when she resembled an entire caravan undulating through a heat-haze across shimmering dunes—I know that of the two of us she was the stronger. I do not mean to say that she was the harder; I am hard, but I was never strong; that is my strength. She took care of me, protected me from the world, and from myself. Under the carapace of her safekeeping I could pretend to be as soft as any milksop in those Restoration comedies that enjoyed one of their recurrent popular revivals in the middle passage of my career. She even had money, eventually, when her dad upped and died one bounteous Christmas Day. Yes, we were a pair, a two-hander, a team. And now, red-eyed and crapulent, standing in my drawers at the window of my boyhood bedroom, above the morning-empty square, in bewilderment and inexplicable distress, I wondered when exactly the moment of catastrophic inattention had occurred and I had dropped the gilded bowl of my life and let it shatter.

Barefoot I made my shaky way downstairs and went into the kitchen and leant infirmly at the table with aching eyes and a frightening pressure in my head. The whiskey bottle, three-quarters empty, stood alone on the table with its shoulders set in what seemed a pointed rebuke. The room in sunlight was a luminous taut tent held down by studs of light reflecting at many corners, that bottle top, the rim of a smeared glass, an unbearably glaring knife blade. What had I said to Quirke? I remembered describing the night the animal made me stop on the road and I knew I must come back and live here. I had recounted to him my dream of being a child on Easter morning; I had even described the plastic chicken, and asked him if he knew what was the difference between a chicken and a hen. This last conundrum he gravely considered for a long moment, without result. Then I heard myself telling him of those afternoons when I would creep off to cry by myself in suburban picture-houses. Under the loosening influence of the whiskey it all came spilling out of me, another version somehow of those very storms of inexplicable sorrow I used to suffer there in the humid darkness, crouched under those vast, shimmering screens. And now in the pitiless light of morning I stood canted by the table with eyes shut fast and felt myself go hot with helpless shame at the thought of that blurted confession.

The telephone began to shrill, giving me a fright. I had not known it was still connected. After a flustered search I found it in the hall, on the floor behind a disembowelled sofa. It was an old-fashioned model made of Bakelite; the receiver had the osseous heft of a tribal artefact, shaped and polished by long and murderous use. I took a moment to register Lydia's voice on the line. I heard her dry laugh.

"Have you forgotten us already?" she said.

"I didn't know the telephone still worked."

"Well, it does." A beat of breathing silence. "And how is the hermit?"

"Hungover." I could see through into the kitchen; the window there had a flaw in one of its panes, and when I made the tiniest movement of my head a tree in the garden seemed to ripple, as if refracted under water. "I was drinking with Quirke," I said.

"With what?"

"Quirke. Our so-called caretaker."

"Much care he's taken."

"He brought a bottle of whiskey."

"To launch you on your new life. Did he break it over your head?"

I could see the scene, the morning light like heavy pale gas and Lydia standing in the living room of the big old dark house by the sea that had been part of her inheritance from her father, with the receiver wedged between shoulder and jaw, a trick that I have never been able to master, talking sideways into it as if it were a sleepy infant cradled beside her face. There is the briny smell of the sea, the far cry of gulls. It all seemed so clear and yet so far away it might have been a vision of life on another planet, unimaginably distant from this one, yet similar in every detail.

"Cass called again," Lydia said.

"Yes?" Slowly I sat down on the sofa, sinking so low my chin almost touched my knees, the sofa's horsehair guts spilling out from underneath and tickling my bare ankles.

"She has a surprise for you."

She breathed a brief laugh.

"Oh?"

"You'll be amazed."

No doubt I shall; a surprise from Cass is a formidable prospect. The tree beyond the flawed pane in the kitchen window rippled. Lydia made a sound that to my consternation seemed a sob; when she spoke again her voice was husky with reproach. "I think you should come home," she said. "I think you should be here when she arrives." I had nothing to say to that. I was remembering the day my daughter was born. She sprang into the world, a smeared and furious fingerling, bearing the generations with her. I had not been prepared for so many resemblances. She was my mother and father, and Lydia's father and dead mother, and Lydia herself, and a host of shadowy ancestors, all of them jostling together, as in the porthole of a departing emigrant ship, in that miniature face contorted upon the struggle for breath. I was present for the birth— oh, yes, I was very progressive, went in for all that kind of thing; it was another performance, of course, inwardly I quailed before the bloody spectacle. By the time the baby came I was in a sort of daze, and did not know where to turn. They put the infant in my arms before they had even washed her. How light she was, yet what a weight. A doctor in bloodied green rubber boots spoke to me but I could not understand him; the nurses were brisk and smug. When they lifted Cass away from me I seemed to hear the twang of an umbilical cord, one that I had paid out of myself, severing. We brought her home in a basket, like some precious piece of shopping we could not wait to unwrap. It was winter, and there was an alpine sting to the air. I recall the pallid sunlight on the car park—Lydia blinking like a prisoner led up from the dungeons— and the cold fresh fragrant breeze coming down from the high hills behind the hospital, and nothing to be seen of the baby but a patch of vague pink above a satin blanket. When we got her home we had no cot for her, and had to put her in the open bottom drawer of a tallboy in our bedroom. I could hardly sleep for fear of getting up in the night and forgetting she was there and slamming it shut. Triangles of watery light from the headlamps of passing motor cars kept opening across the ceiling only to be folded smartly again and dropped, like so many ladies' fans, into the drawer where she was asleep. We had a nickname for her, what was it? Hedgehog, I think; yes, that was it, because of the tiny snuffling noises she made. Bright, innocent-seeming days, in my memory of them, though the clouds were already massing behind the horizon.

"I am talking to myself here," Lydia said, with a tight, exasperated sigh.

I allowed my eyes to close, feeling the rims of the inflamed lids hotly touch. My head ached.

"When is she arriving?" I said.

"Oh, she won't say, of course—that would be too simple." Lydia's voice always takes on a bridling tone when she speaks of our difficult daughter. "She'll probably just appear one day out of the blue."

Another silence then, in which I could hear the rustle of my own breathing in the mouthpiece. I opened my eyes and looked out to the kitchen again. What struck me first about the image, vision, hallucination—I would not have known what to call it, had I thought to call it anything—that I glimpsed out there was the ordinariness of it: the figure of a woman, tall, young, turning from the range, abruptly handing something, it looked like, to what seemed a seated child. Slowly I set the receiver down on the arm of the sofa. No sound at all, except for a faint, a very faint hissing, that might have been no more than the sound of my own self, blood, lymph, labouring organs, making its low susurrus in my ears. I was given only that glimpse—the woman, if it was a woman, turning, the arm extending, the child unmoving, if it was a child—and then it was gone. I squeezed my sore eyes shut again, trying to retain the image. It was all inexplicably, achingly familiar.

I walked softly out to the kitchen and stood and looked about. No one was there. Everything was as it had been a minute ago, before the phone rang, except for a sense of general suspension, as of things holding themselves in stillness, not daring to breathe. I returned to the hall and sat down again on the sofa, a sort of collapse, and exhaled a shuddery sigh. Lydia was still on the line.

"What?" she said snappishly. "What did you say?"

I felt a piercing cold.

"I said, the place is haunted." I was laughing now, unmanageable, feathery gasps of laughter burbling out of me.

Another silence.

"You are your own ghost," Lydia said, with angry haste, and I heard the receiver drop with a crash into its cradle an instant before the connection broke, she too all at once become phantom, fading into air and distance.

It was not the first time I had seen a ghost in this house. One day, when I was a boy, in the dreamy boredom of a summer afternoon I climbed up the unlit steep stairs to the garret, drawn there at who knows what behest. The room was hot under the slanted, low ceiling. Someone, my mother, I suppose, in one of her periodic doomed attempts at thriftiness, had spread shallots on the bare wooden floor to preserve them for a winter that now was long past, and the air was spiced with their sweet decayed dry odour, stirring in me a tangle of indistinct rememberings. There was a single, small window here, round, like a porthole, at which I was leaning, peering out vacantly through the dusty pane into an immensity of dense blue air, when something, not a sound but a sort of tightening in the atmosphere of the room, made me turn my head. I expected it would be one of the lodgers; sometimes on my prowls I would meet one of the more peculiar among them, creeping about, looking for something to spy on or to steal, I suppose. But it was not a lodger. It was my dead father, standing in the open doorway, as real as in life, dressed in striped pyjamas and shoes without laces and an old wheat-coloured cardigan, the same attire that he had worn every day in the long last months of his dying. He held himself stooped in an attitude of indecision, not looking at me, apparently unaware of me, with his head inclined a little, listening, it might be, or trying to recollect something, to capture some stray thought. After a moment he seemed to give up the effort, whatever it was, and shrugged, letting one shoulder droop in that way that he had, and turned and ducked through the doorway out to the stairs and was gone.

I was not frightened. I would have been, I am sure, had he looked directly at me, or given some sign that he knew I was there. As it was, I was only puzzled, and curious, too, of course. Afterwards, I supposed I had been asleep somehow, in some kind of waking sleep, or trance, although there had been no moment at which I had felt myself coming to. I thought of telling my mother what I had seen, and even went down through the house in search of her, but when I found her I was overcome by a sort of shyness, and knew that I must preserve the visit, or haunting, or whatever it had been, against the contamination of a mere recounting of it. For I believed I had been privileged, a privileged witness to some bit of intimate and perhaps momentous business, as when at school one day passing by an empty classroom I had glimpsed a teacher, a youngish man with red hair—I can still see him, so clearly—standing by the blackboard with a letter in his hands, weeping lavishly, his shoulders shaking, with dark stains on his soutane where the tears were splashing.

For a long time after I saw my father everything was bathed in a faint glow of strangeness, an unearthly radiance. The world seemed tilted slightly out of true. Now, all these years later, when I saw the woman in the kitchen, I thought at once that I must have conjured up the apparition in order that it might have the same effect, that is, to make me disoriented, and alienate me from my surroundings and from myself. For I had determined, from the moment Lydia had left me on the doorstep and driven away with tears in her eyes, that I would not let myself become accustomed to the new life I had entered into on the site of the old, and had been angry to discover straight away that I was failing. To be watchful and attentive of everything, to be vigilant against complacency, to resist habituation, these were my aims in coming here. I would catch myself, red-handed, in the act of living; alone, without an audience of any kind, I would cease from performing and simply *be*. And what would be my register of being if not things, the more commonplace the better? Yet almost immediately I found myself settling down in these once familiar surroundings and letting them be so again, with all my plans and pledges forgotten. Even the first sight of my old room had affected me hardly at all; what makes for presence if not absence?—I mean the presence of oneself as a remembered other—and I might as well never have gone away, so little of me was there, to be pondered on or grasped. *Making strange,* people hereabouts say when a child wails at the sudden appearance of a visitor; how was I to make strange now, and not stop making strange? How was I to fight the deadening force of custom? In a month, in a week, I told myself, the old delusion of belonging would have re-established itself irremediably.

So if the purpose of the appearance of this ghost is to dislocate me and keep me thrown off balance, am I indeed projecting it out of my own fancy, or does it come from some outside source? Both, somehow, it seems, although I do not understand how that can be. That glimpse through the kitchen doorway was the first of many such sightings, brief, diaphanous, gleamingly translucent, like a series of photographs blown up to life-size and for a moment made wanly animate. What happens in them continues to be remarkable only in its being unremarkable, the woman going about what seem to be commonplace tasks—nothing is definite in the dimension in which she exists—or just standing, silent, lost in reverie. It is not possible to make out her features properly. That is, I see the scenes in photographic sharpness, but the figures themselves are not finally realised, their features not fully developed, as if they had moved a fraction while the plate was still being exposed. The child in particular is unfixed; I do not know why I even call it a child, so vague and amorphous is its form; it is the mere idea of a child, no more. They are still growing into existence, these shadows made of light, or perhaps they existed once and are fading now. Whatever they are engaged in, whatever attitude they strike, they seem always somehow guardedly at attention. Have they, I wonder, on their side, an intimation of my presence? Am I to them what they are to me, a fleeting brightness glimpsed out of the corner of the eye, through a doorway, or pausing for a second on the stairs and then vanishing with a noiseless sigh? And it is not just these two—that is, they are the ones I see, if see is the word, but there is the sense of others, too, a world of unseen others, through which this woman and her formless child move, and in which they have their life, if life is the word.

I am not afraid of them, just as I was not afraid when my father appeared to me that day in the garret. There is too much the sense of striving, of large and melancholy effort on their part, for them to be truly frightening. Some intricate system, elaborate yet mundane, an unknown unity, some little lost and desolated order, is trying to put itself into place here, to assemble itself within the ill-fitting frame of the house and its contents. I am convinced they are making the effort not only out of an unavoidable compulsion— these creatures are struggling somehow to *come to being*—but that it is for my benefit, too. I believe these phenomena are in some way concentrated on me and my state, intricately involved in the problem of whatever it is that has gone wrong with me. There is pathos in the notion of this poor half-developed world struggling blindly, in bafflement, perhaps in pain, to come fully to life, so that I might . . . what? Have something demonstrated to me? Be a witness? Be instructed? Or is it, I ask myself, is it that something is trying to exist *through me*, to find some form of being, *in me?* For although I speak of them appearing outside of me, a moving spectacle, like figures on a stage, in fact—in fact!—I am amongst them, I am of them, and they are of me, my familiars.

Familiars, yes—that is what is strangest, that I find it all not strange at all. Everything here is twilight and half dream, yet the appearance of these phantoms is naggingly insinuative, as if

I should, or would, know them. There is something in them of those ancestral resemblances that will spring unnervingly up at one from the cradle or the deathbed. They hover maddeningly at the tip of my mind, as a sought-for word will hover on the tip of the tongue. They have that air of inscrutable significance that will surround people encountered the morning after a troubling dream in which they have figured. And indeed, the visions themselves work a similar effect, lending to this or that piece of the humble appurtenances of my new life a passing spectral significance. When I speak of them being at the table, or the range, or standing on the stairs, it is not the actual stairs or range or table that I mean. They have their own furniture, in their own world. It looks like the solid stuff among which I move, but it is not the same, or is the same at another stage of existence. Both sets of things, the phantom and the real, strike up a resonance together, a chiming. If the ghostly scene has a chair in it, say, that the woman is sitting on, and that occupies the same space as a real chair in the real kitchen, and is superimposed on it, however ill the fit, the result will be that when the scene vanishes the real chair will retain a sort of aura, will blush, almost, in the surprise of being singled out and fixed upon, of being lighted upon, in this fashion. The effect soon fades, however, and then the chair, the real chair, will step back, as it were, out of the spotlight, and take its accustomed place in dim anonymity, and I will cease to notice it, try as I might to go on paying deference to this plain thing that has known its numinous moment.

I have come to distrust even the solidest objects, uncertain if they are not merely representations of themselves that might in a moment flicker and fade. The actual has taken on a tense, trembling quality. Everything is poised for dissolution. Yet never in my life, so it seems, have I been so close up to the very stuff of the world, even as the world itself shimmers and turns transparent before my eyes. There are dreams in which one seems to live more vividly than in life. I have my moments of impatient incredulity when, a troubled sleeper, I will seem to struggle out of this dream-world into the sweaty bewilderment of waking. But then one of those translucent images will flash along the edges of my vision and I will realise that I am not awake, or that I am awake and all this that had seemed a dream is no dream at all. The line between delusion and whatever is its opposite has for me grown faint to the point of vanishing. I am neither sleeping nor awake, but in some fuddled middle state between the two; it is like being half tight all the time, a transcendent tipsiness.

The suggestion of the familial the phantoms bring with them makes me wonder if they might be the form of a rejected life coming back to claim me. After all, here I am, living in the house of the dead. It is such a strange sensation, being once more among the surroundings of my growing up. I was never fully at home here. If the lodgers led unreal lives, so too did we, the permanent inhabitants, so called. Doubtless this is a reason why the apparitions do not frighten me, that the place was always haunted. I spent my childhood among alien presences, ghostly figures. How meek they were, our lodgers, how self-effacing, blurring themselves to a sort of murmur in the house. I would meet them on the stairs, squirming sideways as they edged past me and smiling their fixed smiles of pained politeness. In what was called the dining room they would sit stooped over their plates of rashers or meat and mash in the watchful, downcast attitude of children being punished. At night I would seem to hear their presence all around me, a tossing, a shifting, a low, restless sighing. Now here I am, a lodger myself, no more real than the phantoms that appear to me, a shadow among insubstantial shadows.

What is it about the past that makes the present by comparison seem so pallid and weightless? My father, for instance, is more alive to me now than he was when he was living. Even my mother was not wholly there for me until she had safely become a memory. I see them as a sort of archaic double-act, a Baucis and Philemon, bound together here, tending to the needs of others, both of them slowly turning to grey stone as the days rose and fell, each new day indistinguishable from the one that had gone before, slow grains accumulating, becoming the years. As a child I took it that when the time came for me to leave they would stand back, two humble caryatids holding up the portal to my future, watching patiently, in uncomplaining puzzlement, as I strode away from them with hardly a backward glance, each league that I covered making me not smaller but steadily more vast, their overgrown, incomprehensible son. When they died I did not grieve for them. And so I ask myself, are these hauntings now their revenge, a forcing on me of some part of a lost life I did not attend to properly when I had the chance? Are they demanding the due of mourning that I did not pay? For there is a sense of sorrow here, and of regret; of promises unkept, of promise unfulfilled.

In those first days alone here I saw no one, or not in the flesh, at least. After the call from Lydia I would not answer the telephone, and grew so to fear its abrupt harsh summonings that in the end I disconnected it. Such silence after that! I let myself sink down into it as into some motionless warm sustaining stuff. But I did not bask, no, I did not. In the beginning I was all energy, up and doing every day at dawn's first light. I tackled the overgrown garden, ripping up armfuls of scutch grass and hacking at the brambles until my hands bled and sweat ran into my eyes. My mother's rose bushes are still here, all gone wild. The spade turned up ancient potatoes, hollowed-out carcasses that burst under my heel with a plop and oozed a whitish fluid. Spiders scuttled, grubs writhed. I was in my element. Labouring there in the midsummer heat I experienced a demented euphoria. I would find myself muttering snatches of wild talk, or singing, or laughing, and sometimes even

weeping, not in sorrow but a kind of awful glee. I had no aim in
view, I was not going to plant anything; I was just working for the
sake of work, and presently I gave it up, and left the briars and the
mounds of uprooted grass to swelter and rot in the sun until new
growth covered them over.

Now, my fruitless labours abandoned, I felt an unshakeable las-
situde settling on me like a net. At evening, slumped on the sofa in
a daze, I would look back over the eventless day and wonder what
it could have been that had so wearied me. I am calm, if calm is the
way to put it; numb, perhaps, would be a better. My nights are
long, twelve, fourteen hours of turbulent drowsing and dreaming
from which I wake exhausted, cast up on the morning like a sur-
vivor from a shipwreck. I thought that by coming here I would
find a perspective on things, a standpoint from which to survey my
life, but when I look back now to what I have left behind me I am
afflicted by a disabling wonderment: how did I manage to accumu-
late so much of life's clutter, apparently without effort, or even
full consciousness?—so much, that under the weight of it I cannot
begin to locate that singular essential self, the one I came here to
find, that must be in hiding, somewhere, under the jumble of discarded masks. It is a dizzying sensation, as when a word or an
object will break free for a moment from the mind's grasp and
drift out into the empty space of its own utter separateness. Everything is strange now. The most humdrum phenomena fill me with
slow astonishment. I feel at once newborn and immensely old. I
have a dotard's fondness for my chair, my cup of grog, my warm
bed, while in my clumsy groping after things that keep eluding my
grasp I am as helpless as an infant. I have fallen into thrall with
myself. I marvel at the matter my body produces, the stools, the
crusts of snot, the infinitesimal creep of fingernails and hair. I
have as good as given up shaving. I like the scratchy feel of my
face and the sulphur smell of the bristles and the sandpapery rasp
when I run a hand along the line of my jaw. After that short-lived

attempt at gardening my palm turned septic where a thorn from a rose bush had lodged, and I would stand motionless and rapt at the window with my hand held up to the daylight, studying the swelling with its shiny meniscus of purplish skin, taut and translucent as the stuff of an insect's wing; at night, when I woke in the dark, the hand would seem a separate, living thing throbbing beside me. The dull hot pain of it was almost voluptuous. Then one morning when I was getting myself out of bed I stumbled and caught my hand on something sharp, and a tattoo of pain drummed up my arm and the swelling burst and the splinter popped out in a blob of pus. I sank back on the bed clutching my wrist and whimpering, but whether from pain or pleasure I could not exactly say.

There are more well-defined if no less shameful pleasures. I found a cache of dirty pictures thrown on top of a wardrobe in one of the rooms, left behind no doubt by some long-gone travelling salesman. Antique smut it is, hand-tinted photographs of paintings from the last century, postcard-sized but rich in detail, all creams and crimsons and rose-petal pinks. They are mostly oriental scenes: a bevy of pneumatic harem wives in a Turkish bath touching each other up, a blackamoor in a turban doing it from behind to a girl on her knees, a naked wanton on a couch being pleasured by her black slave. I keep them under my mattress, from where in guilty heat I will bring them out and plump up my pillows and sink back with a hoarse sigh into my own vigorous embraces. Afterwards, there is as always a small, sad hollow inside me, that seems in volume to match exactly what I have got rid of, as if the stuff I have pumped out of myself has made a space my body does not quite know how to fill. Yet it is not all anticlimax. There are occasions, rare and precious, when, having brought myself to the last hiccupy scamper, with the pictures fanned out before me and my eyes agoggle, I will experience a moment of desolating rapture that has nothing to do with what is happening in my lap but seems a distillation of all the tenderness and intensity that life can promise. The other day, at one of those moments of swollen bliss, as I lay gasping with my chin on my breast, I heard faintly through the stillness of afternoon the ragged sound of a children's choir in the convent across the way, and it might have been the seraphs singing.

The house attends me, monitoring my movements, as if it had been set the task of keeping track of me and will not let its vigilance slip even for an instant. Floorboards creak under my tread, door hinges squeal tinnily behind me when I walk into a room; if I am sitting at a certain angle by the fireplace in the living room and make some sudden noise—if I cough, or slam shut a book—the whole house like a struck piano will give me back in echo a low, dark, jangling chord. At times I have the feeling that the very air in the rooms is congregating to discuss me and my doings. Then I will jump up and pace about, wringing my hands and muttering to myself, halting to stand motionless, glaring at some object, or into a corner or an open doorway, daring—willing—some hobgoblin to appear there; but the apparitions will never come at my bidding, and at once I am off again headlong, pace and turn, pace and turn. Mostly, though, I am at peace, and want for no one. When I am in the garden and a person goes by on the road, a farmer on his tractor or the postman on his bike, I will turn aside hurriedly, hunching a shoulder, poor Quasimodo, skulking behind the hump of my incomprehensible troubles.

As well as the ghostly ones there are phenomena that seem too solid not to be real, if I may be said to know what real means any more. I hear soft footsteps on the stair, and what seem distant murmurings down in the depths of the house; now and then I have the sense of a general pausing and standing still, as when one stops on a country road at night and the imagined footsteps at one's back stop also on the instant. Surely these are not spirit sounds. The phantom woman appears to me always in a silence deeper than silence, a silence that is an unheard hum. No, these are sounds such as the living make. Is there an interloper in the house, another, or the same one as before, the book-burner come back, some rough brute who might rear up behind me at an unguarded moment and put his terrible hands on my neck or leap from the darkness and dash my brains out with a cudgel? I have taken to keeping a poker by the bed for self-defence. But what if the ruffian were to fall upon me while I was asleep? I have the feeling I am being observed by living eyes. Last evening when I was doing my washing at the kitchen sink I turned my head quickly and caught sight of something in the doorway, not a presence but an intense absence, the vacated air quivering where a second ago I am convinced someone more substantial than a ghost had been standing, watching me.

No, the phantoms will not come when I bid them, and that puzzles me. For I do seem to have some control over them, as one has control, however weak or contingent, over the riotous tumble of happenings in a dream. They depend on me for their autonomy, however paradoxical that may sound. They yearn toward me, one of the living, toward my living light, like invisible plants invisibly at feed on the sky's radiance. This is the pathos of their predicament. I seem to be the engine of action for them, the source that feeds them the sustenance for their frail existence. The woman's manner, if it is possible to speak of such an evanescent being as having a manner, is one of surmise and vague expectation; she is tentative, bemused, uncertain. Oh, I am not so deluded as not to know that these images are the product of my imagination—but they *are* a product; they are not in my head, they are outside; I see them, clear as anything I cannot touch, the sky, clouds, those far blue hills. At night they press into my dreams, wan shades mutely clamouring for my attention. In the daytime there are passages when they will flicker about me like wildfire. As I step through this or that picture of their doings I seem to feel a crackle of faint, falling energy, as if I had broken the tenuous connections of a force field. Something is expected of me here, something is being asked of me. They are not even proper spectres, bent on being terrifying or delivering awful warnings. Shrieks in the darkness, groans and clanking chains, such effects, however exhausted or banal, might at least succeed in frightening me, but what am I to make of this little ghost trio to whose mundane doings I am the puzzled and less than willing witness?

Trio? Why do I say trio? There is only the woman and the even more indistinct child—who is the third? Who, if not I? Perhaps Lydia is right, perhaps I have at last become my own ghost.

Memories crowd in on me, irresistibly, threatening to overwhelm my thoughts entirely, and I might be a child again, and this arid present no more than a troubled foreglimpse of the future. I dare not go up to the garret for fear I might see my father again, still loitering there. Although he does not figure much in the thumbed and dog-eared photo album that passes for my past—he died young, or youngish, after all—one of the earliest mental snapshots I retain is of being taken late one night to meet him at the train station. I do not know where he can have been coming back from, for he was no traveller, my father. He stepped quickly from the train and held me high on his shoulder and laughed. I was no more than, what, four or five? yet I was struck by the unaccustomed gaiety of the moment. Even my mother was laughing. I remember it like a page out of a children's storybook, the station lamps aglow in the misty darkness like the furry heads of dandelions, and the looming black steam engine gasping where it stood, and the licorice smell of smoke and cinders. It was Eastertime. My father had brought me a present. What was it? Some kind of bird, a plastic thing, yellow. We cycled home, my father carrying me on the crossbar of his bicycle inside his buttoned-up overcoat and my mother with his cardboard suitcase strapped to the carrier behind her. The night pressed around us, chill and damp and secret. In the house my father sat by the range in the kitchen smoking a cigarette and talking to my mother. I liked to watch my father smoking. He went at it with a kind of negligent deftness, as if it were a tricky exercise in prestidigitation which he had long ago mastered, tapping and twirling the miniature white baton and rolling it along his knuckles with a magician's fluency. When he put it to his lips he would incline his head sideways and screw up one eye, as if he were taking aim along the barrel of a tiny gun. The smoke that he exhaled—it was blue going in, grey when it came out—had a particular savour that he gave to it, something flat and tarry, the very odour of his insides; I often fancy I can catch a trace of that smell still lingering in odd corners of the house.

But am I rightly remembering that night? Am I remembering anything rightly? I may be embellishing, inventing, I may be mixing everything up. Perhaps it was another night entirely that he brought me home on the bar of his bicycle, under his coat. And how did his bicycle come to be there, at the station, anyway, if he was arriving by train? These are the telltale threads on which memory snags her nails.

Here I am, a grown man in a haunted house, obsessing on the past.

It was summer when my father died. My mother had moved him to the top of the house, to a room across the landing from mine, where he would be out of sight of the lodgers. I would meet him, leaving his tea tray outside his door, or shuffling in his slippers down the hall to the lavatory, and I would avoid his eye, the anguished stoicism of it, like the eye of the Saviour mournfully displaying his pierced heart in the silver and neon-pink picture that hung beside the hatstand in the hall. I see him, ashen, lost inside his clothes, and always, like me now, with a three-day stubble, moving wraithlike without sound through rooms gaunt with summer's stillness, a stooped figure flickering from sunlight into shadow, fading with no footfall, leaving no trace of his passing save a sort of shimmer, a fold in the air, and a coiling question mark of cigarette smoke.

The day of his death is memorable too as the day my mother slapped my face. When she turned from the range I thought she was reaching out quickly to give me something. I can feel still the hard hot quick smack of her hand on my jaw, the jolt of it. She had never hit me before. She did it too not as a parent slapping a child, but as one angry adult turning suddenly on another. I do not remember what I had said or done to provoke her. Her look immediately afterwards was one almost of triumph. She lifted her head back and widened her nostrils, like Snow White's wicked stepmother, and something came at me out of her eyes, sharp and glittering and swift, like a blade shown and promptly pocketed. Then without a word she turned back to whatever it was she had been doing at the range. I did not cry, I was too surprised to cry, but only sat with one hand laid flat before me on the table, feeling the tingle along my jaw where she had slapped me, as if tiny droplets of something scalding were falling on my skin. The oilcloth cover on the table was wonderfully cool and smooth and moist under my hand, almost like something living, almost like skin. Then my father came down, clutching a blanket tight around his drawn, ill-shaven neck. There were shadows in the hollows of his face and feverish red spots on his cheekbones that looked as if they had been painted there. My mother's expression was blank, as though nothing had happened, but my father wrinkled his nose, testing the pressure of her anger on the air, and gave me an odd, sidewise glance, half-smiling, almost sly. Late that night I was wakened by muffled noises outside my room. When I went to the door and looked out I saw my mother in her nightdress crossing the landing hastily with a blue bowl in her hands, and heard through the open

door of my father's room a high whistling noise that was the noise
of him struggling for breath, and I shut my door hurriedly and got
back into bed, and when I woke again it was morning, and I knew
that my father was gone.

At the funeral it rained briefly, as if just for us. A small round
cloud appeared in an otherwise empty sky above the cemetery and
let fall upon the circle of mourners a gentle drizzle, warm and fine.
I watched every step of the ceremony with frowning attention,
determined not to miss a thing. My mother kept glancing off with
a vague, anxious look in the direction of the cemetery gate, as if
there were something far more urgent elsewhere calling out plain-
tively for her attention. Later in the day, when the mourners had
all dispersed, I came upon her sitting on the sofa in the parlour,
weeping, with her face in her hands, and feeling grown-up and
solemnly responsible I walked up quietly and stopped just behind
her and laid a hand gently on her shoulder. I can still feel the cool
smooth brittle texture of her newly bought black dress. She
wrenched herself away from me, making cat noises and scrubbing
at her cheeks, and I had the sense of a small, slightly shameful and
gratifying victory.

Why is it not she who appears to me? Her own last years were
haunted. I would hear her in the night, pacing the floor by her bed,
endlessly pacing. She grew confused, and mistook me for my
father, and would fly into fits of unprovoked rage. Then one
morning I found her lying on her side on the floor in the downstairs lavatory with her bloomers around her knees. Her face had a
bluish cast and there was froth on her lips. I thought she was dead;
I felt strange, very cold and calm and distant from myself. I
flushed the lavatory, careful not to look into the bowl, and knelt
and hauled her up and held her to me. She was warm and flaccid
and faintly atremble, and I was shocked to find myself thinking of
Lydia as she would be at the climax of love-making. Her eyelids

fluttered but did not open, and she sighed as if from a great weariness, and a glistening bubble came out of her mouth and swelled, and swelled, and burst.

For weeks she lay unmoving in a metal-framed bed in a bright room at the corner of the hospital wing that looked out on a cindered pathway and a row of cherry trees. I sat with her through long hours of wakeful dreaming; it was almost restful there. The sunlight threw complicated shapes across the bed that would spend the afternoon inching their way slowly along the blanket and on to the floor like things making an elaborately stealthy getaway. Hospital sounds came to me, soothingly muffled. My mother's hands rested on the sheet, unmoving, pale as paper, impossibly large. She looked like a more than life-sized statue of herself. Some error had been made, some bit of celestial business had gone awry and she had been left like this, felled by death yet still alive, stranded between two imperceptibly darkening shores. When I was leaving at the end of the day's vigil I would lean over her, teetering a little, and kiss her self-consciously on the forehead, smelling her mingled smell of soap and washed-out cotton and dried skin and musty hair.

The cherry trees blossomed, and the blossoms fell, and then the leaves fell. Eventually she regained a sort of consciousness. I arrived one late autumn afternoon and she was sitting up at an angle wearing a pink cardigan that was not hers, with a look of wild enquiry in her eye. When I spoke to her she jerked her head back on its wattled neck like a startled hen. She came home that evening. They brought her in an ambulance, which impressed her, I could see, for all her distractedness; she descended from the wide-flung back doors with an almost queenly step, laying a hand imperiously on my offered arm.

It was strange, the silent clamour of her presence in the house. I felt like an attendant set to watch over a large, dangerous machine that had seized up and that no one knew how to set going

again. It was always there, under everything, the sense of her, all
that stalled potential, the house hummed with it. Inside her somewhere the dynamo was still spinning; where did the energy go to,
what invisible elaborations was it generating? She unnerved me.
She seemed no longer human, she seemed something more than
that, ancient and elemental. I tended her like a priest at a shrine,
with weary reverence, resignedly, stooping under that silent stare,
that mute mixture of pleading and disdain. She took to pushing
things off the bedside table, pill boxes, the night-light holder, the
glass for her false teeth; she even developed a knack of overturn-
ing her chamber pot. Word of her condition got round among the
lodgers, and soon the commercial travellers stopped coming and
the clerks and secretaries found digs elsewhere. Now the deserted
house became her shell, her sounding-box. Despite the ruin of her
mind I credited her with uncanny powers of perception. I fancied
I could hear her breathing wherever I was in the house, even down
in the back scullery, where I brewed her tea and mashed the slops
for her that were all she could manage now. She seemed never to
sleep. I would look into her room and there she would be, no matter how late the hour, sprawled in the foul roost of her bed,
propped up crookedly in the corner against a bank of pillows, in
the tallowy glow of the night light, an elbow wedged against the
wall, grey hair a fright and her jaw set and the little hard blue teary
eyes fixed on me furiously, brimming with all that was pent in her,
the years. Despite myself, I would step inside, and shut the door,
and the flame of the night light would waver and the room would
lurch and immediately right itself again. Sometimes I would talk
to her, not knowing if she could hear me, or if she did, that she
could understand what I was saying. I was prey to an oppressive
self-awareness. Listening shadows hung in the high room. The tall
black wardrobe had a curved front, more like a lid than a door, and
always reminded me of a sarcophagus. She would stir, or rather,
something would stir in her, one of those interior tremors, barely

detectable, that I had learned to interpret, I do not know how, and I would sigh, and lift the teacup and cracked jug that stood with her rosary beads and prayer book on the bedside table, and pour out a draught of water, marvelling vaguely at the undulant rope of liquid coiling into the cup, gold-coloured in the candlelight. I would sit down beside her on one haunch on the side of the bed, the bed in which I had been born—had been got, too, most likely—and put an arm around her shoulders and draw her forward and look on as she drank, her puckered, whiskery lips mumbling the rim of the cup, and feel the water going down her gullet in hiccupy swallows. Then I would see myself here as a child, kneeling on the floor in the rain-light of a winter afternoon, lost in my solitary games, my mother lolling in bed with her magazines and her chocs, and the wireless whispering and the rain tapping on the windowpanes, and now I would shake her a little, not roughly, feeling the bones of her shoulders shift inside their parcel of loose flesh, and at last, surrendering, she would lay her raddled old head against my shoulder and exhale a long, slow, whistling sigh. Look at us there, a deposition scene in reverse, the dying hunched old woman cradled in the arm of her living son, in our dome of candlelight, lapped in our noisome, ancient warmth.

Presently she died. It was, as they say in these parts, a great release.

It is late, the light is going. My mind aches from so much futile remembering. What does it signify, this chapter of family accidents? What is it I hope to retrieve? What is it I am trying to avoid? I see what was my life adrift behind me, going smaller and smaller with distance, like a city on an ice floe caught in a current, its twinkling lights, its palaces and spires and slums, all miraculously intact, all hopelessly beyond reach. Was it I who took an axe to the ice? What can I do now but stand on this crumbling promontory and watch the past as it dwindles? When I look ahead, I see nothing except empty morning, and no day, only dusk thickening into night, and, far off, something that is not to be made out, something vague, patient, biding. Is that the future, trying to speak to me here, among these shadows of the past? I do not want to hear what it might have to say.

II

There is pandemonium among the seagulls, great events seem to be taking place. Before my arrival a flock of them had come in from the sea and settled on the house, building their nests in the chimneys and the valley of the roof. Why they chose this spot I do not know; perhaps they liked the calm and quiet of our little square. They are anything but calm themselves. From earliest morning the sky is filled with their tumult. They clamour and shriek and make an angry rattling with beaks agape. Their favourite noise, however, is a staccato yacking, like a hyena's laugh or baboon's hoot, that decelerates gradually while simultaneously rising in pitch. Even at night they are restless, I hear them flopping about on the roof, grumbling and threatening each other. At dawn every day they set up a deafening racket. Why such uproar? Surely the mating season is well over—certainly there are young already being taught to fly, ugly, awkward, dun-coloured things that waddle to the edge of the roof and perch there, peering down at the drop and swallowing hard, or looking all about with a show of unconcern, before launching themselves out shakily on to the air currents. At certain times their elders all together will take to the sky and wheel and wheel in majestic slow circles above the house, screaming, whether in panic or wild exultation it is impossible to know.

Yesterday I looked up from where I was sitting and saw one of the adults standing outside on the window sill. I am always startled by the great size of these birds when seen up close. They are so menacingly graceful in flight, yet when they land they become sadly comical, perched on their spindly legs and ridiculous flat feet, like the botched prototype of some far more handsome, far more well-fashioned species. This one just stood there beyond the glass, doing nothing except opening wide its beak in what seemed a yawn or a soundless cry. Curious, I put down my book and went outside. The bird did not fly away at my approach, but held its place, shifting ponderously from foot to foot and regarding me with wary deprecation out of one large, pale, lustrous eye. I saw at once what the matter was: on the ground below the window sill a dead fledgeling lay. It must have fallen from the roof, or failed in flight and plummeted to earth and broken its neck. Its look was glazed already, its plumage dulled. The parent, for I have no doubt that is what it was, made its beak gape again in that odd way, with no sound. It might have been a threat, to warn me off, but I am inclined to believe it was a sign of distress. Even seagulls must have expressions of sorrow or of joy recognisable at least to their fellows. Probably they see our visages as just as blank and inexpressive as theirs seem to us. A man numb with inexplicable misery, for instance, I am sure to them would be merely another dead-eyed dullard gazing pitilessly upon a scene of incommensurable loss. The bird was male, I think; I think, yes, a father.

I left it to its silent vigil and, prompted somehow by the encounter, made my way down to the sea. I have hardly left the house since coming here, and I went forth almost fearfully, casting an anxious backward look about my little world, like a medieval explorer about to take ship for Cathay. The trek took a good half-hour. I went by what I thought would be a short cut across the fields, and got lost. At last, sweating and shaken, I came out through a hazel wood on to a shingly strip of beach. The usual mingled iodine and cat-piss smell was very strong. Is there anywhere more evocative than these tawny fringes of our dry-land world? At the first crunching footstep I might have been walking these sands all my life, despite the surly and unwelcoming aspect of the spot, that would have been fitted more to brigandage than bathing. The dunes were low, and there was no grass, only a tough, thorny stuff that crackled underfoot. The beach was steeply shelved, and in places the top layer of sand had blown away, exposing striated ridges of a scaly, shale-like stuff that would cut the soles of any swimmer foolhardy enough to venture barefoot over it.

I wonder if my ghosts would have known I was not in the house. Do they appear when I am not present? Is a rose red in the dark—who said that?

Not a soul was to be seen on the shore, except, a little way out, a very large black seabird standing motionless on a black rock. It had a long slender neck and a slender body, and seemed unreal in its stillness, more an artist's stylisation than a living bird. I sat down on one of the exposed ridges of shale. Curious stuff it was, like crumbly stone, and greasy to the touch. The morning was still, under a seamless white sky. There was a full tide, and the surface of the water, taut and burnished like billowing silk, seemed higher than the land, and on the point of spilling over. The waves were hardly waves at all, more a wrinkle running along the edges of a sluggishly swaying vast bowl of water. Why do I find the thought of the sea so alarming? We speak of its power and violence as if it were a species of wild animal, ravening and unappeasable, but the sea does nothing, it is simply there, its own reality, like night, or the sky. Is it the heave and lurch and sudden suck of it that frightens? Or is it that it is so emphatically not our medium? I think of the world beneath the ocean, the obverse of ours, the negative of ours, with its sandy plains and silent valleys and great sunken mountain ranges, and something fails me in myself, something that is mine draws away from me in horror. Water is uncanny in the way, single-minded and uncontrollable, it keeps seeking its own level, like nothing else in the world that we inhabit. There are storms, yes, and tidal waves, and even in these temperate zones the estuarial bore, or eagre, but such phenomena are not due to any inherent qualities of water itself, for water, though fluid and eerily always beyond our grasp, surely is essentially inert. Yet it puts us off balance; one is always at an angle to the ocean—keeping one's head above water ensures that. To wade into the waves is to seem to fall without falling, feeling the steep squirming sandy incline under one's slowed-down, leaden tread. Yes, the inhuman constant levelling, and the two-dimensional, angled aspect which we see of it, these are the characteristics of water that unnerve us. And drowning, of course, drowning is strange, I mean strange for those on shore. It all seems done so discreetly. The onlooker, attention caught by a distant feathery cry, peers out intently but sees nothing of the struggle, the helpless silencing, the awful slow-motion thrashing, the last, long fall into the bottomless and ever-blackening blue. No. All that is to be seen is a moment of white water, and a hand, languidly sinking.

The sea was not blue now, though; it hardly ever is. In our latitudes it is more often a gleaming grey, or purplish, like a bruise, or, after the churnings of a gale, marl-coloured. But rarely, rarely blue.

The black bird on the rock opened wide its wings and shook them vigorously and after a long moment of absolute, cruciform stillness carefully refolded them.

When I was young I had no fear of the sea, and loved the beach. Disporting myself on that narrow strip of not-quite-land wedged between sky and water, I would feel all down the imperceptibly declining curve of the afternoon a sense of the great world's glamour. Some girl in cheap sunglasses and crimpled swimsuit would catch my attention and seem a glimmering naiad. The yard of undersprung soft sand at the edge of the waves was a trampoline on which I trod with a gracefulness not to be achieved elsewhere in the gawky world of boyhood. And then the sea itself, running off flat to the low horizon, like a limitless promise—no, I had no dread of it, then. As a boy I was a fair swimmer, in my unruly way, all splash and thrash. Especially I loved to dive, loved that moment of breathless almost-panic under water, the eerie greenish glow, the bulging silence, the sense of slide and shift and sway. My father too was fascinated by things maritime. He did not swim, had never been out on the ocean, but he was irresistibly drawn to its margins. He would roll up the bottoms of his trousers and paddle in the shallows, like all the other fathers, but away from them, keeping himself to himself. In my memory it is like a scene in one of those gaudy seaside postcards of the time, him there in his sleeveless pullover and sun hat made from a white handkerchief knotted at the corners, paddling in the running surf, while up the beach my mother sits on a towel with her embarrassingly bare legs stuck straight out before her, deep in a novelette. Later, when the sun lost strength and the light grew heavy, and we collected our things and mashed our way back through the dunes in the direction of the train station, my father would maintain a remote, frowning silence, which even my mother would not try to break, as if he had been away somewhere distant, and had seen incommunicable things.

A shimmer, a shiver in the air. Uncanny sensation, as of a chill presentiment. I peered about the beach. Still there was no one, yet I seemed not alone. I felt a sudden, familiar cold, and scrambled to my feet and at a half-crouch scuttled up the beach in fright. Had my phantoms followed me? At the edge of the hazel wood there was a sort of hut part sunk in the sand, a hide for hunters, I suppose, made of tarred planks warped by sunlight and the salt winds, just three walls and a leaning roof and a board wedged lengthwise to make a bench for sitting. The thing was so old and weathered it had lost almost all trace of human industry, and seemed one with the gnarled trees massed behind it, with the scaly sand and clumps of podded seaweed and strewn driftwood. I went inside and sat down, out of sight of that inhospitable shoreline and the sighing waves. There was the usual litter of cigarette ends and rusty cans and yellowed scraps of newsprint. I imagined myself a fugitive landing up here out of the way of the world's harm. Perhaps, I thought, perhaps this is what I need to do, finally to give it all up, home, wife, possessions, renounce it all for good, rid myself of every last thing and come and live in some such unconsidered spot as this. What would I require for survival, except a cup, a dish, a blanket? Free then of all encumbrance, all distraction, I might be able at last to confront myself without shock or shrinking. For is this not what I am after, the pure conjunction, the union of self with sundered self? I am weary of division, of being always torn. I shut my eyes and in a sort of rapture see myself stepping backward slowly into the cloven shell, and the two halves of it, still moist with glair, closing around me . . .

When I came out of the hut and looked about again the day seemed different, as if the light had shifted, as if a shadow had swept across the sand and left something behind it, a darkening, a chill. Beyond the little waves a patch of water grew a hump, and then there was a heave, and a brief churning, and a figure reared up, clad all in black, with a flashing mask for a face and carrying in one hand what seemed a slender trident. My heart reared on its tethers, bumping like a wind-tossed balloon. The seabird rose from its rock and flew away with a lazily majestic motion. Then Poseidon pulled off his mask and spat, and, seeing me, waved his harpoon gun and flip-flopped away over the shingle. His rubber suit had the same thick dull sheen as the seabird's plumage. I turned and plunged into the wood, blunderingly. Coming, I had got lost, and now I thought I knew the straight way back, but I was wrong.

I am thinking of my daughter. At once an angry buzzing of emotions starts up in my breast. She exasperates me, I confess it. I do not trust her. I know, I know, there is even a name for the syndrome from which she suffers, yet half the time I think there is nothing at all the matter with her, that her fits and fallings, her obsessions, her black days and violent sleepless nights, are all no more than a strategy to make me pay for some enormity she imagines I visited on her in the far past. At times she has a look, a fleeting, sidelong, faintly smiling look, in which I seem to glimpse a wholly other she, cold and sly and secretly laughing. With such ingenuity does she connect the workings of the world to her own fate. Everything that happens, she is convinced, carries a specific and personal reference to her. There is nothing, not a turn in the weather, or a chance word spoken in the street, that does not covertly pass on to her some profound message of warning or encouragement. I used to try to reason with her, talking myself into spluttering, head-shaking, wildly laughing transports of frustration and rage, while she stood silently before me, as if in the stocks, shoulders up and arms hanging and her chin drawn down to her collarbone, frowning in sullen refusal and defiance. There was no keeping track of her moods, I never knew when she might veer aside and turn and confront me with a new version of herself, a whole new map of that strange, intense and volatile world that she alone inhabits. For that is how she makes it seem, that she lives in a place where there is no one else. What an actor she is! She puts on a character with an ease and persuasiveness that I could never match. Yet perhaps she is not feigning, perhaps that is her secret, that she does not act, but variously *is*. Like the sorcerer's assistant, she steps smiling into the spangled casket and comes out the other side transfigured.

Lydia never shared my doubts. This is, of course, another source of annoyance to me. How she would run to Cass, breathless with forced enthusiasm, and try to press her into the latest game she had devised to divert the child's attention from herself and her manias. And Cass would play along for a while, all smiles and trembling enthusiasm, only to turn away in the end and retreat again listlessly into herself. Then Lydia would seem the crestfallen child and Cass the withholding adult.

She was five or six when she displayed the first symptoms of her condition. I came home late one night after a performance and she was standing in her nightdress in the darkness at the top of the stairs, talking. Even yet, as I remember her there, a slow shiver crawls across the back of my scalp. Her eyes were open and her face was empty of expression; she looked like a waxwork model of herself. She was speaking in a low, uninflected voice, the voice of an oracle. I could not make out what she was saying except that it was something about an owl, and the moon. I thought she must be rehearsing in her sleep a nursery rhyme or jingle out of infancy. I took her by the shoulders and turned her about and walked her back to her room. She is the one who at such times is supposed to experience strange auras, but that night it was I who noticed the smell. It was the smell, I am convinced, of what was, is, wrong with her. It is not at all extraordinary, just a dull flat grey faint stink, like that of unwashed hair, or a garment left in a drawer and gone stale. I recognised it. I had an uncle, he died when I was young, I barely remember him, who played the accordion, and wore his hat in the house, and walked with a crutch. He had that smell, too. The crutch was an old-fashioned one, a single thick rough stave and a curved crosspiece padded with sweat-stained cloth; the part of the upright where his hand grasped it was polished to the texture of grey silk. I thought it was this crutch that smelled, but now I think it was the very odour of affliction itself. Cass's room in the lamplight was obsessively neat, as always— there is a touch of the nun to our Cass—yet to my alarmed heart it seemed a site of wild disorder. I made her lie down on the bed, still murmuring, her eyes fixed on my face, her hands clutching mine, and it was as if I were letting her sink into some dark deep pool, under a willow, at dead of night. Sleepily Lydia appeared in the doorway behind us, a hand in her hair, wanting to know what was the matter. I sat down on the side of the narrow bed, still holding Cass's cold pale hands. I looked at the toys on the shelves, at the lampshade stuck with faded transfers; on the wallpaper, cartoon characters pranced and grinned. I felt the darkness pressing around our cave of lamplight like the ogre in a fairy tale. A gloating moon hung crookedly in the window above the bed and when I looked up it seemed to tip me a fat wink, knowing and horrible. Cass's voice when she spoke was scratchy and dry, a fall of dust in a parched place.

"They're telling me things, Daddy," she said, and her fingers holding mine tightened like wires. "They're telling me things."

What things the voices told her, what actions they urged, she would never say. They were her secret. She had periods of respite, weeks, months, even, when of their own accord they would go silent. How still the house seemed then, as if a clamour audible to all had lapsed. But presently, when my ears had adjusted, I would become aware again of that sustained note of anxiety that was always there, in every room, thin and piercing enough to shatter the frail glass of any hope. Of the three of us, Cass was the calmest in face of these disorders. Indeed, such was her calm at times that she would seem to be not there at all, to have drifted off, lighter than air. It is a different air in which she moves, a separate medium. For her I think the world is always somewhere other, an unfamiliar place where yet she has always been. This is for me the hardest thing, to think of her out there, standing on some far bleak deserted shore, beyond help, in unmoving light, with an ocean of lostness all before her and the siren voices singing in her head. She was always alone, always outside. One day when I was collecting her from school I came upon her looking down the length of a long, green-painted corridor to where at the far end a raucous group of girls was gathered. They were preparing for some game or outing, and their laughter and sharp cries made the deadened air ring. Cass stood with her schoolbag clasped to her breast, leaning forward a little, with her head on one side, frowning, helplessly eager, like a naturalist glimpsing some impossible, brilliant-hued new species that had alighted on the far bank of an unfordable river and in a moment would rise and fly away again, into the deeps of the forest, where she could not hope to follow. When she heard my step she looked up at me and smiled, my Miranda, and her eyes did that trick they had of seeming to turn over in their sockets like two flat metal discs to show their blank, defensive backs. We walked together in silence out to the street, where she stopped and stood for a moment motionless, looking at the ground. A March wind grey as her school overcoat whipped up an eddy of dust on the pavement at our feet. The cathedral bell had been ringing, the last reverberations fell about us, wrinkling the air. She told me how in history class they had learned about Joan of Arc and her voices. She raised her eyes and narrowed them and smiled again, looking off toward the river.

"Do you think they'll burn me at the stake, too?" she said. It was to become one of her jokes.

Memory is peculiar in the fierce hold with which it will fix the most insignificant-seeming scenes. Whole tracts of my life have fallen away like a cliff into the sea, yet I cling to seeming trivia with a pop-eyed tenacity. Often in these idle days, and in the wakeful nights especially, I pass the time picking over the parts of this or that remembered moment, like a blackbird grubbing among dead leaves, searching for the one telling thing lurking in the clay, among the wood-scurf and dried husks and discarded wing casings, the morsel that will give meaning to a meaningless remembrance, the fat grub concealed in open sight under the camouflage of the accidental. There are times with Cass that should be burned into the inner lining of my skull, times that I thought as I endured them I would never be so fortunate as to forget—the nights by the telephone, the hours spent watching over the crouched unmoving form under the tangled sheets, the ashen waits in anonymous consulting rooms—that yet seem to me now no more than the vague remnants of bad dreams, while an idle word of hers, a look thrown back from a doorway, an aimless car journey with her slumped silent beside me, resonate in my mind, rife with significance.

There is the icy Christmas afternoon when I took her to the park to try out her first pair of roller skates. The trees were white with hoar-frost and a crepuscular pinkish mist hung in the motionless air. I was not in a pretty mood; the place was full of screaming children and their irritatingly forbearing fathers. Cass on her skates clung to me with trembling fierceness and would not let go. It was like teaching a tiny invalid the rudiments of mobility. In the end she lost her balance and the edge of her skate struck me on the ankle and I swore at her and furiously shook off her clutching hand and she teetered this way and that for a moment and then her legs shot out from under her and she sat down suddenly on the cindered path. What a look she gave me.

There was another day when she fell again, a day in April, it was, and we were walking together in the hills. The weather was wintry still. There had been a brief fall of soft wet snow, and now the sun had come infirmly out, and the sky was made of pale glass, and the gorse was a yellow flame against the whiteness, and all about us water was dripping and trickling and covertly running under the lush, flattened grass. I remarked that the snow was icy, and she pretended to think I had said icing, and wanted to know where the cake was, and held her sides in exaggerated hilarity, doing her snuffly laugh. She was never a gainly girl, and that day she was wearing rubber boots and a heavy padded coat that made the going all the harder, and when we were coming down a stony track between two walls of blue-black pines she tripped and fell over and cut her lip. The drops of her blood against the patchwork snow were a definition of redness. I snatched her up and held her to me, a bulky warm ball of woe, and one of her quicksilver tears ran into my mouth. I think of the two of us there, among the shivering trees, the birdsong, the gossipy swift whisperings of trickling water, and something sags in me, sags, and rebounds with a weary effort. What is happiness but a refined form of pain?

The route I took coming back from that unsettling visit to the beach brought me upland somehow. I was not aware of climbing until at last I came out on the hill road, at the spot where I had stopped in the car that winter night, the night of the animal. The day was hot; light hummed above the fields. I stood on the brow of the hill and the spired town was there below me, huddled in its pale-blue haze. I could see the square, and the house, and the shining white wall of the Stella Maris convent. A little brown bird flitted silently upward from branch to branch of a thorn tree at the side of the road. Beyond the town the sea now was a mirage-like expanse that merged into the sky without horizon. It was that torpid hour of afternoon in summer when all falls silent and even the birds cease their twitterings. At such a time, in such a place, a man might lose his grip on all that he is. As I stood there in the stillness I became aware of an almost imperceptible sound, a sort of attenuated, smoothed-out warbling. It puzzled me, until I realised that what I was hearing was simply the noise of the world, the medleyed voice of everything in the world, just going on, and my heart was almost soothed.

I walked down through the town. It was Sunday and the streets were empty, and the glossy black windows of shut shops stared at me disapprovingly as I went past. A wedge of inky shadow sliced the main street neatly into halves. On one side parked cars squatted hotly in the sun. A small boy threw a stone at me and ran off laughing. I suppose I was a motley sight, with my nascent beard and unkempt hair and no doubt staring eyes. A dog came and sniffed at the cuffs of my trousers with fastidious twitchings of its snout. Where am I here, boy, youth, young man, broken-down actor? This is the place that I should know, the place where I grew up, but I am a stranger, no one can put a name to my face, I cannot even do it myself, with any surety. There is no present, the past is random, and only the future is fixed. To cease becoming and merely be, to stand as a statue in some forgotten dead-leafed square, released from destruction, enduring the seasons equably, the rain and snow and sun, taken for granted even by the birds, how would that be? I turned for home, with a bottle of milk and a brown-paper bag of eggs bought from a crone in a hole-in-the-wall down a lane.

Someone was in the house, I knew it as soon as I crossed the threshold. With the milk and the bag of eggs in my hands I stood motionless, not breathing, nostrils flared and one ear lifted, an animal invaded in its lair. Calm summer light stood in the hall and three flies were circling in tight formation under a peculiarly repulsive, bare grey light-bulb. Not a sound. What was it that was amiss, what scent or signal had I caught? There was a flaw in the atmosphere, a lingering ripple where someone had passed through. Cautiously I moved from room to room, mounted the stairs, the tendons in my knees creaking, even peered into the damp-smelling broom cupboard behind the scullery door, but found no one lurking there. Outside, then? I went to the windows, checking the co-ordinates of my world: the square in front, innocent of any sign that I could see, and at the back the garden, tree, fields, far hills, all Sunday-still in the cottony light of afternoon. I was in the kitchen when I heard a sound behind me. My scalp tingled and a bead of sweat came out at the hairline and ran a little way swiftly down my forehead and stopped. I turned. A girl was standing in the doorway with the light of the hall behind her. The first impression I had was of a general slight lopsidedness. Her eyes were not quite level, and her mouth drooped at one side in the slack lewd way of the bored young. Even the hem of her dress was crooked. She said nothing, only stood there eyeing me with dull candour. Some moments of uncertain silence passed. I might have taken her for another hallucination, but she was far too solidly herself for that. Still neither of us spoke, then there was a shuffle and a cough, and behind her Quirke appeared, stooping apologetically, the nervous fingers of one hand jiggling at his side. Today he was wearing a blue blazer with brass buttons and a high shine on the elbows, a shirt that had once been white, narrow tie, grey slacks sagging in the rear, grey leather slip-ons with buckles on the insteps, white socks. He had cut himself shaving again, a bit of bloodstained toilet paper was stuck to his chin, a white floweret with a tiny rust-red heart. Under his arm he carried a large scuffed black cardboard box tied with a black silk ribbon.

"You asked about the house," he said—had I? "I have it all"—bending a glance in the direction of the box—"here."

He stepped past the girl and came forward eagerly and put the box on the kitchen table and undid the ribbon and with loving deftness set out his documents, fanning them like a hand of outsize cards, talking the while. "I'm what you might call a spoilt solicitor," he said with a melancholy leer, showing big, wax-coloured teeth. He was leaning across the table, holding out to me a sheaf of yellow-edged pages crawled all over by elaborate sepia script. I took them and held them in my hands and looked at them; they had the flat, mildewed fragrance of dried chrysanthemums. I scanned the words. *Whereas . . . hereinunder . . . given this day of . . .* A gathering yawn made my nostrils tighten. The girl came and stood at Quirke's shoulder and looked on in listless curiosity. He had launched into an elaborate account of a historic, long-running and intricate dispute over land rent and boundaries and rights of way, illustrating each stage of the wrangle with its piece of parchment, its deeds, its map. As he spoke I saw the players in the little drama, the shovel-hatted fathers and long-suffering mothers, the hothead sons, the languishing consumptive daughters with their needlepoint and novels. And I pictured Quirke, too, got up in fustian, like them, high-collared in a dank attic room, crouched over his papers by the glimmer of a guttering candle stub, while the night wind sighed through the slates and cats prowled the cramped back gardens under a moon like a paring of polished tin . . . "The son got hold of the old one's will and burned it," he was saying in a husky, confiding whisper, shutting one eye and portentously nodding. "And that of course would have left *him* . . ." He reached out a tapered and faintly trembling forefinger and tapped the top page of the papers where I held them. "Do you see?"

"I do," I said, earnestly, though I lied.

He waited, scanning my face, then sighed; there is no satisfying the hobbyist's hunger. Dispirited, he turned aside and gazed morosely through the window out to the garden with unseeing eyes. The sunlight was turning brazen as the afternoon lost strength. The girl nudged him with a lazy sideways movement of her hip and he blinked. "Oh, yes," he said, "this is Lily." She gave me a cheerless down-turned smile and made a mock curtsey. "You'll be in need of help around the house," he said. "Lily will see to it."

Peeved and doleful, he gathered up his papers and put them into the box and shut the lid and knotted the black silk ribbon; I noticed again the deftness of those maidenly fingers. He fished his bicycle clips from his blazer pocket and bent and put them on, grunting. The girl and I together looked down at the top of his head and the slick of sandy hair and the bowed shoulders with their light snowfall of dandruff. We might have been the parents and he the overgrown, unlovely son of whom we were less than proud. He straightened, now suggesting for a second a pan-talooned palace eunuch, with his yeasty pallor and his white socks and slips-ons upturned at the toes.

"I'll be off," he said.

I walked with him down the hall to the front door. Outside, his bicycle was lying against its lamppost in a state of exaggerated collapse, front wheel upturned and handlebars askew, like a comic impersonating a drunk. He righted it and clipped the document box to the carrier and in moody silence mounted up and rode away. He has a manner of cycling that is all his own, sitting far back on the saddle with shoulders drooping forward and paunch upturned, steering with one hand while the other rests limply in his lap, his knees going up and down like pistons that are not working but merely idling. Halfway across the square he braked and stopped and put a balletic toe to the ground and turned and looked back; I waved; he went on.

In the kitchen the girl was standing at the sink lethargically going through the motions of washing up. She is not a pretty child, and not, by the look of her, particularly clean, either. She kept her head down when I came in. I crossed the room and sat at the table. Butter in its dish had separated in the sun, a greasy puddle of curds; a slice of staling bread was scalloped decoratively along its edges by the heat. The milk and the bag of eggs were there where I had left them. I looked at the girl's pale long neck and rat's tails of colourless hair. I cleared my throat, and drummed my fingers on the table.

"And tell me, Lily," I said, "what age are you?"

I detected a sinister, oily smoothness in my voice, the voice of a sly old roué trying to sound harmless.

"Seventeen," she answered without hesitation; I am sure she is far younger than that.

"And do you go to school?"

A crooked shrug, the right shoulder rising, the left let fall.

"Used to."

I rose from the table and went and stood beside her, leaning back against the draining board with my arms and ankles crossed.

Stance, and tone, these are the important things; once you have the tone and the stance the part plays itself. Lily's hands in the hot water were raw to the wrists, as if she were wearing a pair of pink surgical gloves. They are Quirke's hands, shapely and delicate. She set a mug upside down on the board in a froth of opalescent bubbles. I enquired mildly if she did not think she should rinse off the suds. She went still and stood a moment, looking into the sink, then turned her head slowly and gave me a dead-eyed stare that made me blench. Deliberately she picked up the mug and held it under the running tap and thumped it down again. I tottered hurriedly back to my place at the table, feathers all awry. How do they manage to be so discomfiting, the young, with no more than a glance, a grimace? Presently she finished the dishes, and dried her hands on a rag; her fingers, I noticed, were nicotine-stained. "I have a daughter, you know," I said, sounding the fond old fumbling booby now. "Older than you. Catherine is her name. We call her Cass." She might not have heard me. I watched her as she stored away the still-damp cups and saucers; how well she knows their places, it must be a female instinct. When she was done she stood a moment looking about her dimly, then turned to go, but paused, as if she had just remembered my existence, and looked at me, wrinkling her nose.

"Are you famous?" she said, in a tone of arch incredulity.

It has always seemed to me a disgrace that the embarrassments of early life should continue to smart throughout adulthood with undiminished intensity. Is it not enough that our youthful blunders made us cringe at the time, when we were at our tenderest, but must stay with us beyond cure, burn marks ready to flare up painfully at the merest touch? No: an indiscretion from earliest adolescence will still bring a blush to the cheek of the nonagenarian on his deathbed. The moment is here when I must bring out into the light one of those scorched patches from my past that I would far prefer to leave in the cool dark of forgetfulness. It is that I began my career, not in a polo-neck part in some uncompromisingly avant-garde production in a basement twenty-seater, but on the amateur stage, in an echoing community hall, in my home town, before an audience of gaping provincials. The piece was one of those rural dramas that were still being written at the time, all cawbeens and blackthorn sticks and shawled biddies lamenting their lost sons beside fake turf fires. I redden even yet when I recall the first night. The comic lines were received in respectful silence while the moments of high tragedy provoked storms of mirth. When the curtain had finally fallen, backstage had the air of an operating theatre where the last of the victims of some natural disaster have been swabbed and sewn and trolleyed away, while we actors stood about like walking wounded, squeezing each other's upper arms in sympathetic solidarity and hearing ourselves swallow.

I wish I could say we were a colourful troupe, all charming scamps and complaisant local beauties, but in truth we were a sad and shabby little lot. We met for rehearsals three times a week in a freezing church hall lent us by a stage-struck parish priest. I had the part of the brawny hero's younger brother, the sensitive one, who planned to be a teacher and set up a school in the village. I had not known that I could act, until Dora took me in hand and led me forward into the limelight. Dora: my first manifestation of the muse. She was a stocky, compact person with short-cropped wiry hair and spectacles with frames of clear pink plastic. I recall her provocatively meaty smell, which even the strongest perfume could not entirely overcome. She had joined the Priory Players in search of a husband, I suspect, and instead found me. I was seventeen, and although she cannot have been more than thirty she seemed immensely old to me, excitingly so, a sort of inverted mother, carnal and profane. I thought she had hardly noticed me, until one blustery October evening when we had broken early from rehearsals and she invited me to come with her to the pub for a drink. We were the last to leave the hall. She was busy putting on her raincoat and did not look at me directly. There are occasions when one catches memory at its work, scanning the details of the moment and storing them up for a future time. As she struggled with a recalcitrant sleeve, I noted the oleaginous slither of light down the side of her plastic coat, and the paraffin stove that was ticking in a corner of the hall behind her as the expiring flame ran around the turned-down wick with ever more desperate haste, and the door in the vestibule blowing, and through the doorway massed dark trees and a jagged cleft of molten silver in the stormy western sky. At last she got her arm into that sleeve and looked up at me with a wry half-smile, one defensively ironical eyebrow lifted; a woman like Dora learns to anticipate refusals.

We walked in silence together through a livid twilight down to the quays, where tethered trawlers lurched in the swell and a bell on a buoy out in the harbour clanged and clanged. Dora kept her eyes fixed firmly on the way ahead, and I had the worrying suspicion that she was trying not to laugh. In the pub she sat on a high stool with her legs crossed, displaying a glossy knee. She asked for a gin and tonic and allowed me to strike a match with a shaky hand and hold it to the elusive tip of her cigarette. I had never been in a pub before, had never ordered a drink, or lit a lady's cigarette. As I sought to catch the barman's eye I was aware of Dora's candid gaze roaming over my face, my hands, my clothes. When I turned back to her she did not look away, only lifted her chin and gave me a hard, brazen, smiling stare. I cannot remember what we talked about. She smoked her cigarette like a man, pulling on it with violent concentration, her shoulders hunched and eyes narrowed. Her bust and hips were full, the flesh packed tight inside her short grey dress. The smoke and the silver-sweet fumes of the gin worked on my senses. I would have liked to put my hand on her knee; I could almost feel the taut, silky stuff of her stocking under my fingers. She was still looking into my face with that challenging, half-mocking smile, and I grew flustered and kept trying to avoid her eye. She finished her drink with a toss of the head and got down from the stool and put on her coat and said that she had to go. When we were at the door of the pub she paused, allowing me time to . . . I did not know what. As she turned away I thought I heard her heave a small sharp sigh. We parted on the quayside. I stood and watched her stride off into the darkness, head down and shoulders braced against the cold. The wind from the sea buffeted her, making her wiry curls shake and plastering her coat against her body. The click of her high heels on the pavement was like the sound of something walking up my spine.

After that she went back to ignoring me, until one night I met her coming through from the lavatory at the back of the hall, frowning to herself and carrying a glass of water, and in an access of daring that made my heart set up a panic-stricken knocking I pushed her into the woolly dark of the alcove where the coats were kept and kissed her clumsily and put a hand on her disconcertingly armoured, firm hot breast. She took off her spectacles accommodatingly and her eyes went vague and swam in their sockets like dreamy fish. Her mouth tasted of smoke and toothpaste and something feety that made my blood flare. After a long, swollen moment she did her throaty chuckle and put a hand against my chest and pushed me away, not ungently. She was still holding the glass; she looked at it, and laughed again, and the surface of the water tinily trembled, and a drop of moisture quick as mercury ran zigzag down the misted side.

So began our liaison, if that is not too large a word. It was hardly more than a matter of a few crushed kisses, a tremulous brushing of hands, a flash of whey-white thigh in the gap between two cinema seats, a silent tussle ending in a hissed *No!* and the melancholy snap of released elastic. I suppose she could not take me entirely seriously, callow youth that I still was. "I'm a cradle-snatcher," she would say, shaking her head and heaving an exaggeratedly rueful sigh. I never felt I had her full attention, for she seemed always faintly preoccupied, as if she were listening past me, intent on some hoped-for response from elsewhere. When I held her in my arms I would have the eerie sensation that she was looking past my shoulder at another presence standing behind me, someone there whom only she could see, watching us in anguish, it might be, or helpless fury. She had too an unsettling way of smiling to herself when we were alone together, her lips twitching and eyes slitted, as if she were enjoying a secret, spiteful joke. I think now there must have been something in her past—dashed hopes, betrayal, an absconded fiancé—for which through me she was taking a phantom revenge.

She would tell me nothing about herself. She lived in the north end of town, in a rough hinterland of council houses and Saturday-night fights. Only once did she allow me to walk her home. It was deep winter by now, and there was a heavy frost and the darkness glistened and everything was very still and silent, and our footsteps rang on the iron of the frozen pavements. There was hardly a soul abroad. The few night walkers we met seemed to me the very picture of loneliness, huddled into their coats and mufflers, and I felt an uneasy sense of pride, going along with this mysterious warm provoking woman on my arm. The icy air was like a shower of tiny needles against my face, and I was reminded of the slap my mother had given me all those years before, on the day of my father's death. When we were near her house Dora made me stop and kissed me brusquely and hurried on alone. In the stillness of the vast cold night I stood and heard the scrape of coins as she fished in her purse for her key, heard the key going into the lock, heard the door open and then close behind her. A wireless set was playing somewhere, dance band melodies, a tinny music, quaint and mournful. Above me a shooting star whizzed through its brief arc and I fancied I heard it, a rush, a swish, a sigh.

It was for Dora, offstage, that I gave my first real performances, filled my first authentic roles. How I posed and preened in the mirror of her sceptical regard. Onstage, too, I saw my talent reflected in her. One night I turned in the midst of my curtain speech— *"And which of us, brother, will Ballybog remember?"*—and caught the flash of her specs in the wings from where she was watching me narrowly, and under the heat of her sullen envy something opened in me like a hand and I stepped at last into the part as if it were my own skin. Never looked back, after that.

The curtain goes down, the interval bar is invaded, and in the space of the huge silence that settles on the briefly emptied auditorium, thirty years fleet past. It is another first night and, for me, a last. I am at what the critics would call, reaching down again into their capacious bag of clichés, the height of my powers. I have had triumphs from here to Adelaide and back. I have held a thousand audiences in the palm of my hand, ditto a bevy of leading ladies. The headlines I have made!—my favourite is the one they wrote after my first American tour: *Alexander Finds New World to Conquer.* Inside his suit of armour, however, all was not well with our flawed hero. When the collapse came, I was the only one who was not surprised. For months I had been beset by bouts of crippling self-consciousness. I would involuntarily fix on a bit of myself, a finger, a foot, and gape at it in a kind of horror, paralysed, unable to understand how it made its movements, what force was guiding it. In the street I would catch sight of my reflection in a shop window, skulking along with head down and shoulders up and my elbows pressed into my sides, like a felon bearing a body away, and I would falter, and almost fall, breathless as if from a blow, overwhelmed by the inescapable predicament of being what I was. It was this at last that took me by the throat onstage that night and throttled the words as I was speaking them, this hideous awareness, this insupportable excess of self. Next day there was a great fuss, of course, and much amused speculation as to what it was that had befallen me. Everyone assumed that drink was the cause of my lapse. The incident achieved a brief notoriety. One of the newspapers—in a front-page story, no less—quoted a disgruntled member of the audience as saying that it had been like witnessing a giant statue toppling off its pedestal and smashing into rubble on the stage. I could not decide whether to feel offended or flattered by the comparison. I should have preferred to be likened to Agamemnon, say, or Coriolanus, some such high doomed hero staggering under the weight of his own magnificence.

I see the scene in scaled-down form, everything tiny and manically detailed, as in one of those maquettes that stage designers love to play with. There I am stuck, in my Theban general's costume, mouth open, mute as a fish, with the cast at a standstill around me, appalled and staring, like onlookers at the scene of a gruesome accident. From curtain-up everything had been going steadily awry. The theatre was hot, and in my breastplate and robe I felt as if I were bound in swaddling clothes. Sweat dimmed my sight and I seemed to be delivering my lines through a wetted gag. *"Who if not I, then, is Amphitryon?"* I cried—it is now for me the most poignant line in all drama—and suddenly everything shifted on to another plane and I was at once there and not there. It was like the state that survivors of heart attacks describe, I seemed to be onstage and at the same time looking down on myself from somewhere up in the flies. Nothing in the theatre is as horribly thrilling as the moment when an actor dries. My mind was whirling and flailing like the broken belt of a runaway engine. I had not forgotten my lines—in fact, I could see them clearly before me, as if written on a prompt card—only I could not speak them. While I gagged and sweated, the young fellow playing Mercury, who in the guise of Amphitryon's servant Sosia was supposed to be cruelly taunting me on the loss of my identity, stood transfixed behind plywood crenellations, looking down at me with terrified eyes in which I am convinced I could see myself doubly reflected, two tiny, bulbous Amphitryons, both struck speechless. Before me, in the wings, my stage-wife Alcmene was trying to prompt me, reading from the text and frantically mouthing my lines. She was a pretty girl, preposterously young; since the beginning of rehearsals we had been engaged behind the scenes in an unconvinced dalliance, and now as she writhed there in the looming half-darkness, her mouth working mutely like the valve of an undersea creature, I felt embarrassed less for myself than for her, this child who that very afternoon had lain in my arms weeping sham tears of ecstasy, and I wanted to cross the stage quickly and put a restraining finger tenderly to her lips and tell her that it was all right, that it was all all right. At last, seeing in my face, I suppose, something of what I was thinking, she let the text fall to her side and stood and looked at me with a mixture of unconcealable pity, impatience and contempt. The moment was so grotesquely apt to the point we had arrived at in our so-called love affair—both silent, lost for words, confronting each other in dumb hopelessness—that despite my distress I almost laughed. Instead, with an effort, and with more fondness than I had managed to show to her even in the intensest toils of passion, I nodded, the barest nod, in apology and rueful gratitude, and looked away. Meanwhile, behind me in the auditorium the atmosphere was pinging like a violin string screwed to snapping point. There was much coughing. Someone tittered. I glimpsed Lydia's stricken white face looking up at me from the stalls, and I remember thinking, *Thank God Cass is not here.* I turned about and with funereal tread, seeming to wade into the very boards of the stage, made a grave, unsteady exit, comically creaking and clanking in my armour. Already the curtain was coming down, I could feel it descending above my head, ponderous and solid as a stone portcullis. From the audience there were jeers now, and a scattering of half-heartedly sympathetic applause. In the dimness backstage I had a sense of figures running to and fro. One of the actors behind me spoke my name in a furious stage whisper. With a yard or two still to go I lost my nerve entirely and made a sort of run for it and practically fell into the wings, while the gods' vast dark laughter shook the scenery around me.

I should have had another Dora, to mock me out of my malady of selfness. She would have grasped my neck in a wrestler's hold—she could be rough, could Dora—and rubbed her rubbery breasts against my back and laughed, showing teeth and gums and epiglottis with its quivering pink polyp, and I would have been cured. As it was, I had to flee, of course. How could I show my face in public, to my public, after the mask had so spectacularly slipped? So I ran away, not far, and hid my head here in shame.

Before I fled I did seek help in discovering what might be the exact nature of my malady, though more out of curiosity, I think, than any hope of a cure. In a drinking club late one gin-soaked night I met a fellow thesp who some years previously had suffered a collapse similar to mine. He was far gone in drink by now, and I had to spend a grisly hour listening to him pour out his tale of woe, with many slurs and wearisome repetitions. Then all at once he sobered up, in that disconcerting way that unhappy drunks sometimes manage to do, and said that I must see his man—that was how he put it, in a ringing, cut-glass voice that silenced the surrounding tables, *"Cleave, you must see my man!"*—and wrote down on the back of a cardboard beer mat the address of a therapist who, he assured me, tapping a finger to the side of his nose, was the very soul of discretion. I forgot all about it, until a week or two later I found the beer mat in my pocket, and looked up the telephone number, and found myself one glassy April evening at the unmarked door of a nondescript red-brick house in a leafy suburb, feeling inexplicably nervous, my heart racing and palms wet, as if I were about to go onstage in the most difficult part I had ever played, which was the case, I suppose, since the part I must play was myself, and I had no lines learned.

The therapist, whose name was Lewis, or Louis—I never did discover whether it was a first or surname—was an oldish young man with very beautiful, dark-brown, haunted eyes. He gave me an undertaker's handshake and led me up carpeted stairs that made me think of my mother's lodging house, and deposited me in a cramped and faintly smelly waiting room looking through net curtains down into a yard with dustbins and a cat. A quarter of an hour passed. The house around me had a funereal, tensely waiting atmosphere, as if in certain expectation of frightful occurrences about to take place. Not a sound stirred the silence. I imagined Lewis locked in terrible, wordless commune with some hapless wretch far sicker than I was, and I saw myself a fraud, and was tempted to run away. Presently he came and fetched me to his consulting room on the first floor—gunmetal desk, two armchairs, porridge-coloured carpet—and I launched at once into a gabbling and faintly hysterical confession of how fraudulent I felt. He held up a fine, hairless hand and smiled, closing his eyes briefly, and shook his head. I suppose it was the kind of thing he heard from all first-timers. I could not let it go, however, and said I really did not know why I was there, and was startled when he agreed and said that he did not know, either. I had not realised he was being humorous. "Why don't you try to tell me," he said gently, "and then maybe we'll both know." My wariness deepened, for I suspected he knew very well who I was, and what the matter was, for it was only a week or two since my disgrace had been splashed, liked vomit, all over the newspapers. I supposed it might be bad manners on his part, professionally speaking—indeed, bad ethics—to admit to any knowledge gathered outside this room. Anyway, so far as our hour together was concerned there *was* no outside. The therapist's room, where even the silence is different, is a world to itself. Certainly, my experiences with Cass were of no help to me here. Indeed, Cass did not enter my thoughts at all. One's troubles are always unique.

We sat in the armchairs, facing each other, with the desk to one side of us like a watchful referee. I have only the haziest recollection of what things I told him. There were frequent, awkward silences. At one point, to my annoyance, though not unexpectedly, tears came into my eyes. He contributed little, in the way of words, though his attendance on mine had a marked if enigmatic eloquence. Two things that he said I do clearly remember. I had complained that I was not happy, and hastened to laugh and say I supposed he was about to ask me why I thought I should be, but to my surprise he shook his head, and turned aside and looked out through the bay window behind the desk into the boughs of the chestnut tree outside that was coming into leaf, and said that no, on the contrary, he believed that joy is the natural state of human beings. He went on to refine this statement, acknowledging that of course we do not always know what is natural or best for us, but I was hardly listening, for the notion was so amazing to me it left me speechless, literally, and the session ended early that day.

The other thing I remember him saying is that I seemed to him to be overwhelmed—that was the word he used. I thought this fanciful, even a touch melodramatic, and said so. He persisted, however, by which I mean that he did not argue or protest, but only sat in silence, watching me with an alert, calm gaze, and after a moment's consideration I had to agree with him, and said, yes, overwhelmed, that was exactly how I felt. "But what is it that is overwhelming me?" I said, more in impatience than entreaty. "That is what I want to know." Needless to say, he did not offer an answer. I did not go to him again after that, not because I was disappointed, or angry that he had not been able to help me, but simply because there seemed nothing more for me to say to him. I suspect he felt this too, for when I was leaving that day he shook my hand with a warmer pressure than usual, and his smile was weighed with melancholy sadness; it was the smile of a father seeing his troubled son step out into the world to fend for himself. I think of him with nostalgia, almost with a sense of loss. Perhaps he did help me, without my realising it. The silence in that room of his was like a balm. I wrote to Cass and told her about him. It was a kind of confession, ill-masked with facetious humour; a kind of apology, too, as I took my place shamefacedly in the lower ranks of the high consistory of which she was an adept of long standing. She did not reply. I had signed myself The Overwhelmed.

What am I to do about this girl, this Lily? She preys on my mind, which has, I know, too little to occupy it. I feel like an impotent satrap presented by his subjects with yet another superfluous concubine. Her presence makes the house seem impossibly overcrowded. She has upset the balance of things. My phantom woman and her more phantasmal child were quite enough without this all too corporeal girl to dog my doings. I edge around her presence as though it might explode in my face at any moment. On her first full day in my employ she scrubbed half the kitchen floor, took everything out of the refrigerator and put it all back again, and did something to the downstairs lavatory so that even still it will not flush properly. After these labours her enthusiasm for housework waned. I could get rid of her, of course, could tell Quirke I do not need her, that I can care for the house myself, but something prevents me. Is it that I have been unconsciously pining for company? Not that Lily could be said to be companionable, exactly. She sulks about the place as if she were under house arrest. Why does she stay, if she is so discontent? I pay her a pittance, hardly more than pocket money, so there is no profit in it for her, or for Quirke, either. And anyway, why did he foist her on me in the first place? Perhaps he feels guilty for the years of neglect of the house, although I suspect guilt is not one of the more burdensome affects under which Quirke chafes. She stays late into the evening, asprawl in an armchair in the parlour reading glossy magazines, or brooding chin on fist beside a window, following with inexpectant gaze the few passers-by in the square. It is twilight by the time Quirke comes to fetch her, wobbling to the door on his bike and looming in the hallway in his bicycle clips, uneasy and humble-seeming as a poor relation. I note the heavy hand he lays on her shoulder and the way she tries half-heartedly to squirm out from under his grasp. I do not know where it is they go to at close of day; they trail off aimlessly together into the night, seemingly without fixed direction. I watch the fitful glow of the rear light of Quirke's bicycle dwindling in the darkness. What sort of life do they lead away from here? When I enquired one day about her mother, Lily's expression went blank. "Dead," she said flatly, and turned away.

She is constantly bored; boredom is her mode, her medium. She gives herself up to inaction almost sensuously. She is a voluptuary of indolence. In the midst of performing some common task—sweeping the floor, polishing a windowpane—she will droop gradually to a stop, her arms falling limp, her cheek languishing toward her shoulder, her lips gone slack and swollen. At those moments of stillness and self-forgetting she takes on an unearthly aura, exudes a kind of negative radiance, a dark light. She reminds me of Cass, naturally; in every daughter I see my own. They could not be more different, in almost all ways, this dull slattern and my driven girl, and yet there is something essential that is common to them both. What can it be? There is the same deadened, disenchanted glance, the same way of slowly blinking, and focusing with a frowning effort, that Cass at Lily's age would turn on me when I tried to cajole or hector her out of one of her melancholy moods. But there must be more than that, there must be something deeper than a look, that makes me tolerate this invasion of my solitude.

I cannot think how Lily fills her day. I find myself straining to monitor her movements. I will stop and stand listening for her, not breathing, in a sort of anxious expectancy, in the same way that in the early days here I would wait for my phantoms to appear. She will be silent for hours, not a sound, and then suddenly, just when I have relaxed my vigilance, there will be a ripping blare of music from her transistor radio—it goes everywhere with her, like a prosthesis—or a bedroom door will bang open and shut, followed by the clatter of her heels on the stairs, like the sound of a window cleaner falling down his ladder. I will come upon her practising her dance steps, shaking and shuffling to the tinny beat in her earphones and singing along to the melody in a bat-squeak nasal falsetto. When she sees me observing her she will snatch off the earphones and turn aside, directing a surly backward glance in the region of my knees, as though I had taken unfair advantage of her. She pokes about the house as I used to do when I was a child here. She has been in the garret—I trust she did not meet my Dad—and in my room, too, I suspect. What secrets does she think she will uncover? There are no more bottled frogs for her to find. My stash of pornography has gone too, thrown out one day in a sudden attack of self-disgust—I think I have at last cured myself of sex; certainly the symptoms are clearing up nicely.

She gets up to things. She started a scrapbook in one of my mother's old cloth-bound account books, sticking photographs of her pop idols over the columns of pencilled figures with paste that she made herself from flour and water; afterwards I had to call in Quirke to unblock the kitchen sink. I think he hit her for that, for next day she had an angry blue and yellow bruise on her cheekbone. I do not know if I should speak to him about this. Certainly I shall not tell tales on her again. She lay low for a day or two, then yesterday a wall-shaking crash, like that of a heavy piece of furniture falling over, made me leap out of my chair and hare off upstairs three steps at a time, expecting disaster. I found her standing in the middle of my mother's room with her hands behind her back, grinding the toe of her sandal into an imaginary hole in the linoleum. "What noise?" she said, giving me a look of offended innocence. And indeed, I could find nothing amiss in the room, although there was a strong whiff of stale wood dust, and the sunlight at the window was aswirl with motes. If things go on like this she will have the place down about our ears.

She seems to eat nothing but potato crisps and chocolate bars. The latter come in a baffling variety of flavours and fillings. I find discarded wrappers all over the house, torn and twisted like pieces of shrapnel, and read them, marvelling at the confectioners' inventiveness. The chocolate seems to be not chocolate at all, but a blend of unpronounceable multisyllabic chemicals. How did I miss all this, the jungly music, the gaudy, fake food, the clumpy shoes and skimpy, acid-coloured skirts, the hairstyles, the vampire make-up, the livid lipsticks and nail polish shiny and thick as clotted blood? Was Cass never young like this? I cannot recall her adolescence. She must have gone straight from stormy childhood to being the mysterious young woman she is now, with nothing in between. I have suppressed the second act, with its cast of consultants and therapists and mind-menders, charlatans all, in my not unbiased opinion. She passed through their ministrations like a sleepwalker pacing the roof's leads and guttering, beyond the urgent reaching out of hands from attic windows to restrain her. Despite everything, despite all my suspicions, disappointment, fury, even—why could she not be *normal?*—I always secretly admired her intensity, her drivenness, the unrelenting using up of the store of herself. There were moments onstage, sadly rare, when I felt in my own nerves something of her irresistible repeated compulsion to risk the self's stability.

As the days progress I have noted a modulation in the jaded indifference with which Lily at first regarded me. She has even initiated a rudimentary attempt at what in other circumstances might be called communication. That is, she asks short questions in expectation of long answers. What can I tell her? I have not mastered the language of Lilyland. It seems she looked me up in a reference book in the town library. I am impressed; a girl of Lily's tastes and attitudes does not venture lightly among the stacks.

When she confessed to these researches she blushed—quite a thing, to see Lily blush—and then was furious with herself, and frowned fiercely and bit her lip, and gave her hair a hard toss, as if she were giving herself a slap. She marvels at the number of productions I have been in; I tell her I am very old, and that I started young, which bit of winsome bathos makes her curl her lip. She asked if the awards that *Who's Who* says I have garnered had a cash element, and was disappointed when I told her sadly no, only useless statuettes. Nevertheless, she has obviously begun to take me for a person of at least some consequence. Her interest in the possibility of knowing someone famous is tempered by her scepticism that anyone famous would choose to come to this dump, which is how she invariably refers to her birthplace, and mine. I asked if she has ever been to the theatre and she narrowed her eyes defensively.

"I go to the pictures," she said.

"So do I, Lily," I said, "so do I."

Thrillers she likes, and horror movies. What about romances? I asked, and she snorted and mimed sticking two fingers down her throat. She is a bloodthirsty child. She recounted in yawn-inducing detail the plot of her favourite film, an action picture called *Bloodline*. Although I probably saw it, refracted through tears, on one of my clandestine afternoons in the cinema—I must have seen every feature shown in those three or four months—I could not follow her account of it, for the story was as populously complicated as a Jacobean tragedy, though with a far higher quotient of corpses. In the end the heroine drowns.

Lily is sorely disappointed, I can see, that I have not starred in a picture. I tell her of my triumphs and travels, my Hamlet at Elsinore, my Macbeth in Bucharest, my notorious Oedipus at Sagesta—oh, yes, I could have been an international star, had I not been at heart afraid of the big world beyond these safe shores—but what is any of that to her compared with a lead role on the silver screen? I demonstrate the lurch I devised for my Richard the Third at Stratford—Ontario, that is—of which I used to be very proud, though she thinks it comic; she says I look more like the Hunchback of Notre-Dame. I suspect she finds me generally hilarious, my poses, my actor's burr, all my little tics and twitches, too funny for laughter. I catch her watching me, mooneyed with expectation, waiting for me to perform some wonderful new foolishness. Cass used to look at me like that when she was little. Perhaps I should have gone in more for comedy. I might have been a—

Well. I have made a momentous discovery. I hardly know what to think of it, or what to do about it. I should be angry but I am not, although I confess I do feel something of a fool. It might have been ages before I found out had I not decided on a whim to follow Quirke when I spotted him in the town today. I have always been a secret stalker. I mean I follow people, pick them out at random in the street and shadow them, or used to, anyway, before I became what the newspapers, were they still to be interested in me, would call a recluse. It is a harmless vice, and easy to entertain—human beings have scant sense of themselves as objects of speculation in the world outside their heads, and will rarely notice a stranger's interest in them. I am not sure what it is I hope to find, peering hungrily like this into other lives. I used to tell myself that I was gathering material—a walk, a stance, a way of carrying a newspaper or putting on a hat—some bit of real-life business I could transfer raw on to the stage to flesh out and lend a touch of verisimilitude to whatever character I happened to be playing at the time. But that is not it, not really, or not entirely. And besides, there is no such thing as verisimilitude. Do not misunderstand me, I am no Peeping Tom, hunched over in a hot sweat with throbbing eye glued to keyhole. It is not that kind of gratification I am after.

When Lydia and I were first married we lived in a cavernous third-floor flat in a crumbling Georgian terrace, with a bathroom up a short flight of stairs, through the small high window of which, if I craned, I could see down into the bedroom of a flat in the house next door, where often of a morning, when the weather was clement, I would glimpse a naked girl getting herself ready for her day. Through a whole spring and summer I watched for her there each morning, one knee pressed tremblingly on the lavatory seat and my tortoise neck straining; I might have been an Attic shepherd and she a nymph at her toilet. She was not particularly pretty: red-haired, I remember, rather thick in the waist, and with an unhealthy pallor. Yet she fascinated me. She was not aware of being spied on, and so she was—what shall I say?—free. I had never before witnessed such purity of gesture. All her actions—brushing her hair, pulling on her pants, fastening a clasp behind her back—had an economy that was beyond mere physical adroitness. This was a kind of art, at once primitive and highly developed. Nothing was wasted, not the lift of a hand, the turn of a shoulder; nothing was for show. Without knowing, in perfect self-absorption, she achieved at the start of each day there in her mean room an apotheosis of grace and suavity. The unadorned grave beauty of her movements was, it pained the performer in me to acknowledge, inimitable: even if I spent a lifetime in rehearsal I could not hope to aspire to the thoughtless elegance of this girl's most trivial gesture. Of course, all was dependent precisely on there being no thought attached to what she was doing, no awareness. One glimpse of my eager eye at the bathroom window, watching her, and she would have scrambled to hide her nakedness with all the grace of a collapsing deck chair or, worse, would have slipped into the travesty of self-conscious display. Innocent of being watched, she was naked; aware of my eye on her, she would have turned into a nude. What was most intensely striking, I think, was her lack of expression. Her face was an utter blank, an almost featureless mask, such that if I had encountered her in the street—which I am sure I must have, often—I would not have recognised her.

It is this forgetfulness, this loss of creaturely attendance, that I find fascinating. In watching someone who is unaware of being watched one glimpses a state of being that is beyond, or behind, what we think of as the human; it is to behold, however ungraspably, the unmasked self itself. The ones I fixed on to trail about the streets were never the freaks, the cripples or dwarves, the amputees, the unfortunates with limps or squints or port-wine stains; or if I did choose some such afflicted wretch, it was not his affliction that drew me but what in him was utterly commonplace and drab. In my table of types, beauty does not make eligible nor ugliness disqualify. Indeed, ugliness and beauty are not categories that apply here—my questing gaze makes no aesthetic measurements. I am a specialist, with a specialist's dispassion, like a surgeon, say, to whose diagnostic eye a girl's budding breasts or an old man's sagging paps are objects of equal interest, equal indifference. Nor would I bother with the blind, as might be expected of a stalker as timid as I am, as leery of notice and challenge. Despite his blank or downcast gaze, the blind man is always more alert than the sighted one—more watchful, even, one might say— unable for an instant to relax his awareness of the self as it negotiates its fastidious way through this menacing, many-angled world.

Among my favourite quarries were the derelicts, the tramps and reeling winos, of whom we have always boasted a thriving community. I knew them all, the fat fellow in the knitted tricolour cap, the one with the look of an anguished ascetic whose left hand was a permanently outstretched begging bowl, the sauntering flâneurs with crusted bare feet, the raging tinker-women, the drunkards spouting obscenities or scraps of Latin verse. This is true theatre of the streets, and they its strolling players. What fascinated me was the distance between what they were now and what they must once have been. I tried to imagine them as babes in arms, or toddling about the floor of some loud tenement or sequestered cottage, watched over by fond eyes, borne up by loving hands. For they had to have been young once, in a past that must seem to them now as far off and impossibly radiant as the dawn of the world.

Apart from their intrinsic interest as a species, I favoured outcasts because, being outcasts, they were not liable suddenly to elude me by disappearing into a smart boutique, or turning in at a suburban garden gate, frowningly fishing for a key. We had the freedom of the streets, they and I, and for hours I would follow after them—an actor, especially in his early years, has a lot of time on his hands—along the dreamy pavements, through the faintly sinister orderliness of public parks, as the afternoons grew loud with the clamour of paroled schoolchildren, and the broad strips of sky above us turned mussel-shell blue, and the evening traffic started up, scurrying in herds through the dusk, hunched and bleating. Along with the peculiar pleasure I derive from this furtive hobby goes a certain melancholy, due to what I think of as the Uncertainty Principle. You see, as long as I only watch them without their knowing, I am in some sense intimately in touch with them, they are in some sense *mine*, whereas if they were to become aware of me dogging their steps, that which in them is of interest to me—their lack of awareness, their freedom from self-consciousness, their wonderful, vacant ease—would instantly vanish. I may observe, but not touch.

One day one of them confronted me. It was a shock. He was a drinker, a rough, vigorous fellow of about my own age, with a bristling rufous jaw and the stricken eyes of a saint in quest of martyrdom. It was a raw day in March, but I stuck with him. He favoured the quays, I do not know why, for there was a cutting wind from the river. I skulked behind him with my collar turned up, while he went along at a stumbling swagger, his coat-tails billowing and his filthy shirt collar open—do they somehow develop an immunity to the cold? In a pocket of his coat was stowed a large fat bottle, wrapped in a brown-paper bag, the neck exposed. At every dozen paces or so he would stop and with a dramatic sweep bring out the bottle, still in its bag, and take a long slug, rocking back on his heels, his throat working in coital spasms as he swallowed. These mighty quaffings had no discernible effect on him, except perhaps to lend a momentary faltering jerkiness to his stride. We had been promenading like this for a good half-hour, down one side of the quays and up the other—he seemed to have his beat marked out in his head—and I was ready to abandon him, for it was apparent he was going nowhere, when at one of the bridges he swerved aside on to the footway, and when I hastened to catch up I found myself abruptly face to face with him. He had turned back and stopped, and was standing with a steadying hand pressed on the parapet, head lifted and mouth sternly set, regarding me with a challenging glare. I experienced a thrill of alarm—I felt like a schoolboy surprised in a prank—and looked about hurriedly for a way of escape. Yet although the path was wide, and I could easily have sidestepped him, I did not. He continued to look at me out of those imperiously questioning, agonised eyes. I do not know what he expected of me. I was scandalised, it is the only word, to be thus accosted by a quarry, yet partly I was excited, too, and partly—odd though the word will seem—flattered, as one would be flattered to win the attention of some fierce creature of the wild. A blast of wind made the flap of his coat crack like a flag and he gave himself a shuddery shake. I dithered. Passers-by were glancing at us with curiosity and disapproval, suspecting the nature of the commerce they imagined we were engaged in. I reached fumblingly into my pocket and found a banknote and offered it to him. He looked at the money with surprise and even, I thought, a touch of umbrage. I persisted, and even went so far as to press the note into his hot and mottled hand. His demeanour now turned positively patronising; he had the large, half-smiling, half-surprised look of an opponent into whose power I had clumsily allowed myself to fall. I might have spoken, but what would I have said? I stepped past him quickly and hurried on, across the bridge, without daring to look back. I thought I heard him say something, call out something, but still I did not turn. My heart was racing. On the other side of the bridge I slowed my steps. I was badly shaken, I can tell you. Despite the fellow's fierce appearance there had been something cloyingly intimate in the encounter, something from which my mind's eye insisted on averting its gaze. Rules had been broken, a barrier had been transgressed, an interdiction breached. I had been forced to experience a human moment, and now I was confused, and did not know what to think. Strange bright fragments of lost possibilities flashed about in my mind. I regretted not having asked the fellow's name. I regretted not telling him mine. I wondered, with a pang that startled me, if I would ever come across him again. But what did I imagine I would do, if he were to step out boldly into my path on some other bridge, on some other day, and challenge me?

Anyway, as I was saying, today in town I was in a telephone box, calling Lydia, when I spotted Quirke coming out of the solicitor's office where he works—although the word is, I am sure, overly strong for what he does in the way of earning a living. He was carrying a clutch of manila envelopes under his arm, and wore an aspect of sullen duty. "There's Quirke," I said into the phone, in one of my lapses into the inconsequential that Lydia finds so irritating. It was the first time we had talked since I disconnected the telephone in the house, and it felt strange. There was the distance between us—she might have been speaking from the dark side of the moon—yet more marked was the unshakeable sensation I had that it was not really she on the line, but a recording, or even a mechanically generated imitation of her voice. Have I sunk so far into myself that the living should sound like automata? The booth smelled strongly of urine and crushed cigarette ends, and the sun was hot on the glass. I had telephoned to enquire as to Cass's whereabouts. Although Cass is what I must think of as a grown woman—she is twenty-two, or is it twenty-three? the calendar is a little indistinct, from where I am positioned at present—part of my peace of mind depends on always knowing at least approximately where she is. My peace of mind, that's a good one. The last I knew of her she was doing research of an unspecified and no doubt arcane—not to say, hare-brained—nature in some unpronounceable declivity of the Low Countries; now, it seems, she is in Italy. "I had a peculiar call from her," Lydia was saying, as if a call from Cass could be anything other than peculiar. I asked if she was all right. It was what we used to ask each other in the old days, with an unstillable, apprehensive tremor: *Is she all right?* Lydia's brief silence on the line was the equivalent of a shrug. For a moment we said nothing, then I began to describe Quirke's odd, small-footed lope—how daintily he moves, for one so large and top-heavy—and Lydia became angry, and her voice thickened.

"Why are you doing this to me?" she almost wailed.

"Doing what?" I asked, and immediately, without another word, she hung up. I put in more coins and began to dial the number again, but stopped; what more was there to say?—what had there been to say in the first place?

Quirke had not seen me there behind the grimed glass of the booth, crouched over the receiver in the attitude of a man nursing a toothache, and I decided to follow him. But I should not say that I decided. I never do set out wholly consciously to stalk anyone. Rather, I will find myself already on the way, absent-mindedly, as it were, half thinking of something else, yet with my . . . my *victim*, I was about to say, firmly fixed in view. It was a morning of warm wind and heavy sunlight. Quirke was going along on the shady side of the street and almost at once I nearly lost him, when he ducked into a post office, but there was no mistaking that broad stooped back and its following down-at-heel grey shoe and grubby white sock. I dawdled at the window of a chemist's shop opposite, waiting for him. How hard it is, as I the stalker know from long experience, to concentrate on a reflection in a shop window without letting one's attention drift to the wares on offer, however less solid they may seem than the fleeting, burnished world mirrored on the surface of the glass behind which they stand in uneasy display. Distracted by posters of bathing beauties advertising sun creams, and in particular a coy arrangement of gleaming steel pincers designed, I believe, for castrating calves, I almost missed Quirke's reappearance. Empty-handed now, he bustled off with accelerated step and turned a corner on to the quays. I hurried across the road, making a delivery boy on a bike swerve and swear, but when I rounded the corner there was no sign of Quirke. I stood and surveyed the scene with a narrowed eye, searching for a sign of him among wheeling gulls, those three rusted trawlers, a bronze statue pointing with vague urgency out to sea. When a stalkee vanishes like this the uncanniness of ordinary things is intensified; a telltale gap opens in the world, like the chink of blue evening sky the Chinaman in the fable spots between the magic city and the hill on which it is supposed to be standing. Then I noticed the pub, wedged into a corner between a fish shop and the gate of a motor car repair yard.

It was an old-style premises, the nicotine-brown varnish on the door and window sills combed and whorled to give the illusion of wood grain, and the window painted inside an opaque sepia shade to a filigreed six inches of the top. The place had somehow the mark of Quirke about it. I went in, stumbling on the worn threshold. The place was empty, the bar untended. In an ashtray on the counter a forgotten cigarette was smoking itself in surreptitious haste, sending up a quick straight plume of blue smoke. On a shelf an old-fashioned wireless muttered. Behind the usual pub smells there was a mingled whiff of machine oil and brine from the next-door premises on either side. I heard from somewhere in the shadowed rear a lavatory flushing and a rickety door opening with a scrape, and Quirke came shambling forward, hitching up the waistband of his trousers and running a quick finger down the flies. I turned aside hastily, but I need not have bothered, for he did not even glance at me, but walked straight past and out the door with a self-forgetting look, squinting into the light.

I am still wondering which of the world's secret administrators it was who left that cigarette burning on the bar.

In the minute that I had been in the pub the morning had clouded over. A great grey bank of cumulus fringed in silver hung above the sea, moving landward with menacing intent. Quirke had crossed to the wooden quay and was walking along with what seemed a blundering step, like that of a man purblinded by tears. Or was he tipsy, I wondered? Surely he had not been long enough in the pub to drink himself drunk. Yet as I followed along behind him I could not rid myself of the notion that he was somehow incapacitated, in some great distress. All at once I was seized on violently by the memory of a dream that I dreamed one recent night, and that I had forgotten, until now. In the dream I was a torturer, a professional of long experience, skilled in the art of pain, whom people came to—tyrants, spy-catchers, brigand chiefs—to hire my unique services, when their own efforts and those of their most enthusiastic henchmen had all failed. My current victim was a man of great presence, of great resolve and assurance, a burly, bearded fellow, the kind of high-toned hero I used to be cast to play in the latter years of my career, when I was judged to have attained a grizzled majesty of bearing. I do not know who he was supposed to be, nor did I know him in the dream; seemingly it was a condition of my professionalism not to know the identity or the supposed crimes of those on whom I was called to work my persuasive art. The details of my methods were vague; I employed no tools, no tongs or prods or burning-irons, but was myself the implement of torture. I would grasp my victim in some special way and crush him slowly until his bones buckled and his internal organs collapsed. I was irresistible, not to be withstood; all succumbed, sooner or later, under my terrible ministrations. All, that is, except this bearded hero, who was defeating me simply by not paying me sufficient attention, by not acknowledging me. Oh, he was in agony, all right, I was inflicting the most terrible torments on him, masterpieces of pain that made him writhe and shudder and grind his teeth until they creaked, but it was as if his sufferings were his own, were generated out of himself, and that it was himself and not I that he must resist, his own will and vigour and unrelenting force. I might not have been part of the process at all. I could feel the heat of his flesh, could smell the fetor of his anguish. He strained away from me, lifting his face to the smoke-blackened ceiling of the dungeon, where a fitful light flickered; he cried out, he whimpered; sweat dripped from his beard, his eyeballs bled. Never had the person I was in the dream experienced so strongly the erotic intimacy that binds the torturer to his victim, yet never had I been so thoroughly shut out from my subject's pain. I was not there—simply, for him I was not there, and so, despite the intensity, despite the passion, one might say, of my presence in the midst of his agony, somehow I was absent for myself as well, absent, that is to say, from myself.

Caught up as I was in trying to recapture this dream, in all its cruelty and mysterious splendour, I almost lost Quirke a second time, when just as we were coming to the edge of town he veered off and plunged down a laneway. The lane was narrow, between high whitewashed walls with greenery and clumps of buddleia sprouting along their tops. I knew where it led. I allowed him to get a good way on, so that if he turned and I had nowhere to hide myself he still might not know me, at such a distance. He had quickened his pace, and kept glancing at the sky, which was growing steadily more threatening. A dog sitting at a back-garden gate barked at him and he made an unsuccessful kick at it. The lane dipped and turned and came to a sort of bower, with a pair of leaning beeches and a lichen-spattered horse trough and an old-fashioned green water pump, at which Quirke paused and worked the handle and bent over the trough and cupped the water in his hand and drank. I stopped, too, and watched him, and heard the plash of the water falling on the stone side of the trough, and the murmurous rustling of a breeze in the trees above us. I did not care now that he might see me; even if he had turned and recognised me I think it would not have made any difference, we would have gone on as before, him leading and me following after him with unflagging eagerness, though for what, or with what cause, I could not tell. Still he did not look back, and after a moment of silent pondering, leaning there in the greenish gloom under the trees, he was off again. I went forward and stood where he had stood, and stooped where he had stooped, and worked the handle of the pump and cupped my hands and caught the water and drank deep of that uncanny element that tasted of steel and earth. Above me the trees conferred among themselves in fateful whispers. I might have been an itinerant priest stopping at a sacred grove. Abruptly then it began to rain, I heard the swish of it behind me and turned in time to see it coming fast along the lane like a blown curtain, then it was against my face, a vehement chill glassy drenching. Quirke broke into a canter, scrabbling to turn up the collar of his jacket. I heard him curse. I hastened after him. I did not mind the wetting; there is always something exultant about a cloudburst. Big drops batted the beech leaves and danced on the road. There was a crackling in the air, and a moment later came the thunderclap, like something being hugely crumpled. Now Quirke, head down, his sparse hair flattened to his skull, was fairly sprinting up the last length of the lane, high-stepping among the forming puddles like a big, awkward bird. We came out into the square. I was no more than a dozen paces behind Quirke now. He

went along close under the convent wall, clutching the lapels of
his jacket closed at his throat. He stopped at the house, and opened
the door with a key, slipped into the hall, and was gone.

I was not surprised. From the start I think I had known where
our destination lay. It seemed the most natural thing that he should
have led me home. I stood shivering in the wet, uncertain of what
would come next. The rain was pelting the cherry trees; I thought
how patient they were, how valiant. For an instant I had a vision of
a world thrashing without complaint in unmitigable agony; I
bowed my head; the rain beat on my back. Then gradually there
arose behind me the muffled sound of hoofs, and I looked up to see
a young boy on a little black-and-white horse trotting bareback
toward me across the square. At first I could hardly make out
horse and rider, so thick was the web of rain between them and
me. It might have been a faun, or centaur. But no, it was a boy, on a
little horse. The boy was dressed in a dirty jersey and short pants,
with no shoes or socks. His mount was a tired poor creature with a
bowed back and distended belly; as it clopped toward me it rolled
a cautiously measuring eye sideways in my direction. Despite the
downpour the boy seemed hardly to be wet at all, as if he were
protected within an invisible shell of glass. When they were almost level with me the boy hauled on the length of rope that was
the reins and the animal slowed to a wavering walk. I wanted to
speak but somehow felt that I should not, and anyway I could not
think what I might say. The boy smiled at me, or perhaps it was a
grimace, expressing what, I could not guess. He had a pinched pale
face and red hair. I noticed his belt, an old-fashioned one such as I
used to wear myself when I was his age, made of red-and-white
striped elastic with a silver metal buckle in the shape of a snake. I
thought he would say something but he did not, only went on
smiling, or grimacing, and then clicked his tongue and heeled the
horse's flanks and they went on again, into the lane whence I had
come. I followed. The rain was stopping. I could smell the horse's

smell, like the smell of wetted sacking. Hard by the side gate into the garden of the house they halted, and the boy turned and looked back at me, with a calm, impassive gaze, bracing a hand behind him on the horse's spine. What passed between us there, what wordless intimation? I was hungry for a sign. After a moment the boy faced forward again and gave the bridle rope a tug, and the little horse started up, as if by clockwork, and off they went, down the lane's incline, and presently were gone from sight. I shall not forget them, that boy, and his pied nag, cantering there, in the summer rain.

I examined the gate. It is what I think used to be called a postern, a wooden affair, very old now, dark and rotted to crumbling stumps at top and bottom, set into the whitewashed wall on two big rusted rings and held fast with a rusted bolt. Often as a boy I would enter by this gate when coming home from school. I tried the bolt. At first the flange refused to lift, but I persisted and in the end the cylinder, thick as my thumb, turned in its coils with a shriek. Behind the gate was a mass of overgrown creeper and old brambles, and I had to push hard to make a gap wide enough to squeeze through. The rain had fully stopped now and a shamefaced sun was managing to shine. I shoved the gate to behind me and stood a moment in survey. The garden was grown to shoulder-height in places. The rose trees hung in dripping tangles, and clumps of scutch grass steamed; there were jewelled dock leaves big as shovels. The wet had brought the snails out, they were in the grass and on the briars, swaying on the tall thorned fronds. I set off toward the house, the untidy back of which hung out in seeming despair over this scene of vegetable riot. Nettles stung me, cobwebs strung with pearls of moisture draped themselves across my face. All of childhood was in the high sharp stink of rained-on weeds. The sun was gathering strength, my shirt clung wetly warm to my back. I felt like a hero out of some old saga, come at last, at the end of his quest, unhelmed, travel-worn

and weary, to the perilous glade. The house out of blank unrecog-
nising eyes watched me approach, giving no sign of life. I came
into the yard. Rusted bits of kitchen things were strewn about, a
washboard and mangle, an old refrigerator with its eerily white
innards on show, a pan to the bottom of which was welded a
charred lump of something from an immemorial fry-up. On all
this I looked with the eyes of an expectant stranger, as if I had seen
none of it before.

Now, through the top part of the barred basement window, I
caught sight of Quirke, or of his head at least, turned away from
me, in quarter-profile. It was an uncanny sight, that big round
head resting there behind bars at ground level, as though he were
interred up to the neck in the floor of a cage. At first I could not
make out what it was he was up to. He would lean his head forward
briefly and then straighten again, and would seem to speak in some
steady, unemphatic way, as if he were delivering a lecture, or com-
mitting lines to memory. Then I stepped forward for a better look
and saw that he was sitting at table, with a plate of food before
him, on which with knife and fork he was methodically working.
The sun was burning the back of my neck now, and my skin
smarted from thorns and nettle stings, and the rich deep gloom in
which Quirke sat seemed wonderfully cool and inviting. I crossed
to the back door. It had the look of a square-shouldered sentry
standing in his box, tall and narrow, with a many-layered impasto
of black paint and two little panes of meshed glass set high up that
seemed to glare out with suspicion and menace. I tried the knob,
and at once the door opened before me, smoothly silent, with
accommodating ease. Cautiously I crossed the threshold, eager
and apprehensive as Lord Bluebeard's wife. At once, as if of its
own volition, the door with a faint sigh closed behind me.

I was in the kitchen. I might never have been here before. Or I
might have been, but in another dimension. Talk about making
strange! Everything was askew. It was like entering backstage and

seeing the set in reverse, all the parts of it known but not where they should be. Where were my chalk-marks now, my blocked-out map of moves? I was seized by a peculiar cold excitement, the sort that comes in dreams, at once irresistible and disabling. If only I could creep up on the whole of life like this, and see it all from a different perspective! The door to the basement scullery was shut; from behind it could be heard the faint clink and scrape of Quirke at his victuals. Softly I stepped into the passageway leading out to the front hall. A gleam in the lino transported me on the instant, heart-shakingly, to a country road somewhere, in April, long ago, at evening, with rain, and breezes, and swooping birds, and a break of brilliant blue in the far sky shining on the black tarmac of the road. Here is the front hall, with its fern dying in a brass pot, and a broken pane in the transom, and Quirke's increasingly anthropo-morphic bike leaning against the hatstand. Here is the staircase, with a thick beam of sunlight hanging in suspended fall from a window on the landing above. I stood listening, and seemed lis-tened back to by the silence. I set off up the stairs, feeling the faintly repulsive clamminess of the banister rail under my hand, offering me its dubious intimacy. I went into my mother's room, and sat on the side of my mother's bed. There was a dry smell, not unpleasant, as if something ripe had rotted here and turned to dust. The bedclothes were awry, a pillow bore a head-shaped hol-low. Through the window I looked out to the far blue hills shim-mering in rain-rinsed air. So I remained for a long moment, listening to the faint sounds of the day, that might have been the tumult of a far-off battle, not thinking, exactly, but touching the thought of thought, as one would touch the tender, buzzing edges of a wound.

Cass was good with my mother. It always surprised me. There was something between them, a complicity, from which I was irri-tated to find myself excluded. They were alike, in ways. What in my mother was distraction turned out in Cass to be an absence, a lostness. Thus the march of the generations works its dark magic, making its elaborations, its complications, turning a trait into an affliction. Cass would sit here for hours with the dying woman at the end, seeming not to mind the smell, the foulings, the impenetrable speechlessness. They communed in silence. Once I found her asleep with her head on my mother's breast. I did not wake her. Over the sleeping girl my mother watched me with narrow malignity. Cass was always an insomniac, worse than me. Sleep to her was a dry run for death. Even as a toddler she would make herself stay awake into the small hours, afraid of letting go, convinced she would not wake up again. I would look into her room and find her lying big-eyed and rigid in the darkness. One night when I—

The door was opened from without and Quirke cautiously put in his head. When he saw me his Adam's apple bobbed.

"I thought I heard someone, all right," he said, and let a grey tongue-tip snake its way from one corner of his mouth to the other.

I went down again to the hall and sat on the sofa there with my hands in my lap. I could hear Quirke moving about upstairs. I stood up and walked into the kitchen and leaned at the sink and poured a glass of water and drank it slowly, swallow by long swallow, shivering a little as the liquid ran down through the branched tree in my breast. I glanced into the scullery. On the table were the remains of Quirke's lunch. What pathos in a crust of bread. I heard him come along the hall and stop in the doorway behind me.

"You're living here," I said, "aren't you?"

I turned to him, and he grinned.

III

I pause, as a chronicler should, to record the imminence of a great event. There is to be a solar eclipse. Total occlusion is predicted, though not for all. The Scandinavians are not to get a look-in, likewise the inhabitants of the Antipodes. Even within the relatively narrow band over which the moon's cloak will sweep, there are to be appreciable variations. In this latitude it is expected we shall have about ninety-five per cent coverage of the disc. For others, however, notably the beggars on the streets of Benares, a treat is in store: they are to enjoy approximately two and a half minutes of noontime night, the longest to be experienced anywhere on the globe. I deplore the lack of precision in these forecasts. Today, when there are clocks that work on the oscillations of a single atom, one surely might expect better than *about* ninety-five per cent, or *approximately* two and a half minutes—why are these things not being measured in nanoseconds? Yet people are agog. Tens of thousands are said to be already on the move, flocking to the rocky coasts of the south, on which the full shadow will fall. I wish I could share their enthusiasm; I should like to believe in something, or at least be in expectation of something, even if only a chance celestial conjunction. I see them, of course, as a great band of pilgrims out of an old tale, trudging down the dusty roads with staff and bell, archaic faces alight with longing and hope. And I, I am the scoffer, lounging in doublet and hose in an upstairs window of some half-timbered inn, languidly spitting pomegranate seeds on their bowed heads as they pass below me. They yearn for a sign, a light in the sky, a darkness, even, to tell them that things are intended, that all is not blind happenstance. What would they not give for a glimpse of my ghosts? Now, there is a sign, there is a portent, of what, I am still not sure, although I am beginning to have my suspicions.

I was right, they have been here all along, the two of them, Quirke and the girl. I am more baffled than indignant. How did they manage it without my noticing? Haunted, I was ever on the watch for phantoms, how then could I overlook the presence of two of the living? But perhaps the living are not my kind, any more, perhaps they do not register with me as once they would have done. Quirke of course is embarrassed to have been found out, but I can see from his look that he is amused, too, in a rueful sort of way. When I confronted him there in the kitchen he looked me boldly in the eye, still grinning, and said he had considered it a perk of the job of caretaker that he and his girl should be allowed to live on the premises. I was so taken aback by the brazenness of this that I could think of nothing to say in reply. He went on to assure me that he had kept up the charade only out of a desire that I should not be disturbed; I would have laughed, in other circumstances. Nor has he offered to move out. He sauntered off, quite breezy, whistling through his teeth, and presently appeared at the door on his bicycle as usual, and he and Lily straggled away into the twilight quite as they have done every evening. Later, when I was in bed, I heard them stealthily returning. These must be the sounds I have been hearing every night since I came here, and which I failed to interpret. How simple and dull and disappointing things become when they are explained; maybe my ghosts will yet step forward, bowing and smirking, and I shall be allowed to see the mirrors and the smoke.

How the two of them—Quirke and Lily, I mean—how they pass the hours between their twilight departure and their return in the dark I cannot say. Lily goes to the pictures, I suppose, or to the disco—there is one somewhere nearby, half the night I feel its dull pulse drumming through the air—while Quirke haunts the pub; I can see him, with his pint and his cigarette, chaffing the barmaid, or gloomily ogling the bare-chested lovelies in someone else's discarded newspaper. I asked him where it is in the house that he and Lily sleep and he shrugged and said with deliberate vagueness that they bunk down wherever is handy. I believe it is the girl who sometimes uses my mother's bed. I do not know what to think of this. It is not yet acknowledged, between Lily and me, that I know her secret. Something prevents me from mentioning it, an obscure squeamishness. There are no rules of etiquette to cover a situation such as this. Although Quirke must have told her I am on to them, for her part she goes on just as before, with the same air of general resentment and bored disinclination.

What is most remarkable to me is the transformation my discovery has wrought in the house, or at least in my attitude toward it. That sense of goggle-eyed alienation that came over me yesterday when I stalked Quirke into the kitchen still persists. I have stepped through the looking-glass into another world where everything is exactly as it was and at the same time entirely transformed. It is a disconcerting sensation, but not, I discover, unwelcome—after all, this is exactly the kind of dislocated stance to things that I had hoped but failed to maintain by my own efforts. So really, Quirke and his girl have done me a service, and I suppose I should be grateful. True, I could have wished for more stimulating sharers of my solitude. I have the uneasy feeling that I should assert my rights. For a start I shall stop paying Lily for her domestic services, such as they are, and performed with such ill grace. Quirke too must be required to fill some necessary function. He could be my major-domo; I have always wanted a major-domo, even though I am not entirely certain what duties such a personage performs. I amuse myself by imagining him, pigeon-breasted in frock coat and striped trousers, creaking about the place on those dainty pigeon feet. I doubt that he can cook; on the evidence of that plate he left on the scullery table he is strictly a sausage-and-egg man. The matter, I can see, is going to take some pondering. And to think I feared an excess of solitude!

My discovery has made me look anew not only at the house, but at my two houseguests, also. I feel that I am seeing them, too, for the first time. They have come into focus, in a way that I am not sure I like, and that certainly I did not expect. It is as if they had stood up in their seats and ambled on to the stage while the play was going on, interrupting me in the middle of an intense if perhaps overly introspective soliloquy, and to save the show I must find a means somehow of incorporating them into the plot, despite their incurious and lackadaisical and wholly unprofessional air. It is the kind of thing an actor has nightmares about, yet I am strangely calm. Of course, the son of lodging-house keepers will necessarily have a diminished territorial sense, but there is more to it than that. I am puzzled, as I am when I try to identify what it is of Cass that I detect in Lily. She is a strange girl. This morning when I came down, a little bunch of wild violets was set in a jam jar beside my place at the kitchen table. There was still dew on the petals, and the stems were crushed where she had clutched them. At what time did she get up to go out and pick flowers?—for I assume it was she, and not Quirke, whom I cannot see tiptoeing out to the dewy fields of morn to pluck a nosegay, for me or anyone else. How does a girl like Lily know where to find wild violets? But I must bethink myself and stop these generalisations into which I have always fallen too easily. It is not a girl like Lily I am dealing with—it is Lily herself, unique and mysterious, for all her ordinariness. Who knows what longings burn in that meagre breast?

I study her now with an almost ogreish intensity. She is an animate riddle that I have been set to solve. I watch her painting her nails. She attends to the task with stern concentration, dabbing and smoothing with her little brush, careful as a medieval miniaturist. Often when she is finished she will hold her hands splayed out before her and, spotting some failure of execution, some flaw in the glaze, she will wrinkle her nose in annoyance and bring out her bottle of remover and wipe off every speck of the polish she has just finished applying and start all over again. She pays an equal attention to her toes. She has long, slender, lemur feet, not unlike Lydia's, roughly callused along the outer edges. On each foot the littlest toe is turned in under its neighbour like the handle of a little cup. She perches on the edge of the big winged armchair in the parlour with her leg up and her chin pressed on her knee and the oily coils of her hair hanging down about her face; the room smells like a spray-painter's workshop. I wonder if she is aware of my gaze idly roving the shadowed, mossy places under her uplifted skirts. Sometimes I catch her eyeing me with a heavy-lidded something that I cannot allow myself to believe is tumescence. I recall those violets, and contemplate with mild unease the milk-blue backs of her knees, each with its parallel pair of hairline cracks, her coarse dark hair that seems always in need of washing, and the outlines of her shoulder blades, like little stunted wings, printed on the skimpy stuff of her summer dress. She is, I have found out, fifteen.

The phantoms work their immanent magic on her. She reclines in the places where they appear, in their very midst, a grubby and all too actual odalisque, scanning her mags, and sipping her cola with subdued snorkelling noises. Does she sense their presence? Yesterday she looked up quickly from her comic, frowning, as if she had felt a ghostly touch on her shoulder. Then she glared at me suspiciously, chin tucked into her throat and brows drawn darkly down, and demanded to know what I was smiling at. Had I been smiling? She thinks me a fond old fool; she is right. I wonder if the ghost woman, on her side, registers the living girl? Am I right in feeling I detect in the ghostly one's appearances now a growing sense of puzzlement, of faint dismay, even? Can she be jealous? I await the moment, which is bound to come, when she will exactly coincide with Lily, will descend on her like the annunciatory angel, like the goddess herself, and illumine her with the momentary benison of her supernatural presence.

Here now in this for me transfigured house I have an inkling of how it must be for Cass, moving always in the midst of familiar strangers, uncertain as to what is real and what is not, unable quite to recognise the perfectly recognisable, spoken at by voices out of the air. The presence of living people in it has robbed the house for me of an essential solidity. The Quirkes have made me too into a ghost—I am not sure I would not be able to walk through walls, now. Does my daughter, I wonder, have this abiding sensation of lightness, of volatility, of there being always a sustaining skim of nothingness between foot and floor? Yet everywhere around me there is substance, eminently tangible stuff, the common old world itself, hard and dense and warm to the touch. The other night, instead of taking the girl away with him as usual, Quirke parked his bicycle in the hall and came into the kitchen and boldly brought a chair up to the table and sat down. There was a momentary pause while he waited to see what I would do. I did nothing, of course, only sat down, and we played cards, the three of us. I am no good at cards, never was. I sit and frown wildly at my hand, making a lunge for the dwindling deck when it seems required of me, uncertain even as to what suit or value I should be hoping to draw. Quirke plays with elephantine circumspection, holding the cards close up to his face and peering over them craftily at Lily and at me, one eye shut and the other a slit. He loses too, though. Lily is the one who wins. In the excitement of the game she is transformed, becomes a different child, whooping and cackling when she picks the right card, groaning at reverses and rolling her eyes and banging her forehead dully on the table in simulated despair. When she has assembled the winning trick she slams the cards

down with a Red Indian ululation of triumph. We are too slow for
her, Quirke and I, as we fumble and sigh over our hopeless hands.
She screams at Quirke to hurry up, shaking her head disgustedly,
and when I am being particularly dilatory she punches me in the
small of the back, or painfully on the upper arm, with her hard
little pointed fist. Waiting for the last required card she goes silent,
fixing her eye on the deck, watchful as a vixen. She calls the three
a trey, and what I know as knaves are jacks to her. We play by
candlelight, at Lily's insistence; she says it is romantic, pronounc-
ing the word with a deep-voiced trill— *"soo romawntic"*—in a way
that I suspect is meant to be a parody of me. Then she crosses her
eyes and lets her mouth sag in an idiot leer. The weather is still
warm, we leave the windows open on the vast soft star-struck
night. Moths come in and do their drunken clockwork spirals
around the candle flame, and the dust of their wings falls into the
shivering, soot-black puddle of shadow in which the candle
stands. Tonight when the game was over and Lily was gathering
up the cards and Quirke sat vacantly at gaze I heard an owl out in
the darkness, and I thought of Cass, and wondered where she
might be at that moment, and what doing, my Minerva. Perilous
speculation. Even in the softest lee of summer night the mind can
conjure horrors.

I was right again, Lily is sleeping in my mother's room. I
looked in early this morning and there she was, in the smouldering
dawn light, crouched in a heap in a corner of the big bed, snoring.
She did not wake up, even when I came to the side of the bed and
put my face down close to hers. What a strange spectacle it is, the
slumbering human. She smelled of sleep and young sweat and that
sickly sweet cheap perfume that she douses herself with. Except
for the scent and the snores it might have been Cass. Whole days
my girl would keep to her bed, ignoring all entreaties, all reproaches. I would tiptoe into her room and lift a corner of the
sheet and there she would be, like something that had crept in from

the wild, stark pale and tousled, lying stiffly on her side and staring at nothing, a knuckle pressed against two bared front teeth. Then at dead of night she would drag herself up at last and come down and sit with her knees against her chest in front of the television with the sound turned off, watching the flickering images with a fixed, hungry stare, as if they were so many hieroglyphs she was struggling to decipher.

Over our nightly card games Quirke has been telling me his life story, such as it is: mother ran a pub, father drank it dry, Quirke *fils* sent to work at fourteen as a solicitor's runner, been there ever since; wife, child; later, dead wife, widower. He recounts all this with a bemused air, shaking his head, as if these were things that had happened to someone else, someone he had heard of, or read about in the papers. The family home he lost through legal finagling of some kind, whether by him or another he does not say, and I do not press for details. From an inner pocket he produced a creased and yellowed newspaper cutting announcing the sale of a house by auction. "Ours," he said, nodding. "Went for a song." The paper is warm from being close to his chest with its womanly bubs; squeamishly, between thumb and forefinger, I hand the clipping back to him, and he studies it a moment, making that clicking noise in his cheek, then stows it and turns his attention to the cards again.

The future he seems to regard as an entirely improbable prospect, like a win of the sweepstakes, or the promise of eternal life. How long does he think I will allow him to live here, I wonder? I marvel at his equanimity. His mother knew my mother, he says. He remembers well this house when there were lodgers here, claims he was brought on visits with his Ma. He says he remembers me, too. I find all this obscurely disquieting. It is like being told of indecent things that had been done to one in sleep, or under anaesthesia. I trawled and trawled my memory and at last obligingly the deeps gave up an image that might be him, not as he would have been then but, ludicrously, as he is now, got up in a schoolboy's outfit bursting at the buttons, with a skullcap perched on his big round head, a Tweedledum to my identically attired Tweedledee. We have been sent into the garden to play, while our mothers sit in the parlour murmuring over their tea and fairy cakes. We stand in moody silence, the man-child Quirke and I, looking away from each other and kicking holes in the lawn with the toecaps of our school shoes. Even the sunlight seems bored. Quirke treads on a slug and squashes it, leaving a long smear like snot on the grass. I would have been his senior by some years, yet we seem to be the same age. From the back pocket of his short trousers he brings out a photograph, which shows a fat girl in a cloche hat and flapper's silks lolling on a kitchen chair with her legs wide open, insouciantly inserting a cucumber into herself; he says I can keep it, if I want, he is fed up looking at it. A thunderhead is forming in the sky above the garden. We stand with heads bent, gazing down at the picture of the girl. I can hear him breathing. "Some tart," he says, "what?" A first fat splash of rain falls on the photo. The day is darkening like a bruise.

Is it Quirke I am remembering, really, or another, for instance that boy who was my first love? Have I mentioned him? I cannot remember his name. He lodged at our house one summer with his mother. They were English, or Welsh, maybe: I recall some oddity of accent. The mother must have been in some terrible trouble, fleeing debts, perhaps, or a brutal husband. She would spend entire days in bed, not making a sound, until my mother, unable any longer to stand the suspense, would go up to her with the excuse of a cup of tea, or a vase of roses from the garden. The boy and I were of an age, nine, I suppose, not more than ten, certainly. He was not good-looking, or striking in any particular way. He had thin, reddish hair and freckles and weak eyes, and big hands, I remember, and big, bristly, porcine knees. I adored him; I would lie in bed at night and think about him, devising adventures in which he and I joined forces against robbers and bands of Red-skins. My love for him was innocent of all carnal yearnings, of course, and went undeclared; I would not even have known to call it love, would have been shocked at the word. Nor did I know if he knew what I felt for him, nor what he might feel for me, if he felt anything. One day when we were walking through the town together—I was always brimmingly proud to be seen in his company, thinking everyone was noticing and admiring us—all casually I linked my arm in his, and he stiffened and frowned, and looked away, and after a step or two, keeping up a carefully preoccupied air, withdrew his arm delicately from mine. On his last night I crept down, in a fever of sorrow already, and stood outside the door of the room he shared with his mother and tried to hear him breathing as he slept or, better still, as he lay awake, thinking of me, as it might be, and presently, to my dismay and joy, I heard from within the sound of jagged, muffled sobs, and hoarsely I whispered his name, and a moment later the door opened an inch and not his but his mother's blotched and tear-stained face appeared in the crack. She said nothing, only looked at me, a novice in the art of sorrow, and gave a grim, shallow sigh and without a word withdrew and shut the door. Next morning they left early, and he did not come to say goodbye. I stood at my window and watched them struggling across the square with their bags, and even when they were gone from sight I could still see him, his big feet in cheap sandals, his rounded shoulders, the back of his head with its whorl of colourless hair.

We turn away from the sunlight, from the squashed slug, the dirty picture, turn back to the house, and decades flash past.

"Ever see a ghost here?" Quirke asked. "They used to say this place was haunted."

I looked at him. He was absorbed in his cards.

"Haunted?" I said. "By what?"

He shrugged.

"Just old stories," he said. "Old pishogues."

"What sort of stories?"

He sat back on his chair, which gave a shriek, and squinted up into a far corner of the darkness beyond the candlelight. Now Lily was looking at him too, her mouth crookedly open a little way; I wish she would not do that, it makes her look like a retard.

"Don't remember," Quirke said. "Something about a child."

"A child."

"That died. The mother, too. Probably one of the ones that was lodging here . . ." He looked at me and indicated the girl and let an eyelid flicker.

"He means," Lily said to me with ironic emphasis, "someone that got pregnant. I, of course, don't know where babies come from."

Quirke ignored her.

"Always queer goings-on, in an old house, like this," he said mildly. "I'll play the seven."

Life, life is always a surprise. Just when you think you have got the hang of it, have learned your part to perfection, someone in the cast will take it into her head to start improvising, and the whole damned production will be thrown into disorder. Lydia turned up today, unannounced. "Well, how could I let you know I was coming," she snapped, "since you seem to have torn the telephone out of the wall?" When she arrived I was sitting in my eyrie, scribbling away. Have I described this little room, my hidey-hole and refuge? It is at the back of the house, up three high concrete steps, and through a little arched, green-painted door that gives a queer monastic effect. I judge that the room was built on after the house was finished, as a *chambre de bonne*, though any maid the builder had in mind would have had to be a midget. Only in the middle of the room is there space to stand upright, for the ceiling slopes down steeply, almost to the floor at one side. It is like being in a tent, or the attic of a big doll's house. I have a little bamboo table at which I write, and a straw-bottomed chair brought up from the scullery. At my elbow, in the end wall opposite the door, a single small square window gives on to a sunny corner of the garden. Outside, just below the window, there is a clump of old geraniums, whose blossoms when the sun is at a certain angle throw a pinkish cast across the pages of my notebook. In the mornings I clamber in here as into a diving bell and shut myself away from the Quirkes, and brood, and dream, and remember, now and then setting down a sentence or two, a stray thought, a dream. There is a distinct rhetorical cast to the tone of these jottings, inevitable, I suppose, given my actor's training, yet often I catch myself speaking the words aloud as I write them, as if I were addressing them directly to some known and sympathetic ear. Since I found out that the Quirkes are living in the house I have been spending more and more of my time here. I am happy, or happiest, at least, in this sealed chamber, suspended in the tideless sea of myself.

My wife is a considerable person in many ways. She has been a staunch defence against whatever arrows and bomb-balls the world outside might sling into the compound of our lives together. You should have seen the first-night critics shrink when they beheld her descending on them armed with cigarette and wineglass. However, she is not at her best in emotional adversity. Daddy was too indulgent toward her, I believe, with the result that she has never lost the expectation that there will always be someone in charge who will deal with, for instance, the unanticipated eventualities of marriage and its inevitable woes. Not that she would be incapable of handling such things herself; as I say, she is far more formidable than I am when it comes to practical matters. It is just that she has the queenly conviction that she should not be compelled to spend from her store of strength, which she maintains as if for the commonweal, against the day when a real crisis shall arise, and she will be called upon to burst forth in breastplate and plumed helmet, all pennants flying. When I heard her voice today from far off beyond my little green door I experienced a moment of panic, as if I were a fugitive in hiding behind a false wall and she the head of the secret police. Venturing down from my lair I found her striding about the hall in an angry fluster. She was wearing black leggings and a bright-red, hip-length smock that gave her an ungainly and unbecomingly corpulent aspect. When she is angry a high warbling tearful note rises in her voice.

"Where were you, for God's sake?" she said when she saw me. "What's going on? Who is this girl?"

Lily, barefoot, in her crooked dress, was standing at a slouch some way behind her in the hall, chewing on a wad of gum and wearing a sullen look. The panic I had felt a minute ago was now replaced by a chilly calm. I have a gift, if gift it is, of quenching in myself at a stroke any fever of the blood or brain. There are, I mean there were, nights when I would cower in the wings, shaking, in a wet funk, as I awaited my cue, only a moment later to step forward in perfect poise, thundering out my lines without trace of tremor or fluff. A floating sensation comes over me at such moments, as if I were being buoyed up on some dense, fluent medium, a Dead Sea of the emotions. From out of this state of almost pleasant detachment I regarded Lydia now with a mild, enquiring air. I noticed my fountain pen was still in my fingers, cocked like a pistol. I almost laughed. Lydia stood with her head held up and to one side, in the attitude of a startled thrush, staring at me, her face set in a sort of rictus of baffled incredulity.

"That's Lily," I said lightly. "She's the housekeeper."

It sounded improbable even to me.

"The *what?*" Lydia cried, an avian squawk. "Have you gone completely off your head?"

"Lily," I called, "this is Mrs. Cleave." Lily said nothing, and did not stir, except to shift her slouch from one hip to the other, still rhythmically chewing. Lydia went on looking at me with that large surprised angry expression, leaning backward a little now as if to avoid the possibility of a wildly thrown punch.

"Look at you, the state of you," she said, wonderingly. "Is that a beard?"

"Lily takes care of me," I said. "Of the house, that is. She came most opportunely. I had been about to ask the nuns across the way if they might have a couple of orphans to spare." This time I did laugh, an unfamiliar sound. "I could have dressed them up in knee breeches and powdered wigs," I said, "my Justine and Juliette." I once played the divine Marquis, in a headband and flounced shirt open to the navel; I quite fancied myself in the part.

A hurt helpless something came into Lydia's look and it seemed for a moment she might cry. Instead she sighed heavily down her nostrils and tightened her mouth into a grim line, and turned on her heel and stalked off into the parlour. Lily's eyes met mine and she could not suppress a little grin, showing the glint of an eye-tooth.

"Some tea, Lily," I said softly, "for Mrs. Cleave and me."

When I followed her into the parlour Lydia was standing at the window as she had that first day we had come here, with her back to the room and one arm tightly folded across her chest, smoking a cigarette in short, violent puffs.

"What are you doing, Alex?" she said, in a quavery voice. She did not turn. I hate it when she tries to act, it is embarrassing. She only addresses me by name when she is being theatrical. I let a moment lapse.

"You'll be glad to hear," I said in a bright voice, "that the house is known to be haunted. So you see, I am not losing my marbles after all. Quirke says some child—"

"Stop," she said, holding up a hand. "I don't want to hear." I shrugged. She turned to the room and looked about vaguely with a frown. "This place is filthy," she murmured. "What does that girl do?"

"I don't pay her much," I said. "In fact, since recently I haven't been paying her at all."

I hoped she would ask why this was, thus giving me the opportunity of breaking to her the delicate news of my uninvited house-guests, but she only sighed again, still with that preoccupied frown, and shook her head. "I'm not interested in your domestic arrangements here," she said, with large but unconvinced disdain. She looked at the cigarette in her hand as if she had not noticed it before now. Her voice grew thick with breathy distress. "I take it you have left me and will not be coming back," she said in a rush, still glaring at the cigarette with glistening eyes.

I made a show of pondering hard.

"Now, was that a line of anapaests, do you think," I said, "or the rarer, shyer amphibrach? I ask out of professional interest. You really should be a poet." I still had that bloody pen in my hand. I put it down on the mantelpiece, concentrating, so as not to forget later where I had left it; I am becoming very absent-minded, in the matter of small, inanimate things. I could see Lydia in the mirror above the mantelpiece, glaring at the back of my neck. "I'm content here, for the moment," I said, in a considered tone, turning to her. "You see, it offers me a way of being alive without living."

"Of course," she said. "You've always been in love with death."

"Spinoza says—"

"Oh, fuck Spinoza," she said, but with little force, almost wearily.

She glanced about for an ashtray, and not finding one shrugged and dropped an inch of ash on the carpet, where it landed softly and did not crumble. I asked if she had heard again from Cass. She shook her head, but I could see she was lying. "Where is she, exactly?" I asked. Again that stubborn shake of the head, as if she were a child refusing to tell on a playmate who has been naughty in the nursery. I tried another approach. "What is the surprise you said she has for me?"

"She told me not to tell you anything."

"Oh, did she."

One of the things, the very few things, I have learned, or realised, about myself since coming here is that I am always on the lookout for someone or something on whom to wreak revenge. I do not know what I might be seeking revenge for, or what form my vengeance would take, exactly. I am like my mother waiting for the world to apologise to her for the nameless wrongs she believed it had done her. Like her, I cannot rid myself of the conviction that there is indeed blame to be apportioned, a score to be settled. I am content to wait, to take things slowly, to bide my time, but I am always sure that I shall be avenged, somehow, sometime. Perhaps when that time comes I shall know what the original insult or injustice was. What confusion there is in me; I really am a stranger to myself.

Out in the kitchen there was a sudden cacophonous blast from Lily's radio, immediately silenced.

Lydia was watching me sidelong now, waiting to see what I would do next. Sometimes, for instance at moments like this one, I allow myself to entertain the notion that for all her strengths she is a little afraid of me. I confess I like to keep her on her toes. I am unpredictable. Perhaps she really does think I am mad, and might do her violence. Behind her in the window the garden was an incongruously Edenic medley of gay greens and shimmering, petrol blues. High summer's abundance is a continuous surprise. "She wants to come home," she said, "but she can't, at the moment." This struck a false note of attempted appeasement, which I refused even to acknowledge. *At the moment*, indeed.

"She confides in you, does she?" I said. "She never used to."

This is true; whatever differences there may be between my daughter and me, we have always been close enough to read each other's minds—and it is always, always the two of us against poor Lydia.

I heard Lily's bare feet slapping along the corridor from the kitchen, and now she came in bearing a tin tray with a teapot and two unmatching mugs, and a plate piled high with thick, crooked slices of haphazardly buttered bread. I noticed Lydia noticing the crusted dirt on the child's callused feet and etched into the wrinkled red backs of her heels. Lily, biting her lower lip at one side, carefully avoided looking at me, and set the tray down on the hearth, bending from the waist and deliberately showing the backs of her thighs, pale as a fish's belly, right up to her narrow behind.

"Will I pour?" she said from under her hanging hair in a voice strangulate with suppressed mirth.

Lydia came forward quickly from the window. "I'll do it."

"Suit yourself," Lily said, and straightened, still not looking at either of us, and sauntered off, twitching her hips.

To pour the tea Lydia was forced to sit on the hearth rug, leaning aslant with her legs draped together at an awkward angle to one side, which gave her the look, not unfetching, of a beached mermaid.

"What age is that child?" she said, frowning at the teak-coloured tea as it glugged into the mugs.

"Seventeen, she claims."

Lydia snorted.

"Fifteen, more like," she said, "if that." There was something about the clumsy, helpless way she was sitting that set up a metronome beat in my blood. "You had better watch out."

"She's practically an orphan," I said. "Do you think I should make Quirke an offer for her? I'm sure it wouldn't take more than a shrunken head and pouch of cowrie shells and she could be mine—ours, I mean. What do you say?"

She brought her legs around in a quick, surprisingly graceful sweep and rose to her knees and offered me the mug. She was very close to me, almost kneeling between my knees. Taking the mug, I allowed my fingers to brush against hers. She went still, her calm gaze fixed on our two hands.

"You already have a daughter," she said quietly.

I took a sip from my mug. I really must instruct Lily in the art of making tea. I am sure she uses tea bags, though I have told her I will not tolerate them, nasty things. Lydia knelt motionless before me, in the attitude of a supplicant, her head hanging.

"I *had*," I said. "Then she grew up. A woman can't be a daughter."

"She needs help, you know."

"When has she ever not?"

She sighed, and transferred her weight from one knee to the other. Thinking she might be about to embrace me I put down my tea mug quickly and rose and walked past her to the window—stepping over that oddly repellent grey worm of ash she had left on the carpet—and stood where she had stood, contemplating the sunlit garden. There is an archaic quality to certain summer days, the ones that come at the close of July especially, when the season has reached its peak and is already imperceptibly in decline, and the sunlight thickens, and the sky is larger and higher and of a deeper blue than before. On such days, autumn is already sounding its first horn-calls, yet the summer still blithely believes it will never end. In that dreamy stillness, like the stillness in the azure distances of a stage set, all the summers back to childhood seem present; to childhood, and beyond childhood, to those Arcadian fields where memory and imagination merge. A breeze will spring up, one of the weather's half-formed thoughts, and something at the corner of your vision will flap once, languidly, and be still again. Confused soft noises mingle in the air, as of a distant revel. There are bee sounds, bird sounds, the needling buzz of a distant tractor. You will catch a fragrance, one that you know but cannot identify, it will remind you of somewhere else, a meadow, with poppies, beside a dusty road, and someone turning to meet you . . . I realised, there at the window, that something had changed, that I had crossed over into a different place. First there had been me, then me and the phantoms, then me and Quirke and Quirke's girl, and now—I did not know what now, except that this now was new. Behind me I could hear Lydia rising from her knees, grunting a little from the effort.

"The thing is, my dear," I said, "I haven't really got the energy to worry about anyone else, just now."

She gave a harsh little laugh.

"When did you ever?"

A slug-coloured cat was wading through the garden, batting aside the long grass with large deft subduing gestures of its paws. Life is everywhere, even in the stones, slow, secret, long-enduring. I turned from the window. I have always disliked this room, this quintessential parlour; there is a touch of the manse about it, with its brownish shadows and lumpy furniture and its cowed, unmoving air. Too many people have been unhappy here. Lydia was sitting now in the old armchair by the fireplace with her joined hands clasped between her knees, staring sightlessly into the grate. In the minute my back was turned she had put on years; in another minute she would throw them off again; it is a thing she does. Those charred books were still in the fireplace. Ashes, ashes everywhere. Lily came in at the door and paused, taking an interested measure of the atmosphere. "Mrs. Cleave and I would like to adopt you," I said to her, summoning up a big, bright smile. "We want to take you away from all this and give you a proper home and turn you into a little princess. What do you think of that?"

Lily looked from me to Lydia and back again and smiled warily, then went forward quickly and picked up the tray. As she was leaving I winked at her and she bit her lip again and smirked again and ducked out the door. Lydia sat on in her chair for a moment, motionless, gazing into the grate, then stirred, and released her hands and clapped them on her knees and stood up briskly with the air of one who has come to a large decision.

"I think the best thing we can do—" she began, when all at once she started to weep. Fast tears coursed down her cheeks, plump and shiny as drops of glycerine. She stood and stared through them for a second, in appalled surprise, then her face collapsed and she made a mewling noise, half in anger and half in woe, and put up her hands helplessly before her face with fingers splayed and hurried blunderingly from the room. That inch of cigarette ash was still where it had fallen, still unbroken.

I found her in the hall, crouched on the old sofa there, furiously rubbing at her tear-stained face with the heels of both her hands, like a cat cleaning its whiskers. I am not good with other people's distress. How often in our life together had I stood like this, watching her dissolve in grief, as a child might watch a sackful of kittens drowning in a pond. I know I have been a trial to her, in one way or another—indeed, in many ways. The fact is, I have never understood her, what she wants, what she expects. When we were first together she used to accuse me of treating her as if she were a child, and it is true that I liked to keep a fatherly eye on day-to-day matters, from the household accounts to her menstrual cycle—people with a lot of daytime on their hands tend to be busybodies, it is a thing I have noticed among my profession—though I say in my defence that I thought this is what would be required, when she was transferred from her Daddy's care into mine. Then one day in the midst of one of our rows she turned on me a frighteningly contorted face and screamed that she was *not my mother!* This was a new one; what was I to make of it? I was nonplussed. I waited until she calmed down and then asked her what she had meant, but that only sent her into another rage, so I dropped the subject, although I did continue to brood on it for a long time. At first I had thought she was accusing me of demanding to be cared for and coddled, but I dismissed that, and in the end decided that what she had most likely meant was that I was behaving toward her as I had toward my real mother, that is, with impatience, resentment, and that tight-lipped, ironical forbearance—the sigh, the small laugh, the upcast eyes—which I know is one of the more annoying ways I have of handling those who are supposedly close to me. A moment's thought showed me, of course, that what she had screamed at me was simply another form of her assertion that I was treating her like a child, for that, as she never tired of pointing out, was exactly how I had treated my mother. How intricate they are, human relations, so called.

"Darling," I said now, in a voice athrob with insincerity, "I'm sorry."

One of the paradoxes of our fights is that almost invariably they do not begin in earnest until the stage has been reached when I first attempt to offer an apology. It is as if some primitive instinct of suppressed female dominance is triggered in Lydia by this hint of weakness on my part. Now she went for my throat at once. It was all the old things, rehearsed so often they have gone stale, for me, certainly, if not for her. I will say one thing, she is comprehensive. She starts off in my infancy, works her way rapidly through youth and early manhood, lingers with loving bitterness over our first years together, takes a diversionary swipe at my acting, both in professional and private life— *"You're never off the stage, we're just the audience"*—then she gets to my relations with Cass and really rolls up her sleeves. Mind you, she is not as savage or relentless as she used to be; the years have tempered her temper. What does not change is the image of me that she propounds. In her version, I have everything all wrong. My mother is sweet-natured, put-upon, long-suffering, her nagging of my father and then of me simply a plea for some demonstration of love or affection, a muffled cry out of a wounded heart. My father, on the other hand, is a secret tyrant, self-muted, vindictive, withholding, whose very death was an act of spite and revenge on the woman who had cherished him. When I remind her, in a tone of no more than mild remonstrance, that my father was dead long before she met me, she brushes the fact aside with a contemptuous gesture; she knows what she knows. In this inverted picture of my family—the Holy Trinity is her sneering nickname for us—I too of course am stood on my head. Did I lead a lonely and puzzled childhood, shocked by the early loss of my father and subject thereafter to the unmeetable emotional demands of a bitterly disappointed mother? No, no: I was the little prince, showered with love, praise, gifts, who quickly saw off a resented father and spent the rest of his widowed mother's life blaming her for all the things she could not be or do. Did I sacrifice the best years of my adult life working dear in cheap theatre to support my wife and her child in the luxury to which a doting father had irresponsibly accustomed his spoilt daughter? Indeed no: I was the typical monster of selfishness who would have prostituted his wife for a walk-on part. Did I love my daughter, try to wean her away from her darkest obsessions, save her from her worst excesses? Not I: she was a trial to me, an irritation, a stumbling block on the road to stage success, a source of shame and embarrassment before my smart friends in the brittle make-believe world in which I was trying to claw my way to fame. So you see: it was all a lie, all a part I was playing, and playing badly, at that. And now I had done the worst of all, had walked out of the production, leaving the rest of the cast to deal with the cat-calls of the audience and the management's fury, while the backers all backed off.

As I say, she is not the lioness she once was. In the old days she would frighten even herself with the vehemence of her denunciations. We would rage at each other late into the night, on a battlefield littered with smashed crystal and swirling with cigarette smoke and the fumes of alcohol, and wake in the ashen light of morning, a salt bitterness in our mouths and our throats raw from drink and shouting, and reach out a hand to each other, tremblingly, under the sheets, not daring to move our heads, and one would make a shaky enquiry and the other would croak some hoarse word of reassurance, and then we would lie there, counting our wounds, surprised that the war was done for another day and we were still breathing.

I could hear Lily in the kitchen listening to us, trying not to make a sound. Exciting for a child, a real adults' fight. Cass used to like to hear us going at it hammer and tongs; perhaps it was a comforting match for the clangour in her own head. Now I waited, and presently Lydia wound down, and leant forward wearily with her arms folded on her knees and her head hanging, great snorting sobs making her shudder now and then, fury's after-tremors. Around us the shocked shadows congregated, like onlookers cautiously closing in on the still-smouldering scene of an explosion. On the lino near my foot a sunburst streamed and shivered. Odd, how distress gravitates to this passageway, the dank umbilicus of the house, with its windowless stretch of brown wall on one side and the overhang of the stairs on the other. Originally, in grander days, way before our time, it led to the servants' quarters at the rear; halfway along there is still the frame of what was no doubt a green baize door, long ago removed. Air stands unmoving here, unchanged for centuries, it seems; vague draughts swim through, like slow fish. There is a stale, brownish smell that haunted me as a child; it was like the smell I made when I cupped my hands over my nose and mouth and breathed the same breath rapidly in and out. My mother it was who put the sofa here, dragged it in by herself from the front room one day when I was at school, another of her whims. The lodgers took to it straight away, there was always one of them sitting on it, this one nursing a disappointment in love, that one the unacknowledged beginnings of a cancer. Cass too would perch there, with her thumb in her mouth and her legs folded under her, especially after a seizure, when the light hurt her eyes and she wanted nothing but solitude, and silence, and shadows.

The fact is, Lydia has always been jealous of Cass and me. Oh yes, she has. That was the way it was right from the beginning. It was into my arms that Cass as an infant would come tottering, no matter what blandishments her mother might be offering, what coos of encouragement or flattering cries. Even later, when her world was steadily darkening, it was I that our daughter would seek out first, it was my hand she would clutch to keep from falling past all help into the abyss of herself. Whose eyes did she seek when she came back from that first seizure, gazing up from the floor beside her bed with the bloody froth still on her mouth and that look on her face we thought was an unearthly smile but was only the effect of the contracted muscles relaxing? Who did she run to, laughing in terror, when she knew an attack was coming on? Who did she describe her aural visions to, the shattering glass cliffs and terrible birds made of metal and rags that flew at her eyes? Who did she turn to one day by that bed of lilies in someone's garden and whisper in the thrilled rush of discovery that that, *that* was the smell, as of some wonderful delicate sweet rotted meat, that filled the air around her in the seconds before a seizure? Who was the one who woke first when that cry rose up through the night, that long high thin ululation, like a nerve being drawn slowly out of its sheath?

I sat beside Lydia on the sofa, easing myself down as if she were asleep and I unwilling to wake her. The sunspot on the lino had shifted a stealthy inch or two. The moon in its course must be swinging ever closer to the sun, homing in on the light, like a moth. A faint whiff of strawy smoke drifted on to the air; a field of stubble somewhere was burning. The silence had a buzz to it, as of harp strings rubbed not plucked. My upper lip was unpleasantly damp. Long ago, when I was a boy, on a summer day like this one, still and hot, I walked across the fields, oh, for miles, it seemed, to a farm, to buy apples. I had brought with me my mother's oilcloth shopping bag; it had an unpleasant, greasy smell. I wore sandals, and a horsefly stung me on an instep. The farmhouse was all overgrown with ivy and had many small dark gleaming windows. It was the kind of place where in a boy's adventure book dark deeds would be afoot, and the farmer would wear gaiters and a waistcoat and carry a menacing pitchfork. In the yard a black-and-white dog growled at me and turned in cringing circles, its belly almost scraping the gravel. I stood in the stone-flagged porch while a fat surly woman in a flowered apron took my bag and went off into the shadowed depths of the house. There were gnarled geraniums in clay pots and a grandfather clock that seemed to hesitate before each tick. I paid the woman a shilling and she said nothing, watching me go. The dog in the yard growled again and licked its lips. The bag was heavy now, and kept bumping against my leg. In a lane I paused beside a soupy pond and watched the water-skimmers; their feet made pewtery dents in the surface; they moved as if worked by wires. The sunlight came through the trees like hot gold smoke. Why that day, that farm, the farmer's wife, the apples, those insects on that pond—why any of it? Nothing happened, no grand vision was granted me, no blinding insight or sudden understanding, yet it is all there, clear as yesterday—clearer!—as if it were something momentous, a key, a map, a code, the answer to a question I do not know how to ask.

"What is it?" Lydia said without looking up, and for a second I thought she had somehow been reading my mind. "What's wrong with you, what is the matter? What"—wearily—"what has happened to you?"

The apples were a pale whitish green and each bite came away with a satisfying, woody snap. I remember them; to this day I remember them.

"I have the feeling," I said, "the conviction, I can't rid myself of it, that something has happened, something dreadful, and I haven't taken sufficient notice, haven't paid due regard, because I don't know what it is."

She was silent, then gave a sort of laugh, and sat up and rubbed her hands vigorously on her upper arms, as if she had become chilled, keeping her face turned away from me.

"Maybe it's your life," she said. "That's disaster enough, isn't it?"

Evening, and she is still here. At least, I have not heard her departing. I do not know what she is up to, there has not been a sound from her, from anyone, for hours. It is worrying. Perhaps she has encountered Quirke, and is with him now, pouring out her troubles. Serve him right. Or she might have cornered the girl, might be quizzing her, wanting to know if I have interfered with her. I am skulking in my hideout, hunched over my bamboo table, feeling cross and ill at ease. Why must I always be the guilty one? I did not ask her to come here, I did not invite her. All I wanted was to be left alone. They abhor a vacuum, other people. You find a quiet corner where you can hunker down in peace, and the next minute there they are, crowding around you in their party hats, tooting their paper whistles in your face and insisting you get up and join in the knees-up. I am sick of them all. I shall not come out until she is gone.

IV

It is the following morning, and there is much excitement. The circus, of all things, has come to town. After a night of disturbed sleep I was woken early by a confusion of noises outside my window, and looked through a crack in the curtains to find a dozen or more trailers drawn up at haphazard angles in the square. The horses were being unhitched, and big-muscled bandy men in striped vests were hurrying to and fro, plying ropes, and hefting things, and calling to each other in sharp, brief barks; it was as if the performance had already started and they were the opening act. As I watched, tent-poles were being assembled, and a big tarpaulin was thrown down and rapidly unrolled. All around the square, at other bedroom windows, other curtains were twitching, and even the odd front door was opened cautiously and a lathered face or curlered head appeared, poking out in groggy wonderment.

"What's going on?" Lydia asked sleepily from the bed behind me, where she had raised herself on an elbow, a hand lifted to shade her eyes.

"It's the circus," I said, and had to laugh, though it came out more like a cough.

In fact, as I later found, it is more than a circus, it is a kind of roadshow, with a shooting gallery, and stalls for shying coconuts and throwing rings, and a cage on wheels containing a family of mangy, purple-bottomed monkeys who gibber and hoot and stare at passers-by with comical malignity. There is even a hall of mirrors: Lily and I were present when it was being put up. The big rippled sheets of glass were taken out of their sacking and lowered from the back of the wagon, and for a few giddy moments a troupe of rubbery dwarves and etiolated giants shimmied and shivered in those depthless caskets of light. Lily pretends to be bored by all this, but behind her arch look there is a glitter of childish excitement she cannot suppress. We had come out to do a tour of inspection while Lydia prepared breakfast. I had that sense of false alertness that comes from the lack of both sleep and sustenance, and in the early sunlight everything around me was unreally clear and sharply defined, like the pieces of a shattered kaleidoscope. On the back steps of a trailer painted in scarlet and midnight blue a man sat, watching us. He was a shabby, skinny fellow with red hair and a thin, foxy face. He wore a loose red shirt and shapeless trousers that were much too big for him, a clownish get-up, and he had a gold ring in one ear. He looked familiar, although I was sure I had never seen him before. He reminded me of a person I used to meet about the streets last winter, at the start of my bad time, whom also I seemed vaguely to know, and who certainly knew me, or of me, at least, for every time we encountered each other, which happened with alarming frequency, he would smile to himself, an awful, smug, lip-biting smile, which he would make a show of trying to hide behind a hand, while sidling quickly past me, with eyes resolutely downcast, as if he thought I might tackle him, might plant myself in his path and make him stop, or try to cuff him on the ear as he went by. He too had red hair, and wore spectacles that flashed at me mockingly, and a duffel coat, and down-at-heel shoes and concertina trousers. I thought perhaps he might be a member of the guild, a spear-carrier who thinks himself a Kean and hates me for my reputation and my successes. After an encounter with him I would have a sense of disquiet that lingered for days. I did think of confronting him, and demanding to know what it was about me that amused him, what secret of mine he thought he had uncovered, but before I could decide to act he would be gone, hurrying off into the crowd, head down and shoulders shaking, so it seemed to me, with secret mirth. This circus fellow had the same look of amused knowingness, though he was even more sure of himself, and was evidently not in the least concerned as to what I might say or do. Nevertheless, as we drew near he stood up, showing a hand-rolled cigarette and patting his scrawny thighs as if in search of matches, and went inside the trailer. Lily, I saw, had spotted him too.

We inspected the monkeys, one of whom rolled back his mouth so far it seemed he would turn himself inside-out, a moth-eaten lion reclining motionless as a sphinx and gazing out upon the world with an expression of unfathomable boredom, and a supercilious and very smelly dromedary tethered to a cherry tree, the lower leaves of which it was tearing with rubbery lips and spitting disdainfully on the ground. Lily stopped to watch in awe a dun mare copiously pissing. Despite my hunger I was not eager to return to the house. I am not sure which I find harder to cope with, Lydia's anger, or that brittle cheerfulness which is its inevitable consequence. After our fight yesterday she sulked throughout the evening, but relented later, as I knew she would. I had made her come with me to the pub, in order, I confess, to allow Quirke and the girl to get themselves settled for the night without her knowing, for I had not yet gathered my courage sufficiently to break to her the news of their permanent residency. We drank too many gins, and fell into amorousness—yes, yes, I have languished off the sexual wagon, I'm afraid, just when I thought I was cured of all that delirium. But we were very tender and forgiving toward each other, and in the glimmering small hours, clasped in her familiar warmth like a marsupial in its mother's pouch, I seemed more nearly sane than I have felt since I cannot remember when. By morning, however, doubts had set in. There is something not quite right, something even mildly disgraceful, in the way she lets her fury be transformed with such apparent ease into a wholly other sort of passion. Intransigent and cold of heart I may be, but when terrible things are said I take them to be at least an approximately accurate expression of true feelings, firm convictions. For instance, when Lydia hurls at me those accusations—that I am a bad husband and neglectful father, that I am a monster of self-regard, that onstage I cannot act and in life never cease from acting—I am impressed, I am cowed, even, despite the flinty exterior I take care to maintain. Not only that, but I bethink myself, even in the heat of battle, and wonder if perhaps these things are true of me, and if so how I should go about trying at least to ameliorate my faults and failings. My wife, on the other hand, judging by the rapidity and thoroughness with which she switches mood, seems to regard these exchanges of heavy fire, which leave me drilled with holes through which the wind of self-recognition whistles unimpeded, as no more than light badinage, lovers' raillery, or even, as last night, a form of sexual foreplay. Where is her sense of duty, I mean the duty to mean what one says, and, having said it, to stand by it?

After spying on the circus through the curtains for a moment longer—I was not entirely certain it was not a dream—I got back into bed, and presently woke, a second time, to the sound of her whistling. Yes, whistling. Have I mentioned that she does not suffer from hangovers? Angry, gin-blue seas were crashing inside my head, but she was sitting naked and unconcerned on a chair by the window, making up her face with the aid of a pocket mirror and doing that tuneless whistling she claims to be unconscious of, and that nearly brought our marriage to an end before the honeymoon was over. I lay for a while and pretended to be still asleep, fearful of being required to be bright, and suffering from that peculiar shyness, amounting almost to shame, that I always feel after those extravaganzas of fighting and reconciliation that I hope are not to become again a frequent feature of our life together, if we are to have a life together. It is at moments such as this, fraught and uncertain, that I understand myself least, seem a farrago of delusions, false desires, fantastical misconceptions, all muted and made manageable by some sort of natural anaesthetic, an endorphin that soothes not the nerves but the emotions. Is it possible I have lived all my life in this state? Is it possible to be in pain without suffering? Do people look at me and detect a slight peculiarity in my bearing, as one notices the stiff jaw and faintly drooping eye of a person lately risen from the dentist's chair? But no, what has been done to me is deeper than dentistry. I am a heart patient. There may even be a name for my complaint. "Mr. Cleave, harrumph harrumph, I'm afraid it's what we doctors call *anaesthesia cordis*, and the prognosis is not good."

Still feigning sleep, I saw through the peacock shimmer of lowered lashes that Lydia, the make-up brush suspended, was regarding my reflection in her mirror with a sardonic eye, knowing full well I was awake. I never was able to fool her; others might be taken in by my subterfuging ways, but never Lydia. I sat up, and she smiled. I did not like that smile, complicit, feline, expressive of that primitive conspiracy of the flesh we had entered upon again in the night. I repeat, how could she so lightly set at naught the appalling things we had shouted at each other—she said I had broken her spirit, as if she were a horse, to which I replied that if she had been a horse I would have had her shot, that kind of thing—before we both fell drunkenly into bed and, later, into each other?

"You look terrible," she said, husky and indulgent.

I did not answer. It is a curious thing about Lydia, that her body has hardly changed with the years. She has thickened somewhat, of course, and gravity is working its gradual, sad effects, yet in essentials she is still the silver-pale, slightly slouchy, excitingly top-heavy spoilt princess that I used to stalk along the quays by the Hotel Halcyon that summer all those years ago. Her flesh has a flaccid, slightly doughy quality that appeals to the pasha in me, suggestive as it is of the seraglio and the veil. She does not take the sun, after a month in the hottest of southern climes her skin will show no more than a faint, honeyed sheen that will fade within a week of her return to the grey north. On the warmest days there will be parts of her—her flanks, her inner arms, the soft flesh of her throat—that will retain a porcelain chill; I used to love to hold her in the clammy afterglow of passion, feeling her against me, the length of her, from brow to instep, that cool dense surface stippled with gooseflesh. Now I looked at her there in the morning light at the window, big and naked, one leg crossed on the other, the freckled shoulders and blue-veined breasts, those three deep folds of flesh at either side of her waist that I used to pinch until she shivered in languorous pain, and the old dog stirred in me and lifted its twitching snout—yes, yes, I am a fine one to talk of standing on principle. I was not so besotted, though, as to fail to note the small but remarkably well-stocked suitcase she had been foresighted enough to bring with her. I fear she is planning a long stay.

No ghosts today, not a single sighting; has Lydia's coming put them to flight for good? I feel uneasy without them. Something worse might take their place.

When Lydia and I came down, Lily was already in the kitchen, sitting at the table head on hand, glued to a comic and spooning up cereal with automated precision. Lydia was startled to see her there, but not so much as she was a moment later when Quirke himself appeared, coming in from the hall in braces and shirt-sleeves, with a loaf and a bottle of milk in a string bag. Seeing Lydia he paused, and his eyes skittered sideways. For a tense moment all was still, and even Lily looked up from her comic. I had an urge to laugh. "This," I said, "this is Mr. Quirke, my dear." Quirke hastily rubbed a hand on his thigh and came forward, offering it, with a queasy grin. A fuzz of reddish hair spilled thickly from the vee of his open shirt collar, which, it struck me, made it seem as if his stuffing were coming out, and I almost did laugh. Lydia allowed her hand to be shaken and immediately withdrew it. "Breakfast?" Quirke said encouragingly, showing the meagre bag of provisions. Lydia shot at me a darkly questioning glance which I pretended not to notice. She is a practical person, however, and saying nothing she took the milk and bread from him and carried them to the sideboard, and filled a kettle at the sink and put it on the range, while behind her back Quirke looked at me with eyebrows lifted and mouth turned down, as if we were a pair of urchins caught out by a grown-up in some prank.

I could not help but be amused by all this—the social predicament was wonderfully laughable. My enjoyment was short-lived, however. Quirke, no doubt seeing his living arrangements in peril, set himself at once, nauseatingly, to the task of charming Lydia. It worked; she always was a pushover for plausible rogues, as I can attest. While she went about preparing our breakfast he followed her around the kitchen, hastening to lend a helping hand when it seemed required, all the while keeping up a stream of fatuous talk. He spoke of the splendid weather she had brought, said he had wondered, coming in, who owned the lovely motor car parked outside—he must have spotted it last night, and prudently stayed away until after lights-out—told her stories from the town, and even launched into a potted history of the house. This was the last straw for me. Feeling an obscure disgust I went to the door, muttering an exit line about taking a stroll, as if I ever strolled anywhere. At once Lily scrambled up, wiping her mouth on her forearm, and said she would come with me. Outside, the early sun had an intense, lemony cast, and the morning was all glitter and glassy splinterings, which did not help my headache, or my mood. Lily stopped and spoke to one of the circus hands, an Italianate type with oiled curls and a gold stud in his nostril, clasping her hands at the small of her back and swaying her meagre hips, the little slut, and came back to me with the eager news that the first performance will be put on this afternoon; I have the grim suspicion that she hopes I will take her to it. Well, why not; we could make a family outing of it, Lydia, and Quirke and the girl, and me, old paterfamilias.

When we returned to the house Lydia had cooked bacon and eggs and fried bread and tomatoes and black pudding; I had not thought there was so much food in the house—perhaps she brought it with her, all parcelled up in that bottomless suitcase of hers—and my stomach heaved at the sight, which was almost as bad as the smells; lately I have pretty well got out of the way of eating. Quirke, with a large and not quite clean handkerchief knotted round his neck for a napkin, was already tucking in, while Lydia, wearing one of my mother's old aprons, was at the range cheerfully dishing up another round of eggs. I took her by the wrist and drew her into the hallway, and demanded to know, in a furious whisper, through gritted teeth, what she thought she was about, setting up this grotesque parody of domestic life. She only smiled benignly, however—she does not realise how close she comes at times to getting a black eye—and touched a hand to my cheek and said with horrible roguishness that she had thought I would surely be hungry this morning and in need of something hot to restore my strength. I feel I am losing control here; I feel that some large thing I have been holding in my hands for so long that I have ceased to notice it has suddenly shifted and become slippery, and may at any moment go tumbling out of my grasp altogether.

"You brought them into the house," she said, nodding toward the kitchen and the Quirkes.

"No, I didn't. They were here when I came."

"But you let them stay." So Quirke had confessed all. She put on a big triumphant smile, into the soft centre of which I pictured myself sinking a fist. "You are the one who seems in need of a family."

Of course, I could think of no reply to that, and came up here to my cubbyhole in a sulk, nursing an irrational and infantile satisfaction at having refused to eat a crumb of breakfast, the foul aromas of which followed me like a taunt up the three steps and through the green door, and which linger faintly even yet. I flung myself down at my bamboo table, ignoring its squeal and crackle of apprehensive protest, and snatched up my pen and scrawled an extended passage of invective against my wife, which when I had finished it I immediately struck out. Terrible things I wrote, unrepeatable, they made me blush even as I set them down. I do not know what it is that comes over me at such moments, this frightening red rage that might make me do anything. What is there for me to be so angry about? I know what Lydia is up to, it is not so reprehensible. She has a great capacity to make the best of the worst predicaments. Finding how things are here, or how she takes them to be, me a landlocked Crusoe, bearded and wild of eye, with not only Quirke as Friday but a surrogate daughter as well—is that what Lily is? the words were written before I had time to think them—she at once set about creating an environment that would simulate, however grisly the likeness, our own dear hearth, which she supposes I am pining for. Ever the home-maker, my Lydia. Well, it will take more than crisped bacon and black pudding to turn this house into a home.

Although I know that nothing can ever be pinpointed so definitively, I date the inauguration of a significant shift in my attitude toward Lydia from the moment, some years back, when I realised that she is mortal. Let me explain, if I can, or let me describe, at least, how the realisation came to me. It was a very odd experience, or perhaps sensation would be a better word. One day, set as usual on the dogged but indisciplined task of self-improvement, I was reading an intricate passage in the work of some philosopher, I forget which one, dealing with the theoretical possibility of the existence of unicorns, when for no reason that I can think of I saw in my mind suddenly the figure of my wife, a very clear and detailed though miniaturised image of her, dressed, most implausibly, in an unbecoming frock of some stiff, brocade-like fabric, which she certainly never possessed in the—what shall I call it?—the empirical world, and with her hair done in that style of frozen rolls of sea-foam so favoured by the second Queen Elizabeth in her latter years, but which Lydia, the living Lydia, would never dream of adopting; I mention these details only in a spirit of scientific rigorousness, for I can think of no explanation for them; in this peculiar image of her—my wife, that is, not the English monarch—she was suspended in a fathomless dark space, a region of infinite emptiness wherein she was the only and only possible specific point, and in which she was receding backwards, at a steady but not rapid rate, with her hands vainly lifted before her as if holding an invisible orb and sceptre—there is the royal note again—wearing an expression of puzzlement and as yet mild though deepening consternation, and it came to me, with ghastly, breathtaking certitude, that one day she would die. I do not mean to suggest, of course, that before then I had imagined her to be somehow immortal. Despite the absurdity of it, what I had understood in that vision of her, simply, astonishingly, was her absolute otherness, not only from me, but from everything else that was in the world, that *was* the world. Up to then, and, indeed, as I have done most of the time since, the mind being a lazy organ, I had conceived her, as I did so much else, to be a part of me, or at least of my immediate vicinity, a satellite fixed and defined within the gravitational field of the body, of the planet, of the red giant that is my being. But if she could die, as I saw now she most certainly could, and would; if some day I was destined to lose her, even in that awful dress and gruesome perm, into the unknowable depths of eternity; if she was to be taken back, bouncing away from me like a ball that has snapped free at the end of its elastic, then how could she be said to be here, fully, palpably, knowably, now? I even saw the circumstances of her death, if I may use that verb of so nebulous a vision. In it, there was a room, in what seemed to be a large apartment, not a remarkable room, rather low-ceilinged, but wide and deep and well appointed. It was night, or late evening, and although there were many lamps about, on tables and bookshelves and even standing, set in heavy broad bases, on the floor, none of them was lit; what light there was came down from the ceiling, a thickish, worn yet unforgiving light that threw no shadows. The atmosphere was heavy, airless, lifeless, though not in any way threatening or distressed. Someone was reclining in a deep armchair, a person whom I could not see, but who I am certain was not Lydia, and someone else was walking past, a woman, a woman I did not know, nondescript and plainly dressed; she had stopped, and turned to ask a question, and waited now, but no answer came, and it was understood that none would come, that there was no answer, and somehow that was death, Lydia's death, even though Lydia was not there, not there at all. Understand, this was not a dream, or at least I was not asleep. I sat with the book still open in my hands, my eyes still fixed on the page, and went back over it all, carefully, the room, and the tired light, and the woman, and the unseen figure in the chair, and, before that, Lydia herself, still suspended in space, ridiculously coiffed, with her hands held up, but it had all gone inert now, inert and flat, without movement, like a series of badly proportioned photographs, taken by someone else, in places where I had never been. Do not ask me where it came from, this image, illusion, hallucination, call it what you will; I only know what I experienced, and what, for no good reason, it signified.

I have just heard, from down in the house, a sound that for a second I did not recognise. Laughter. They are laughing together, my wife and Quirke. When is it exactly that I last saw my phantoms? Not today, as I have noted, but did I see them yesterday, or even the day before? Perhaps they really have gone for good. Yet somehow I do not think so. The traces of them that persist are all impatience, resentment, envy, even. What there is of them is so little, so faint and insubstantial, that what they leave behind them, their affects, seems more than they are, were, themselves.

An accusation Lydia flung at me last night is that I have always had a deplorable weakness for strays. This was in connection with the Quirkes, obviously, yet I am not clear why she thinks it such a deplorable flaw. After all, I enquired of her, in my most reasoning tone, is not hospitableness a virtue urged on us even by the unaccommodating God of the desert tribes? She laughed at this, one of her large, would-be pitying laughs. "Hospitable?" she cried, throwing back her head. "Hospitable?—You?" What she believes is that I take to strays not out of any charitable urge, but in the spirit of the anthropologist, or, worse, the vivisectionist. "You want to study them," she said, "take them apart, like a watch, to see how they work." Her eyes had a malignant gleam, and there was a speck of white spit at one corner of her mouth, and a flake of ash on her sleeve. We were in my bedroom by now, with no lamp lit and the last grainy glow of twilight from the window making the air seem a box full of agitated, wanly illumined dust. The boy and the watch: how often have I heard that tired formulation flung at me, by a succession of disenchanted lovers, each one imagining she has new-minted it. Yet I did once do it, in fact, took a watch apart, when I was a boy. After my father's death, it was. He had given it to me, brought it home one birthday in a box, with a bow that the girl in the shop had tied for him. A cheap model, Omega, I think the brand was. It boasted seven rubies in the mechanism; I could not find them, search as I would, with my little screwdriver.

Lydia now was speaking of that young fellow who used to come into the house, and how it infuriated her that I would try to talk to him. At first I did not know whom she meant, and said she must be raving—I thought she might hit me for that—but then I remembered him. A big strapping fellow he was, with a shock of yellow hair and amazing big white teeth gapped with caries at regular intervals, so that when he smiled, as he frequently and frighteningly did, it looked as if a miniature piano keyboard had been set into his mouth. He was autistic, although at the outset we did not know it. He first appeared one drowsy hot day in late summer, just walked in through the door with the wasps and the rank tarry stink of the sea. By then we were living in the house above the harbour, where my late father-in-law's spirit still reigned, keeping a beady eye on me in particular. The boy was sixteen or seventeen, I suppose, the same age as Cass at the time. I met him in the hall as he was coming from the open front doorway with the light behind him, shambling along purposefully with his wrestler's arms bowed. I thought he must be a delivery boy, or the man to read the gas meter, and I stood back to let him pass, which he did without giving me a glance. I noticed his eyes, flinty blue and alive with what seemed fierce amusement at some private joke. Straight into the drawing room he went, appearing to know exactly where he was going, and I heard him stop. Curious now, I followed him. He was standing in the middle of the floor, big leonine head thrust forward on its thick-veined neck, looking about him slowly, scanning the room, still with that humorous light in his eye but with an air of knowing scepticism, too, as if things were not as they should be, as if he had been here yesterday and come back today to find everything completely changed. From the doorway I asked him who he was and what he wanted. He heard me, I could see that, but as something he did not recognise, a noise from way out beyond his range. His moving glance glided over me, his eyes meeting mine without any sign that he knew who or even what I was, and fixed on something I was holding in my hand, a newspaper, or a tumbler, I cannot remember what it was, and he gave his head a

rueful little shake, smiling, as if to say, *No, no, that is not it at all,*
and he came forward and pushed past me and strode off quickly
down the hall to the front door and was gone. I stood a moment in
mild bewilderment, unsure that he had been there at all, that I had
not imagined him; thus Mary must have felt when the angel spread
his gold wings and whirred off back to Heaven. I went and told
Lydia about him, and of course she was able at once to tell me who
he was, the retarded son of a fisher family down on the harbour,
who now and then eluded the watchful guardianship of his many
brothers and roamed the village harmlessly before being recap-
tured, as he always was, eventually. Security must have been very
lax at the end of that summer, for he visited us again two or three
times, coming and going as abruptly as he had the first time, and
with as little communication. I was fascinated by him, of course,
and tried all ways I could think of to provoke a response from
him, without success. Why these attempts to communicate, to get
through to him, as they say, should so irritate Lydia I could not
understand. It happened that at the time I was preparing to play
the part of an idiot savant, in an overblown and now long-
forgotten drama set in a steamy bayou of the Deep South, and here
was a living model, wandering about my own house, as if sent by
Melpomene herself—how would I not, I demanded of Lydia, how
would I not at least try to get him to babble a sentence or two, so
that I might copy his cadences? It was all in the cause of art, and
what would it matter to him? She only looked at me and shook her
head and asked if I had no heart, if I could not see the poor child
was helplessly beyond contact. But there was more than this, I
could see, there was something she was not saying, prevented by
an embarrassment of some kind, or so I felt. And it is true, my
interest in him was not entirely professional. I confess I have
always been fascinated by nature's anomalies. Mine is not the
eagerness of the prurient crowd at a freak-show, nor is it, I insist

again, the anthropologist's cold inquisitiveness or the blood-lust of the pitiless dissector; rather, it is the gentle dedication of the naturalist, with his net and syringe. I am convinced I have things to learn from the afflicted, that they have news from elsewhere, a world in which the skies are different, and strange creatures roam, and the laws are not our laws, a world that I would know at once, if I were to see it. Stranger far than Lydia's irritation at my efforts to provoke the boy was Cass's anger at me for having anything whatever to do with him, for not bolting the door against him and calling for his keepers. He was dangerous, she said, violently picking at her fingernails, he might fly at any one of us and tear our throats out. Once she even made a go at him herself, confronted him in the garden as he was making his dementedly determined way toward the back door, and went at him with fists flailing. What a sight they were, the pair of them, like two animals of the same implacable species attempting to fight their way past each other on a forest track wide enough only for one. She had been in her room and looked out the window and spied him. My heart had set up its accustomed warning throb—perpetually switched on, that old alarm, when Cass is about—before my ears had properly registered the quick, hollow patter of her bare feet going down the stairs, and by the time I got to the garden she was already locked in a grapple with him. They had collided under the arbour of wisteria, of which Lydia is so proud; odd, in my memory of that day the bush is prodigiously in flower, which it cannot have been, so late in the season. The sun of noon was shining, and a white butterfly was negotiating its drunken way across the burnished lawn, and even in my anxiety I could not help but note the strikingly formal, the almost classical, composition of the scene, the two young figures there, arms hieratically lifted between them, his hands clasping her wrists, with the garden all around them, in the blue and gold light of summer, two wild things, nymph and faun, struggling in the midst of subdued nature, like an old master's illustration of a moment out of Ovid. Cass was at her most feral, and I think the poor fellow was more than anything amazed to be so violently tackled, otherwise God knows what he might have done, for he looked to be as strong as an ape. I was still sprinting down the garden path, bits of gravel flying out from under my heels like bullets, when with a great heave he lifted her bodily by the wrists and set her behind him like a sack of not very heavy stuff, and resumed his dogged way toward the house. For the first time then they both noticed me. Cass gave an odd sharp cough of laughter. The boy's step faltered, and he stopped, and as I drew level with him he moved aside deferentially on to the grass to let me go past. As I did, I caught his eye. Cass was trembling, and her mouth was working in that awful sideways shunting movement that it did when she was most intensely agitated. Fearing a seizure was imminent I put my arms about her and held her, resisting, against me, shocked as always by the mixture of tenseness, of fierceness and of frailty that she is; I might have been embracing a bird of prey. The boy was looking all about the garden now, at everything except us, with what in another would have been an expression of profound embarrassment. I spoke to him, something foolish and stilted, hearing myself stammer. He made no response, and suddenly turned and loped away, silent and swift, and leapt the low wall on to the harbour road, and was gone. I led Cass to the house. The crisis in her had passed. She was limp now, and I almost had to hold her up. She was muttering under her breath, inveighing against me, as usual, swearing at me and weeping in fury. I hardly listened to her. I could only think, in pity and a kind of crawling horror, of the look I had caught in the boy's eye when he had stepped aside to let me pass. It was a look such as one might receive out of a deep-sea diver's helmet when the air pipe has been severed. Way down in the dazed depths of that murky sea in which he was trapped, he knew; he knew.

I think that was the day Cass cut off her hair, standing in front of the bathroom mirror, with her mother's big sempstress's scissors. It was I who found the shorn tresses strewn on the tiles; I would not have been more shocked had they been splashes of blood. I went to her bedroom to find her but the door was locked. By this stage of early womanhood she had discovered scholarship, and spent the most part of her days shut away in her room overlooking the garden and the harbour, reading in her histories, rummaging back and forth in relentless pursuit of facts—I can still hear the flap and shirr of the heavy pages turning—and writing furiously in her notebooks. The labour was at once a torment to her and a palliative. All that summer she had been engaged on a scheme to plot in maniacal detail Kleist's last three hours on earth, then abruptly one day she abandoned that and began instead researching the lives of the five children that Rousseau had by his Thérèse, all of whom, for their own good, he had consigned to foundling hospitals. We spent a pleasant week together in Paris, where I strolled the boulevards and sat at sidewalk cafés while she tried to trace the orphans' fate through old books and documents at the Bibliothèque Nationale. How restful it was to be there, in the autumnal city, with her immured in these safe and pointless labours; I felt like the worldly wise duenna in an Edwardian novel of international manners. In the evenings Cass would come back to our hotel with inky fingers and library dust in her hair, and we would change, and drink an aperitif, and stroll out to a restaurant, the same one every night, run by a studiedly irascible Basque— what a shoulder-shrugging old fraud he was—where we would dine together in companionable silence, making a handsome couple, I don't doubt, me with my profile, and she sitting upright like a watchful sphinx, that fine heart-shaped head of hers poised on its pale and slender neck. Afterwards we would go to the cinema, or is it the Comédie Française, where she would translate the lines for me in a stage whisper that on one occasion almost got us thrown out of the theatre. In the end, of course, her project on the philosopher's misfortunate children came to nothing; the offspring of the great leave scant trace upon the page of history. I still have a bundle of foolscap sheets scrawled with notes in her disordered, very black, barbed-wire hand. They are already decaying at the edges.

Lily has been scrabbling at my door, wanting me to take her to the circus. I can hear faintly the tinny music that has been blaring out from tannoys this past hour, interspersed with frantically enticing announcements of the Grand Opening Performance, which is to begin at noon. I told her repeatedly to go away. The circus, indeed—what next? Perhaps she thinks I really do want to adopt her, not realising that my heart is as hard as Jean Jacques's ever was. She whined and wheedled for a time, then went off muttering. She is a little wary of me, I think, when I am up here in my alchemist's cell, busy about these mysterious scribblings. There is something at once unsettling and tantalising about a locked door with someone sitting behind it hour on hour in silence. When I knocked at Cass's room that day, standing in the corridor clutching a hank of her hair, I had the feeling that I always had on such occasions, a mingling of dread and vexation, and a peculiar, stifled excitedness—Cass, after all, is capable of anything. And I felt foolish, too. A buttery lozenge of late sunlight lay fatly on the carpet runner at my feet. I spoke through the door to her and got no response. There was the circus music—no, no, that is now, not then; things are running together, collapsing into each other, the present into the past, the past into the future. My head feels full of something. It must be the effect of the heat. I wish this oppressive weather would break.

My phantoms were my own, exclusively mine, that was the point of them. We were a little family together, the three of us, the woman, child, and me the surrogate father. And what a fatherhood it was, absolute and unquestioned, for everything, their very existence, depended on me. Why now have they deserted me? More—why have they deserted me and left this air of accusation behind them, as if it were I who had exorcised them, instead of, as it feels to me, the other way about? I know, I know, I let others in, first the Quirkes, now Lydia, but what of it? These interlopers are merely the living, while what *we* shared was a communion of the dead. For I have died, that is what has happened to me, I have just this moment realised it. The living are only a species of the dead, someone has written somewhere, and a rare species, at that. I believe it. Come back, sweet shades! come back.

She cut off all her russet hair and threw it on the floor for me to find. Eventually she unlocked the bedroom door, I heard her do it, and I waited a moment, taking a breath. Inside, she had returned to her table by the open window, and was pretending to write, with books and papers stacked around her in a semicircle on the floor, her little crenellated keep. Bent there over the page she was for me in a flash a child again. I stood behind her. She writes with violent thrusts of her fist, as if she were not writing but, on the contrary, endlessly crossing out. The tufts of hair stood out from her skull like a fledgeling's ruffled feathers. How defenceless seemed the suddenly bared back of her neck. The day had hazed over, and the garden beyond the window lay in silence, leadenly. High up in the dully luminous sky, immensely far, the swifts, those sharks of the air, were acrobatically at feed. At last she paused and looked up, not at me, but at the world outside, her pen suspended aloft like a dart she was about to throw. When she frowns, the pale patch of skin above each ear develops a wrinkle, an effect I had not seen since she was an infant. The swathe of hair I was holding had a cold, silken, inhuman texture; I laid it on the table beside her elbow.

"Did you tell her?" she said.

"Your mother? No."

I was remembering, I am not sure why, the afternoons when I used to collect her from the music academy. She was nine that year. She had decided she wanted to learn to play the piano, it was one of her whims. She had no aptitude. She kept at it through a whole winter, though. I would wait for her in the draughty vestibule, vacantly reading the announcements on the notice board, while other pupils came and went, the quiffed mama's boys with their violin cases like miniature coffins, the girls pasty and glowering, in awkward shoes. Every time the swing door opened a flurry of damp wind would burst in and make a rowdy scene for a moment before being subdued by the gauntly disapproving atmosphere. Now and then one of the teachers would come wandering through, dowdy in tweed skirts and sensible shoes or fingering a despondent tie, distracted, bored, irritable, all of them always seemingly in search of something they had mislaid. There was a touch of bedlam to the place. A soprano's sudden shriek from some high chamber within would rip the air redly, or a drum-roll would come pounding down the stairs like the footfalls of a rotund inmate making a bid for freedom. Five-finger exercises tinkled, precise, monotonous and insane. At the end of her lesson Cass somehow always contrived to appear from an unexpected direction, up the narrow basement steps when I was watching the double doors of frosted glass that led to the concert room, or from the concert room itself when I had thought she would have been upstairs. How small she looked in those surroundings, under the dusty chandelier, glared at from their shadowy niches by laurel-wreathed busts of the great composers. She would advance with a quick yet somehow hesitating step, shyly, wearing an unfocused dreamy smile, as if she had been doing something not quite proper, her music case gripped tightly under her arm. She would slip her hand into mine almost conspiratorially and lead me firmly from the place, and then stop on the granite step outside and look about her in the wintry twilight, seeming to have been half expecting it all not to be there and enchanted that it was, the lighted shop windows, and seal-like cars plunging past, the hurrying office workers making their way head-down for the train station. Then the spring came, and after the Easter break she did not go back to her lessons. No tenacity, that was always Cass's problem, one of her problems. We did not try to force her to continue; provocation was the thing to be avoided above all, even in those early days. I found to my surprise that I missed my twice-weekly dawdles there in that cold bleak ante-room. What is it about such occasions of timeless time that afterwards makes them seem touched with such a precious, melancholy sweetness? Sometimes it seems to me that it is in those vacant intervals, without my being aware of it, that my true life has been most authentically lived.

Cass was watching the swifts. To be in her presence, even when she is at her most calm, is to be always a little on edge. But no, calm is the wrong word, she is never calm. It is as if she is filled to the brim with some highly volatile substance that must not be interfered with, or even subjected to overly close scrutiny. One must watch her sidelong, as it were, drumming one's fingers and nonchalantly whistling; I have been doing it for so long I have developed a cast in my eye, I mean the eye of my heart. In childhood her inner turmoil would manifest itself in a series of physical ailments and minor mishaps; she suffered constantly from nosebleeds, earaches, chilblains, verrucas; she burned herself, scalded herself; she fell down. All this she bore with amused impatience, as if these inflictions were a price she must pay for some eventual blessing, the conferring of which she is awaiting even yet. She bites her nails so deeply that the quicks bleed. I want to know where she is. I want to know where my daughter is and what she is doing. There is something going on, something no one will tell me, I am convinced of it. I shall get it out of Lydia, I shall beat it out of her, if that is what it takes.

"Remember," Cass said, leaning forward a little at the table to get a better look at the bird-specks swooping, "remember the stories you used to tell me about Billy in the Bowl?"

I remembered. She was a bloodthirsty child, was my Cass, as bad as Lily, worse. She loved to hear the ferocious escapades I used to invent for that fabled legless wretch who in olden times went about the city streets at night in a cut-off barrel with wheels and drank the blood of babies, it was said.

"Why do you think of that, now?" I asked.

She rubbed a hand on her shorn pate, making a raspy sound.

"I used to make believe that I was him," she said, "Billy in the Bowl." At last she looked at me. Her eyes are green; my eyes, so they tell me, although I cannot see the resemblance. "Do you like it, my haircut?"

Faintly from on high I could hear the cries of the gorging swifts. One day when she was small she climbed into my lap and gravely said that there were only three things in the world she was not afraid of, toothpaste, ladders, and birds.

"Yes, Cass," I said. "I like it."

Lily is scratching at my door again. The circus is about to start, she says. Well, let it.

When eventually I came down from my ivory tower I found Quirke on his knees in the kitchen, shirtsleeves and trouser bottoms rolled, going at the floor with a scrubbing brush and a bucket of suds. I stood and stared, and he sat back on his heels and gave me back a wry look, not at all abashed. Then Lydia came through from the hall with her hair tied up in a scarf and carrying a mop—yes, a mop—looking every inch the cockney charlady; there was even a cigarette dangling from a corner of her mouth. This really is becoming ridiculous. She frowned at me absently. "When are you going to shave off that awful beard?" she said, the cigarette joggling and letting fall a light spray of ash. If Lydia were ever to become lost, the search party could simply follow her cigarette droppings. Quirke was grinning now. Without a word I turned aside from this absurd scene of domestic industry and went in search of Lily, the only one left in this house, seemingly, whom I can depend on to be as irresponsible as I am. She was in her room—I think of it as hers now, no longer my mother's, which is progress, I suppose, though toward what, exactly, I cannot say— lying on her belly on the bed with her legs up and ankles crossed, reading an inevitable magazine. She was in a sulk, and would not look at me, hesitant in the doorway. Her bare feet were filthy, as usual; I wonder if the child ever bathes. She swayed her legs lightly from side to side in time to some dreamy rhythm in her head. The window was a big gold box of light; the far hills shimmered, dream-blue. I asked if she would care to come for a walk with me.

"We went for one this morning," she answered in a mumble, and still would not lift her eyes from the page.

"Well," I said mildly, "we could go for another." She had been smoking, I could smell it in the air. I picture her Lydia's age, a wizened slattern, hair dyed yellow and those delicate purple veins in her spindle legs all varicosed. "Mrs. Cleave is going to come up any minute and make you scrub the floor," I said.

She snorted softly. She pretends to regard Lydia as a figure of fun, but I think she is jealous of her, and possibly a little afraid of her, too. She can be formidable, can Lydia, when provoked, and I know that she finds Lily provocative. In bored languor Lily rose now and waded on her knees as through water to the edge of the bed and stepped lightly to the floor; the bedsprings gave a dismayingly familiar jangle. Is Lydia right, in that mismatched marriage was my poor mother the injured party, not my father? But then, is there ever an uninjured party? Lily dropped to one knee to fasten the strap of her sandal, and for a moment an Attic light glowed in the room. When we were on the stairs she stopped and gave me an odd look.

"Are you going to let us keep on living here," she said, "my Da and me?"

I shrugged, and tried not to smile—what was it that was making me want to smile?—and she laughed to herself and shook her head and went on quickly, leaving me behind.

Queer, how much of a stranger I am in this town. It was always that way, even when I was a child. I was hardly here at all, just biding my time; the future was where I lived. I do not even know the names of half the streets, and never did. I had a mental map of the place that was wholly of my own devising. I found my way about by designated landmarks: school, church, post office, picture-house. I called the streets by what was in them. My Abbey Street was where the Abbey Cinema stood, my Pikeman Place was where there was a statue of a stylised patriot, whose verdigrised curls and stalwart stare for some reason always made me want to snigger. There are certain parts of the town that are more unfamil-iar to me than others, places I rarely had cause to be in, and which over the years took on in my mind an almost exotic aspect. There was a hill with a patch of wasteland—it is probably built over now—traversed by a meandering track, where tinkers used to let their horses loose to graze; I had a recurring dream of being there, in hazy sunlight, looking down on the town, with something extraordinary about to happen, that never did. A lane that ran behind the back of a public house had a sour green smell of porter that made my stomach heave, reminding me, I don't know why, of a frog I once saw a boy inflate to an eyed balloon by sticking a straw down its gullet and vigorously blowing into it. Buildings, too, gave off an alien air, the Methodist Hall, the old chandlery in Cornmarket, and the malt store, built like a fortress, with a double rank of low, barred windows that at certain times emitted wraith-like clouds of evil-smelling steam, and where I was convinced I could hear rats scampering over the grain. In such places my fancy tarried uneasily, frightening itself with the thought of nameless terrors.

I was describing to Lily the malt store and those rats, making her do her dry-retching routine, when we came into a little open space bounded at the far end by a fragment of the old town wall that Cromwell's cannons missed. There we sat down on a bench beside a disused public lavatory, under the shade of a gnarled tree, and she began to tell me about her mother. The sun was hot, and there was not a soul about save for a lame dog that circled us warily, wagging a limp tail, before mooching off. I suppose it must have been this deserted atmosphere, the noontide stillness, and the tree, and the glare of the whitewashed lavatory wall beside us and the faint understink of drains, that made it seem that we were somewhere in the far south, somewhere hot and dry, on some harsh coast, with peeling plane trees and cicadas chirring under a merciless sky. *What seas what shores what granite islands* ... As she talked, Lily picked at a loose thread in the hem of her dress, squinting in the light. A breeze rattled the leaves above us and then all settled down again, like an audience settling down for the next act.

"Where were you living, when she died," I said, "your mother?" She did not answer, pretending not to have heard.

I have discovered Quirke's lair, did I say that? I stumbled on it in one of my prowls about the house the other day. He picked a modest room, I will say that for him. It is hardly a room at all, up near the attics; my mother would not have offered it to even the most indigent of our lodgers, and used it for storing lumber, and, after his death, my father's old suits and shoes that her sense of thrift would not let her throw away. It is low-ceilinged, and slightly wedge-shaped, with a single, crooked window at the narrower end, long ago painted shut, as the cheesy air attested. There is a camp bed with a thin horsehair mattress, and a blanket but no sheets. He uses a chamber pot, I noticed, the handle of it protruded from under the bed like an ear eagerly cocked. He is not the most fastidious of persons. There was dust on everything, and some worrying smears on the walls, and used plates, and a tea mug that does not seem to have been washed for a very long time, and three far from clean shirts hanging in an overlapping row on the wardrobe door, like a trio of close-harmony singers. I trust he will not invite Lydia up here, no matter how chummy they may become, for she would surely smack him smartly on the wrist and have him down on his knees again with the scrubbing brush and pail. Despite the squalor and the sadness of the place—those shirts, that mug, a pair of cracked shoes, one lying on its side, both with their tongues hanging out, that looked as if they had dropped off a corpse as it was being dragged out—I experienced a childish tingle of excitement. I have always been an enthusiastic snooper; diaries, letters, handbags, nothing is safe from me—why, sometimes, though I should not admit it, sometimes I will even take a peek into other people's laundry baskets, or used to, in the days when Lydia and I had friends, and would go out to their houses, for parties, and dinner, and summer lunches . . . Unimaginable, now. In Quirke's room, though, the tingly sensation I had was more than merely the pleasure of delving into someone else's belongings. I am thinking of the hare's nest I found one day at the seaside when I was a child, a neat deep whorl hollowed out of the coarse grass on the back of a dune, containing three tiny, throbbing leverets huddled so close together they looked like a single animal with three heads. I picked them up and put them inside my jersey and carried them back to the two-roomed wooden chalet where my mother and I were enduring a holiday together. When I showed them to her she gave a small cry of dismay and took a hasty step backward; she was not long a widow, and her nerves were bad. She said the creatures were probably diseased, or had lice, and would I please take the dirty things away this instant. I plodded out to the dunes again, where now a fine rain was slanting in from the sea, but of course I could not find the nest, and in the end I lodged the poor things, unpleasantly slippery now in their wet fur and seeming even tinier than before, in a sandy hollow under a stone, and when I returned the next day they were gone. But I have not forgotten them, their helplessness, the hot soft feel of them against my heart, the faltering way they kept moving their blind heads from side to side and up and down, like those toy dogs that people put in the back windows of motor cars. Quirke, for all his bulk and his sardonic humour, has something of the same motherless lost incompetency about him. I searched his things, of course, but the dearth of secrets, indeed, the absence of anything much of interest, was more dispiriting than would have been the most shaming discovery. As I turned over the bits and pieces of his gimcrack life a bleak awfulness came down on me, and despite myself I felt ashamed, though whether for my prurience or the paltriness of his life I could not rightly tell. In a leather wallet polished with age and shaped to the curve of a buttock I found a photograph, similarly curved, and finely craquelured, in faded shades of pearl and grey. The picture was of a thin, youngish woman with an unfortunate perm, standing in a summer garden smiling bravely into the lens. I took it to the window and scanned it hungrily, cursing the lack of a magnifying glass. The woman was holding herself in an awkward pose before the camera's bulging eye. She had a hand lifted to her forehead against the glare of the sun, so that most of the upper part of her face was in shadow. Minutely I examined what features I could make out—delicate pointed chin, somewhat vapid mouth, her smile disclosing the hint of a discoloured front tooth, that lifted arm, nicely curved but pathetically skinny, the little, weak, defensive hand—searching for the slightest suggestion of familiarity, the faintest echo. In the bottom left corner a part of the photographer's shadow was to be seen, a sloping shoulder and one side of a big round head, Quirke's, most likely. And the garden? At the woman's back there was a tree of some sort, birch, perhaps, in full leaf, and under her a bit of lumpy lawn. Could be anywhere. Discouraged, I pocketed the photo, and with a last gloomy look around I went out softly and shut the door behind me. On the stairs I stopped, struck by a flaw in the stillness, as if someone, fled now, had been listening at the door, or spying on me through the keyhole. Lily, probably; it did not matter.

What I want to know now is, how long exactly have the Quirkes been living here, and, more important, how many of them were there here to start with? Lily clings to a stubborn vagueness on the matter. Yet she claims to remember clearly the circumstances, even if she will not disclose the precise location, of her mother's death—too clearly, I surmise, for it happened many years ago, and I do not see Lily as an infant prodigy, beadily recording the events of family history over the rim of her cradle. Her mother woke one night with a pain, she says. The doctor was sent for, but there was a mix-up and he went to the wrong house, and did not realise the mistake because by chance in the other house there was also a mother in distress, though she was giving birth, and did so, successfully, while Lily's poor Mam was engaged in an opposite exercise, which in time she accomplished, with much anguish. Her Auntie Dora came, Lily says, from the far end of town, wearing a raincoat over her nightdress, but even Auntie Dora, evidently a stalwart among incompetent Quirkes, even she could do nothing to save her sister. She had shouted at Quirke, and said it was all his fault, and said if he was any example of a husband she was glad she had never married, and Quirke had made to hit her and she put up her fists to him, and there might have been a real fight, for Quirke was beside himself and Auntie Dora was ready for him, except that someone else who was there, a neighbour or a family friend, Lily could not recall who it was, had stepped between the opponents and said they should be ashamed of themselves, with Kitty not yet cold. All this I heard, sitting on that bench, in the sun, while Lily picked at that thread in her dress and squinted off. It must have been quite a night, the night that Kitty died. I had the purloined photograph in my pocket. I showed it to Lily, and she looked at it blankly. I asked if it was not her mother. She peered harder and was silent for a long moment.

"I don't think so," she said, tentatively. "I don't think it's her."

"Then who is it?" I asked, in some chagrin. I told her where I had got the picture, thinking she might protest my invasion of her father's privacy, but she only snickered.

"Oh, it's some girl, then," she said. "Da always had girls."

Quirke as Casanova; it does not seem likely, somehow.

"And did you have a brother," I said, "or a sister, that died?"

At that she took on a furtive, rabbity look, and after hesitating for a moment gave a quick little nod, darting her head forward as if to pluck a morsel of something from my hand.

Is it true? Can this be the identity of the ghostly mother and her child who have been haunting me? I want to believe it, but I cannot. I think Lily was lying; I think there is no dead sibling, except in her fancy.

There was a waiting stillness about us now. The air had grown leaden, and the leaves of the tree above us hung inert. A cloud had risen in the sky, blank as a wall, and now there was a hushing sound, and the rain came, hard quick vengeful rods falling straight down and splattering on the pavement like so many flung pennies. In the three hurried steps that it took Lily and me to get to the doorway of the public lavatory we were wet. The door was sealed with a chain and padlock, and we had to cower in the concrete porch, with its green-slimed wall and lingering ammoniac stink. Even here the big drops falling on the lintel above us threw off a chill fine mist that drifted into our faces and made Lily in her thin dress shiver. She wore a black look, huddled there with her head drawn down between her shoulders and her lips set in a line and her thin arms tightly folded. Meanwhile the air was steadily darkening. I remarked the peculiar light, insipid and shrouded, like the light in a dream.

"It's the eclipse," Lily said sullenly. "We're missing it."

The eclipse! Of course. I thought of the thousands standing in silence, in the rain, their faces lifted vainly to the sky, and instead of laughing I felt a sharp and inexplicable pang of sadness, though for what, or whom, I do not know. Presently the downpour ceased and a watery sun, unoccluded, struggled through the clouds, and we ventured out of shelter. The streets that we walked through were awash, grey water with brief pewter bubbles running in the gutters and the pavements shining and giving off wavering flaws of steam. Cars churned past like motorboats, drawing miniature rainbows in their wake, while above us a life-sized one, the daddy of them all, was braced across the sky, looking like a huge and perfect practical joke.

When we came to the square again the circus show was still in progress. We could hear the band inside the tent blaring and squawking, and a big mad voice bellowing incomprehensibly, with awful hilarity, through a loudspeaker. The sun was drying off the canvas of the tent in patches, giving a camouflage effect, and the soaked pennant mounted above the entrance was plastered around its pole. It was not the regular kind of circus tent, what they call the Big Top—I wonder why?—but a tall, long rectangle, suggesting equally a jousting tournament and an agricultural show, with a supporting strut at each of the four corners and a fifth one in the middle of the roof. As we drew near there was a hiatus of some kind in the performance. The music stopped, and the audience inside set up a murmurous buzzing. Some people came out of the tent, ducking awkwardly under the canvas flap in the entrance-way, and stood about in a faintly dazed fashion, blinking in the glistening air. A fat man leading a small boy by the hand paused to stretch, and yawn, and light a cigarette, while the child turned aside and peed against the trunk of a cherry tree. I thought the show was over, but Lily knew better. "It's only the interval," she said bitterly, with revived resentment. Just then the red-haired fellow, the one who had grinned at me from the back step of his trailer, appeared from around the side of the tent. Over his red shirt and clown's trousers he wore a rusty black tailcoat now, and a dented top hat was fixed somehow at an impossible angle to the back of his head. I realised who it was he reminded me of: George Goodfellow, an affable fox, the villain in a cartoon strip in the newspapers long ago, who sported a slender cigarette holder and just such a stovepipe hat, and whose brush protruded cheekily between the split tails of his moth-eaten coat. When he saw us the fellow hesitated, and that knowing smirk crossed his face again. Before I could stop her—and why should I have tried to?—Lily went forward eagerly and spoke to him. He had been about to slip inside the tent, and now stood half turned away from her, holding open the canvas flap and looking down at her over his shoulder with an expression of mock alarm. He listened for a moment, then laughed, and glanced at me, and said something briefly, and then with another glance in my direction slipped nimbly into the darkness of the tent.

"We can go in," Lily said breathlessly, "for the second half."

She stood before me in quivering stillness, like a colt waiting to be loosed from the reins, hands clasped at her back and looking intently at the toe of her sandal.

"Who is that fellow?" I said. "What did you say to him?"

She gave herself an impatient shake.

"He's just one of them," she said, gesturing toward the caravans and the tethered horses. "He said we could go in."

The smell inside the tent struck me with a familiar smack: greasepaint, sweat, dust, and, underneath all, a heavy wet warm musky something that was as old as Nero's Rome. Benches were set out in rows, as in a church, facing a makeshift trestle stage at the far end. There was the unmistakable atmosphere of a matinée, jaded, restless, faintly violent. People were promenading in the aisles, hands in pockets, nodding to their friends and shouting jocular insults. A gang of youths at the back, whooping and whistling, was hurling abuse and apple cores at a rival gang nearby. One of the circus folk, in singlet and tights and espadrilles—it was the Lothario with greasy curls and the nostril stud whom Lily had spoken to in the morning—loitered at the edge of the stage, absent-mindedly picking his nose. I was looking about for Goodfellow when he came bustling in from the left, carrying a piano accordion in one hand and a chair in the other. At sight of him there was a smattering of ironic applause, at which he stopped in his tracks and gave a great start, peering about with exaggerated astonishment, as if an audience were the last thing he had expected. Then he put on a blissful smile of acknowledgement, closing his eyes, and bowed deeply, to a chorus of jeers; his top hat fell off and rolled in a half circle around his feet, and carelessly he snatched it up and clapped it on again, and proceeded gaily toward the front of the stage, the accordion hanging down at his side with the bellows at full stretch and emitting tortured squeaks and wheezes. At every other step he would pause, pretending not to know where these cat-call sounds were coming from, and would peer over his shoulder, or glare suspiciously at the people in the front row, and once even twisted himself into a corkscrew shape to stare down in stern admonishment past his shoulder at his own behind. When the laughter had subsided, and after essaying a few experimental runs on the keyboard, head inclined and gaze turned soulfully inward, like a virtuoso testing the tone of his Stradivarius, he threw himself back on the chair with a violent movement of the shoulders and began to play and sing raucously. He sang in a reedy falsetto, with many sobs and gasps and cracked notes, swaying from side to side on the chair and passionately casting up his eyes, so that a rim of yellowish white was visible below the pupils. After a handful of rackety

numbers—"O Sole Mio" was one, and "South of the Border"—
he ended with a broad flourish by letting the accordion fall open
flabbily across his knees, producing from it a wounded roar, and
immediately slammed it shut again. After that for a long moment
he sat motionless, with the instrument shut in his lap, stricken-
faced, staring before him with bulging eyes, then rose, wincing,
and scuttled off at a knock-kneed run, a hand clutched to his
crotch.

Lily thought all this was wonderful, and laughed and laughed,
leaning her head weakly against my shoulder. We were seated near
the front, where the crowd was densest. The atmosphere under the
soaked canvas was heavy and humid; it was like being trapped
inside a blown-up balloon, and my head had begun to ache. Until
it started up I did not notice the band, down at the side of the stage,
a three-piece ensemble of trumpet, drums, and an amplified keyboard on a sort of stand. The trumpet, unexpectedly, was played
by a large and no longer young woman, heavily made up and
wearing a blonde wig, who on the high notes would go into a
crouch and screw shut her eyes, as if she could not bear the intensity of the brassy music she was making. The drummer, a bored
young man with sideburns and an oiled quiff, smoked a cigarette
with negligent ease all the while that he was playing, shifting it
expertly from one corner of his mouth to the other and letting the
smoke dribble out at his nostrils. The player at the keyboard was
old, and wore braces; a wispy fan of hair was combed flat across
the bald dome of his skull. Preceded by a rattle on the kettledrum,
Goodfellow reappeared, bounding into the middle of the stage,
kissing bunched fingers at us and opening wide his arms in a gesture of swooning gratitude, as if it were wild applause that was
being showered on him, instead of howls and lip-farts. Then the
band went into an oily, drunken tango and he began to dance,
sashaying and slithering about the stage on legs that might have
been made of rubber, his arms wrapped about himself in a lascivi-

ous embrace. Each time he passed her by the trumpet player blew a loud, discordant squeal and thrust the bell of her instrument lewdly in the direction of his skinny loins. He pretended to ignore her, and pranced on, with a disdainful waggle of his backside. At the close he did a pirouette, twisting himself into that corkscrew shape again, coat-tails flying and his arms lifted and fingers daintily touching high above his head, then leapt into the air and executed a scissors-kick, and finished in the splits, landing with a thump loud enough to be heard over the music and bringing delighted shrieks of mock agony from the laughing youths at the back. His top hat had stayed in place throughout, and now he skipped nimbly to his feet and snatched it off and made another low bow, the hat pressed to his breast and an arm upswept behind him with rigid index finger pointing aloft. Lily, laughing, said into my ear in a whispered wail that she was sure she was going to wet herself.

The next act was a juggler; it took me a moment to recognise Lothario, got up in a loose red silk shirt open on a perfectly hairless chest. He kept dropping an Indian club and picking it up with forced and scowling insouciance. After him came a magician, even clumsier than he, wearing a crumpled evening suit too long in the leg, and a celluloid dicky that had a habit of snapping up like a roller-blind when he was about to complete a trick. He too was familiar, and sure enough, when I looked to the keyboard it was unattended. The magic feats he performed were old and obvious. When they went wrong and the audience guffawed he would smile shyly, showing the tip of his tongue, and smooth a small plump hand across the oiled hair plastered to his pate. Presently he summoned his assistant—the trumpeter, of course, quick-changed now into a crimson corset affair and fishnet tights and wearing a lustrous black wig that seemed made of plastic—and proceeded laboriously to saw her in half. After that he shuffled off, to derisory applause, while the trumpeter remained behind and did a perfunctory sword-swallowing act. Striking a heroic stance, stout legs braced and back arched, she lowered the blade deftly and daintily down her throat as if it were a long, gleaming silver fish, winning a storm of wolf-whistles from the rear of the tent.

Now Goodfellow came on to the stage yet again, hatless this time, and wearing a spangled waistcoat. I studied him with anxious scrutiny, wondering what it was about him that alarmed me so strangely. His face was stark and waxy white, as if there were no skin at all, just the skull set with a moving mouth and those two darting eyes. He swaggered back and forth before us, chanting in a high, singsong voice a patter he had obviously delivered so often that the words had taken on a rhythm of their own, independent of any sense. He was calling for a volunteer, some stout soul from amongst us brave enough, he said, smirking, to enter into a contest of wills with him. The crowd was quieter now. He cast his dark glance over us with contemptuous enjoyment. Lily sat with a fist clenched in her lap and her legs coiled, one ankle hooked behind the other, her face lifted to the stage in an attitude of awed solemnity, like that of one of the women at the foot of the cross. I could feel the tiny tremors of excitement running through her. Then all at once she was out of her seat and racing forward, fleet as a maenad, and with one skip leapt on to the stage and stopped, and stood, teetering a little, her mouth open in a silent exclamation of surprise and sudden misgiving.

At first, Goodfellow did not look at her at all, but pretended to be unaware of her presence; then, slowly, still keeping his eye on us, he began to circle around her, in a strange, high-stepping, stealthy prowl, approaching a little nearer to her at each pass, until he was close enough to lay a hand lightly on her shoulder. Still he continued to circle about her, gently turning her with him, so that she became the revolving axis around which he moved. Her expression was growing ever more uncertain, and a worried smile kept flickering on and off her face like the light of a faltering bulb.

Her gaze was fixed on Goodfellow's face, though still he had not looked directly at her. Now he began to speak, in the same singsong manner as when a moment ago he had issued his challenge to us, but gently, tenderly, almost, in caressing soft insinuating tones. His was a strange voice, mellifluous yet not pleasant at all, wheedling, suggestive, the voice of a pander. More and more slowly he paced, speaking all the while, and slowly she turned with him, and at last they came to a stop, and something moved over the audience, a wave of something, moved, and was still. In the silence Goodfellow surveyed us with that tight-lipped, foxy smile of his that never reached his eyes. Lily's look had gone entirely blank, and her arms hung at her sides as if there were no bones at all inside them. At long last Goodfellow looked at her. Carefully, as if she were some delicate figure he had just finished fashioning, he lifted his hand from her shoulder and passed it smoothly back and forth in front of her eyes. She did not blink, or stir in any way. Again the audience made that sighing, wave-like movement. Goodfellow turned his head and looked at us with a piercing, narrowed stare. How thin that smiling mouth, how red, a livid cicatrice. He took Lily's hand in his and led her unresisting to the edge of the stage.

"Well?" he said, turning to us in the audience, his voice so soft as to be hardly heard. "What shall we have her do?"

One afternoon, long ago, I caught a glimpse of myself in the mirror in my mother's room. I was on one of my solitary and aimless explorations about the house. The door to the bedroom stood ajar, and as I passed by a movement flashed in the corner of my eye, a glossy start and flinch, so it seemed, knife-coloured, as of an assassin in there surprised at his surreptitious work. I stopped, my heart thudding, and took a wary step backward, and my reflection stepped with me again into the tilted mirror on the dressing table, and I saw myself as someone else, a stranger lurking there, a figure of momentous and inscrutable intent, and an almost pleasurable shiver of horror swarmed briefly across my shoulder blades. I had that same feeling as I rose from my seat now and went forward, light on my feet as Mercury himself, and stepped nimbly on to the stage and stopped, head lifted and my arms swinging a little, in the stance of an athlete at the end of some graceful and strenuous display of skill. Odd, to be treading the boards again. There is only one stage; wherever the venue, it is always the same. I think of it as a trampoline, it has that spring, that queasy-making bounce; at times it sways and sags, at others it is tight as a drum-skin, and as thin, with only an endless emptiness underneath. There is no fear like the fear one knows up there. I do not mean the anxiety of fluffed lines or a wig coming unstuck; such mishaps mean less to us than an audience imagines. No, what I speak of is a terror of the self, of letting the self go so far free that one night it might break away, detach entirely and become another, leaving behind it only a talking shell, an empty costume standing there aghast, topped by an eyeless mask.

I took Lily's hand, the one that Goodfellow was not holding, and pressed it in my own.

"My name is Alexander Cleave," I said, in a loud, firm voice, "and this is my daughter."

Before I rose I had not known what I would do or say, and indeed, I still did not rightly know what I was saying, what doing, but at the touch of Lily's chill, soft, damp hand on mine I experienced a moment of inexplicable and ecstatic sorrow such that I faltered and almost fell out of my standing; it was as if a drop of the most refined, the purest acid had been let fall into an open chamber of my heart. Goodfellow seemed not at all surprised by my sudden appearance there before him. He did not start, or stir at all, but stood in an almost pensive pose, head held a little to one side and eyes downcast, his red mouth pursed in that smile of covert knowing, like the footman who has recognised the king in disguise and keeps the secret to himself, not out of loyalty, but other things.

Did he know me? I do not like to think he did. Lily sighed; she had the intent, turned-in expression of a sleepwalker. I spoke her name and a little languid tremor went through her, and she gave a shivery sigh, and was still again. Goodfellow shook his head once, and clicked his tongue, as if in mild admonition. He had yet to meet my eye. I caught his smell, a thin, rancid, secretive stink. Behind him, off at the entrance to the tent, the canvas flap hung open a little way, framing a tall, thorn-shaped glimpse of the sunlit square outside. In here, the khaki-coloured air was dense, and had a bruised tinge to it. The audience sat in puzzlement, waiting. Throats were cleared, and there was an uneasy laugh or two, and someone said something, asking a question, it seemed, and someone gave what seemed a muffled answer. Lily had begun to sway a little, back and forth, her arms outstretched to Goodfellow and me as we held her between us. Now he looked at me. Yes, yes, I think he knew me, I think he knew who I was, am. I saw myself reflected in his eyes. Then with the faintest of shrugs he let go his hold on Lily's hand. She swayed again, sideways this time, and I put my arm around her shoulders, fearing she might drop. As I led her down from the stage someone booed at the back, and laughed, and the trumpeter leaned out and blew a brassy note at us, but half-heartedly. Heads turned to watch us as we went past. Outside the tent, Lily drew back, blinking in the harsh sunlight. I smelled the tethered horses, and remembered the boy in the square that day, on his pony, in the rain. Lily, with a hand to her face, was quietly weeping. *There there*, I said; *there there*.

I marvel at the superabundance of summer. This evening, leaning chin on fist at my little window, I can see the last of the geraniums and smell their citrusy scent; the air swarms with midges; in the west a fat sun squats in a sky of palest pink and leek-green and Marian blue. These are the dog days, when Sirius rises and sets with the sun. As a boy I knew the stars, and loved to speak their names over to myself, in celestial litany, Venus, Betelgeuse, Aldebaran, the Bears, great and lesser. How I loved the coldness of those lights, their purity, their remoteness from us and all we do and all that befalls us. Where they are is where the dead live. That is what I believed, as a boy. The gulls are making a great to-do. What is it that ails them? Perhaps they are angels who have been sent down here to Hell. There is a commotion in the house, too. I hear what seems to be a woman wailing. It is a cry that unwillingly I recognise. It has been coming to me for a long time, through an immensity of space, like the light of a distant star, of a dead sun.

V

Swish, and the curtain goes up on the last act. Place: the same. Time: some weeks later. I am at my table, as before. But no, nothing is as before. The geraniums are finished, save for a few drooping sprays. The angle of the sun on the garden has shifted, it does not shine in at my window any more. The air has a new chill to it, there are gales, and the skies all day are a deeper blue and piled high with clouds, dense, billowing ranges of copper and chrome. I avoid all that outside stuff, though, when I can. It is too much for me. The world has become a wound I cannot bear to look at. I take everything very slowly, with great care and caution, avoiding all sudden movements, afraid that something inside me might be stirred, or shattered, even, that sealed flask in which the demon lurks, raging to get at me. Throughout the house deep silence reigns, a silence as of the sickroom. I shall not stay long.

The tragedians are wrong, grief has no grandeur. Grief is grey, it has a grey smell and a grey taste and a grey ashy feel on the fingers. Lydia's instinct was to struggle against it, vainly ducking and clawing, as though grappling with an attacker, or trying to fend off a pestilence out of the air. Of the two of us, I was the luckier; I had been in practice, so to speak, and had come to quietude, a kind of quietude. When at last I left the safety of my little room that evening, the evening after the circus, the scene that met me was strikingly reminiscent of the one the day before, when Lydia had arrived and I had found her in the hall and she had shouted at me for not coming sooner to greet her. There she was now, again, in her leggings and smock, and there too was Lily, barefoot, just as they had been yesterday—I think I was even

holding my fountain pen. Lydia still wore her charlady's headscarf, and her smock today was white, not red. Her expression . . .
no, I shall not attempt to describe her expression. When I saw her,
what came into my head immediately was a recollection of something that happened once when I was with Cass, when she was a
child. It was summer, and she was wearing a white dress made of
layer upon layer of some very fine, translucent, gauzy stuff. We
had just stepped out of the house, we were going somewhere
together, I cannot remember where, it was some outing we were
on. The day was sunny, with thrilling gusts of wind, I remember
it, the gulls crying and the mast-ropes of the boats in the harbour
tinkling like Javanese bells. A group of half-drunk loud young
men was in the street, all vests and belt buckles and menacing hair-
cuts. As they went reeling past us, one of them, a blue-eyed brute
clutching himself by the wrist, turned about suddenly and with a
flick of his hand, the palm of which bore a broad gash from knife
or broken bottle, threw a long splash of blood diagonally across
Cass's dress. He laughed, a high, crazed whinny, and the others
laughed too, and they went on, down the road, staggering, and
shouldering each other, like a skulk of Jacobean villains. Cass said
nothing, only stood a moment with her arms lifted away from her
sides, looking down at the crimson sash of blood athwart her white
bodice. At once, without a word, we turned back to the house, and
she went off quickly upstairs and changed her dress, and we set
out again, to wherever it was we had been going, as if nothing had
happened. I do not know what she did with the white dress. It disappeared. When her mother questioned her about it she refused to
answer. I said nothing, either. I think now that what had happened
had happened out of time, I mean had happened somehow not as a
real event at all, with causes and consequences, but in some special
way, in some special dimension of dream or memory, solely, and
precisely, that it might come to me there, as I stood in the hall, in

my mother's house, on an evening in summer, the last evening of what I used to think of as my life.

With three quick, stiff steps Lydia was on me, pounding her fists on my chest, pressing her face close up to mine. "You knew!" she cried. "Blubbering in picture-houses, and coming back to this place, and seeing ghosts—you *knew!*" She was trying to get at me with her nails now. I held her by the wrists, smelling her tears and her snot, feeling against my face the awful furnace heat of her sorrow. I was aware of a low animal wailing somewhere, and looked past Lydia's shoulder and saw that it was Lily, up at the front door, who was keening in this unhuman way—it must have been she, not Lydia, her child's stricken cries, that I had heard from my room. She stood at a crouch, with her fists braced on her knees and her face a crumpled mask, trying not to look at us as we grappled there. I found myself wondering in mild annoyance what it could be that so ailed her, when it was we, Lydia and I, who should have been crying out in anguish and in pain; had Lydia frightened her, or hurt her in some way, by slapping her, perhaps? The door behind her was open a disturbing foot or so. The evening sun shone through the transom window, an ancient light, golden, dense, dust-laden. Now Quirke appeared in the kitchen doorway, carrying a tall glass of water, holding it on the palm of one hand and balancing it with the fingers of the other. Without surprise, almost wearily, he looked at Lydia and me, still locked in struggle. At sight of him Lily abruptly left off her wailing, and something of Lydia's fierceness abated too. I let go of her wrists, and Quirke he came forward with a priestlike mien and did not so much hand her the glass as entrust it to her, as if it were a chalice. The ecclesiastical tenor of the moment was heightened by the paper coaster he had placed under the glass, white and brittle as a Host. All these things I noted with avid attention, as if a record of them must be kept, for evidence, and the task of preserving them had fallen to me. Holding the coaster in place during the handing over of the glass, which both of them seemed to feel was essential, required a complicated pas de deux of swivelling thumbs, and fingertips held delicately en pointe. Lydia took a long deep draught of the water, leaning her head far back, her throat, the new and slightly goitrous pale fatness of which I had not noticed until now, working with a pumping motion, as if there were a fist inside it, going up and down. Having done, she handed back the glass to Quirke, both of them repeating the business with the coaster. Lily at the door had begun to snivel, with every sign of being about to start wailing again, but Quirke made a sharp noise of command in her direction, such as shepherds make at their dogs, and she clapped a hand over her mouth, which made her eyes seem all the more abulge and terrified. Lydia, the fight all gone out of her, had pulled off her headscarf and stood before me dispiritedly now with her head bowed, her splayed fingers pressed to her forehead at the hairline, in the attitude of one who has escaped a catastrophe, instead of being caught in the middle of it. The front door standing open like that was still troubling me, there was something horribly insinuating about it, as if there were someone or something out there waiting for just the right moment to slip inside, unnoticed.

"The tea is on," Quirke said in a sombre, curiously flat voice, like that of the villain in a pantomime.

I could not understand him at all; it was as if the words were all out of order, and I thought he must be drunk, or attempting some sort of hideous joke. Struggling to comprehend, I had that panicky sensation one has sometimes abroad, when a request to a chambermaid or shop assistant spoken three times over in three different languages elicits only the same dull shrug and downcast glance. Then I noticed the sounds that were coming from the kitchen, the homely sounds of crockery being laid out and chairs set in place at table, and when I looked into the room a woman was there whom I did not remember ever having seen before, though yet she seemed familiar. She was elderly, with iron-grey hair, and pink-framed spectacles that were slightly askew. She was wearing my mother's apron, the same one that Lydia had been wearing earlier. The woman looked to be perfectly at ease out there and familiar with everything, and I wondered for a moment if she might be yet another secret tenant of the house whose presence I had not detected. Seeing me looking in, she gave me a warmly encouraging smile, nodding, and wiping her hands on her—I mean my mother's—apron. I turned to Quirke, who only raised his eyes and inclined his head a little to one side. "The *tea*," he said again, with a heavier emphasis, as if the word should explain everything. "You'll be hungry, though you won't know it." I found his flat complacent tone suddenly, deeply, irritating.

It was Quirke who had brought the news. It always falls to a Quirke, to bring news like that. Someone had phoned him at the office, he told me, and looked abashed at the grandly proprietorial sound of that *at the office*. He did not know who the caller was, he said, and had forgotten to ask, and now was very apologetic, as if it really were something that mattered. It had been a woman, he thought, though he was not sure even of that much. Foreign accent, and the line was bad. I never did find out her, or his, identity. Tragedy always has its anonymous messengers, in sandals and robe they run in fleet-footed from the wings and fall to one knee before the throne, heads bowed, leaning on the caduceus. Or do I mean caducous? Words, words. No matter, I have not the energy to look up the dictionary, and anyway, when I think of it, both words apply, in this case.

I am running dry.

The strange woman came forward, still smiling, still nodding encouragement, like the kindly old lady in the gingerbread house in the forest where the babes are lost. I shall call her, let me see, I shall call her—oh, what does it matter, call her Miss Kettle, that will do. She was a Miss, I believe, for I feel, on no evidence, that she was a spinster. I noticed the reason that her specs were askew: the earpiece on one side was missing. She took my hand; hers was warm, and dry, and not at all work-worn, a soft warm pad of flesh, the most real thing I had touched since hearing Lily's cries and coming out of my room. "I'm sorry for your trouble," she said, and I heard myself, out of unthinking politeness, answer her almost airily, "Oh, it's no trouble."

She had prepared one of those quintessential, archaic meals of childhood. There was a lettuce salad with tomatoes and scallions and cut-up hard-boiled eggs, and plates of soda bread, brown and white, and two big pots of tea, each with its pig's-tail of steam curling from the spout, and square slices of that processed ham I did not think they still produced, pallid, marbled, evilly aglisten. For a moment we all stood around the table eyeing the food, awkward as a party of incongruously varied dinner guests—*Whatever will that actress find to talk to the Bishop about?*—then Quirke with a courtly gesture pulled back a chair for Lydia, and she sat, and so did we, clearing our throats and scraping our heels on the floor, and Miss Kettle poured the tea.

This was the first of several sombre repasts that Lydia and I were to be treated to over the following days. At times of bereavement, I have discovered, people revert to a primitive kindliness, which is manifest most obviously in the form of offerings of food. Plates of sandwiches were brought to us, and thermos flasks of chicken soup, and apple tarts, and big-bellied pots of stew, discreetly draped in tea towels that afterwards Lydia washed and ironed and returned to their owners, neatly folded inside the scrubbed pots that I had emptied, every one of them, into the dustbin. We felt like priest and priestess officiating at the place of veneration, receiving the sacrifices of the faithful, which were all handed over with the same sad nodding smile, the same patting of hand or grasping of arm, the same embarrassed, mumbled condolences. I did not weep at all, never once, in those first days—I had done my weeping already, in the luminously peopled darkness of those afternoon cinemas months before—but if I were to break down, it would have been at one of those moments when a plate of fairy cakes or a saucepan of soup was pressed tenderly into my hands. But it all came too late, the muttered invocations, the promised prayers, the funeral baked meats, for the maiden had already gone to the sacrifice.

Grief takes the taste out of things. I do not mean to say merely that it dulls the subtler savours, smoothing out the texture of a fine cut of beef or blunting the sharpness of a sauce, but that the very tastes themselves, of meat, vegetables, wine, ambrosia, whatever, are utterly killed, so that the stuff on the end of the fork might as well be cardboard, the strong drink in one's glass dead water only. I sat and ate like a machine, slow and ruminant; the food went in, my jaws made their familiar figure-of-eight motion, the cud went down, and if it had come out immediately at the other end without pausing on the way I would not have been surprised, or perturbed, for that matter. Miss Kettle in her commonsensical way kept up a conversation, or monologue, really, that was not exactly cheerful but not lugubrious, either. She must have been a neighbour, or one of Quirke's relations he had called on for support and succour in this hour of crisis, though she seemed to disapprove of him, for her lips went tight and deeply striated whenever her unwilling gaze encountered him. She was a descendant and refinement of those professional keeners who in the old days in this part of the world would have been hired in to set the process of mourning properly in motion with their screeches and wailings. In her talk she touched on the matter of death with a skill and delicacy worthy of a society undertaker. The only discordant note in her performance was those crooked spectacles, which gave her something of the look of a Dickensian eccentric. She mentioned repeatedly her sister who had died, though when or in what manner I was not attending closely enough to register; from the way that she spoke of her and her going, it almost seemed that I was expected to be already familiar with the details. These exchanges, if exchanges they could be called, would have had the potential for large confusions and embarrassments, in other circumstances; here, however, nothing seemed required of me in the way of manners or politeness; I felt like some harmless big beast who had been brought in wounded from the wild, to be cared for, and covertly studied. Lydia sat opposite me, like me mechanically eating, in silence, her gaze fixed steadily on her plate. Quirke was at the head of the table, looking quite the man of the house, mild and solicitous of expression, keeping an eye on everything. There are people who are good with death, they positively blossom in the icy breath of mortality, and to my surprise, and obscure displeasure, Quirke was turning out to be one of them. Each time I met his eye, which was as seldom as I could manage, he would give me a half-smile accompanied by a short, encouraging nod, a close relative to the smiling nods Miss Kettle had bestowed on me earlier, when we had first caught sight of each other, and it briefly crossed my addled mind that perhaps all this—the sympathy, the distracting talk, the meat tea—was indeed a professional service they were rendering, and that presently there would be an awkward moment of coughs and apologetic shrugs, and an invoice, and a fee to be paid. I pictured Quirke discreetly passing over the bill, the reverse of a magician palming a card—the envelope no doubt done up with a black silk ribbon—and his appreciative, silent mouthings as I disdainfully handed over a pouch of clinking guineas. Yes, there is definitely something Victorian about Quirke; he has the proprietorial, jauntily insolent air of a retainer who has been retained so long he believes he may count himself part of the family.

Lily was the one who puzzled me. After her earlier outburst in the hall, she was all surliness and feline shrinking now. She sat beside me slumped over her plate, her face hidden by hanging locks of hair. I know very well how death bores the young, like a glum intruder come to spoil finally an already dull party, but the silence that radiated off her like heat had a furious force to it that was, as I could see even in my distress of mind, directed entirely at me. But what injury had I done to her? As a rule I do not understand human beings, as I am sure I have remarked more than once, but the young I find especially baffling, and always have found them so. Later, in the hall, when Lydia and I were leaving, shuffling off in our sodden sorrow, the child appeared out of nowhere and fairly flung herself at me and clung to me for a second in a violent, awkward, damp embrace, before speeding off again, on those swift, bare, filthy feet of hers. Perhaps she really did want me for a Dad.

By now it was almost night, yet it was hard to get away, hard to find a formulation that would bring the occasion to a close. Miss Kettle was smiling and nodding again, and Quirke stood by saying nothing, but looking serious and thoughtfully benign. We might have been children, Lydia and I, tired and sleepy after a day in the country visiting a kindly aunt and uncle. The evening had passed for me in a peculiar, crepuscular gloom, illumined fitfully as by wan and slowed-down flashes of a camera bulb. Certain snapshots remained: Quirke and Lydia away from the table, sitting opposite each other on straight-backed chairs, Lydia weeping without restraint, and Quirke, leaning forward earnestly with his knees open, holding her hands in his and gently flapping them up and down, as if he were out for a drive in a gig and they were the two ends of the reins he was wielding; Miss Kettle laughing at something, and then remembering, and snapping shut her mouth, and apologetically straightening her glasses, which at once went crooked again; Lily's bare arm beside mine, each tiny strand of down on it agleam; the evening sunlight in the window, goldening the draining board and glinting on the rim of a tumbler; my plate, with one limp round of tomato, a bruised lettuce leaf, a smear of crumbled egg yolk. These are the things one remembers.

Our leaving, when we managed it at last, was the beginning of that grotesque parody of a family holiday that Lydia and I were condemned to play out over the coming days. We were all gathered at the front door, us with our bags, and Quirke and Miss Kettle, and even Lily, who had reappeared from wherever she had fled to, and hung back in the shadows of the hall, surly and accusing, like a spoiled young actress who has been upstaged, which I suppose she had been. The last light of evening from the west paled the glow of the street lamps behind us. The lenses of Miss Kettle's spectacles caught a flash of something and for an instant seemed two blank-faced, shining coins laid on her eyes. Quirke in shirt-sleeves stood in the doorway in the pose of Vaublin's Pierrot, trying to find something to do with his hanging hands.

"There was only the one?" he said to me.

"The one?"

"Daughter."

In my mind I clearly saw Goodfellow, who smiled his thin-lipped smile, and winked at me, and faded.

"Only the one," I said, "yes."

There were bizarre gestures of aid and comfort. It will seem strange, perhaps, but these, the most bizarre of them, were the ones that touched me most sharply, striking through the otherwise impenetrable shrouds of grief like little shocks of static electricity. One of Lydia's aunts, a moustached old brute with skin like elephant hide, who I thought had always despised me, clasped me in a mothball-smelling embrace and thrust a wad of banknotes into my hand, croaking hoarsely in my ear that *there would be things that would be needed*. The man who did Lydia's garden—I think of the house by the sea and everything in it as hers, now—volunteered to do the flowers for the funeral. The local tradesmen rallied, too; Lydia had to spend days writing notes of thanks. Her chemist passed us under the counter an insomniac's treasure trove of sleeping draughts that would normally have required a prescription signed by a whole board of doctors, so potent were they. The grocer sent round a box of assorted tinned goods. And there were the letters of condolence, they had to be answered too. Some of these were from people whose names we did not recognise, in places abroad that we had never heard of, academic institutions, research foundations, libraries. They made another version of our daughter, one I did not recognise: the international scholar; I should have paid more attention to what I always winced at when I heard her refer to it as her *work*. I could never believe it was anything more than an elaborate pastime, like thousand-piece jigsaw puzzles, or Chinese patience, something dull but demanding that would soothe her frantic mind. Late one night, when we had finally got to sleep, felled at last by Mr. Finn's knock-out drops, someone telephoned, but he was drunk, and rapturously weeping, and I could make out nothing of what he was saying, except that it was something about Cass, and I was still trying to shake my brain awake when he hung up. I have begun to realise fully at last how little I know about my daughter—how little I had known; I must accustom myself now to the past tenses.

On the endless journey out—in real time it took only from early morning until the middle of an afternoon—woe sat like lumpy satchels on our backs, weighing us down. I thought of a pair of mendicant pilgrims out of a Bible scene, bent under our burdens, making our toilsome way along a hot and dusty road leading off into an infinite perspective. We were so weary; I have never known such weariness, it burned in us like the dregs of a long night's drinking. I felt grimy and sweat-stained and used up. My skin was puffy and hot to the touch, as if it were not blood but acid that was boiling in my veins. I sat slumped in the narrow aeroplane seat, numb of mind and heart, stewing in my crumpled clothes, my bilious frog's stare fixed on the stylised patchwork world slowly passing far below us. I could find no ease for my physical discomforts, and kept involuntarily heaving little fluttery, whimpering sighs. Beside me Lydia wept to herself quietly, almost reflectively, it seemed, and sighing too the while. Yet I wonder if, like me, she felt behind it all, behind the sorrow and the ceaseless tears, hardly palpable yet never fading, the background hum of relief. Yes, there was a kind of relief. For now that the worst had happened, I would no longer have to live in fear of it. Thus reason, stricken, formulates its wounded logic.

A charming spot it was Cass chose to die in, we saw it first from a turn of the coast road, an untidy amphitheatre of white and ochre and terracotta little houses on a stepped hill at the end of a promontory thrusting out into a white-capped sea of a deep, malignant blueness. It was like something in a travel brochure, only a little more wild of aspect. Byron supposedly did one of his marathon swims from here, thrashing away, club foot and all, to another headland a good five miles off across the strait. There were real fishermen on the harbour mending real nets, and real bars with bead curtains and men in white shirts playing clackety board games, and real *ragazzi* kicking a soccer ball under the dusty lime trees in the Piazza Cavour. Lydia parked our hired car outside the police station—at the airport I had realised that I had lost the ability to drive, simply could not work the pedals, change the gears—and we sat for a moment motionless side by side gazing blankly through the windscreen at a torn advertising poster from which an unreally perfect young woman poutingly proffered her half-naked breasts. "I can't," Lydia said, without emphasis. I laid a hand on her wrist but she shrugged it off, jadedly. We got out of the car, unfolding ourselves from our seats with the caution and infirm laboriousness of the sole survivors of a fatal accident. The square was strikingly familiar—that tree, that stark white wall—

and I felt all this had happened before. There was the usual smell of fish and oil and dust and bad drains. A neat little man in a neat, expensive suit came out on the steps of the police station to meet us. Everything about him was made in miniature. He had a small moustache, and wonderfully small feet shod in spotless patent-leather pumps, and very black hair oiled and combed smooth and severely parted at the side. He shook hands gravely with both of us, his mouth pursed in a sympathetic moue, and ushered us inside the station. The building was incongruously grand, an echoing high square temple with pillars of pitted stone and a chequered black-and-white marble floor. Heads were briefly lifted from desks, dark eyes looked on us with remote inquisitiveness. The little man was skipping ahead, urging us on with soft clickings of tongue and lips, as if we were a pair of prize horses. I was never to make out exactly who or what he was; he may have been the chief of police, or the coroner, or Death himself, even. He could not be still, even when we had come to the mortuary and were standing helpless by the bier, but kept bowing from the shoulders, and reaching out but not quite touching Lydia's hand, or my elbow, and stepping back quickly and delicately clearing his throat behind the raised first knuckle of a tiny brown fist. It was he who took me aside, out of Lydia's hearing, and told me in a hurried whisper, husky with embarrassment, that my daughter had been pregnant when she died. Three months gone, as they say. He clapped a hand histrionically to his breast. *"Ah, signore, mi dispiace . . ."*

The sheet was drawn back. *Stella maris.* Her face was not there, the rocks and the sea had taken it. We identified her by a ring, and a little scar on her left ankle that Lydia remembered. But I would have known her, my Marina, even if all that was left of her was the bare, wave-washed bones.

What was she doing in this place, what had brought her here? As if the mystery of her life were not enough, now I must deal with the mystery of her death. We climbed the narrow streets to the little hotel where she had stayed. It was the siesta hour, and all was eerily still in the flat, airless heat, and as we laboured up those cobbled steeps we gaped about in a blear of disbelief, unable to credit the cruelty of the picturesqueness all around us. There were sleepy cats in doorways, and geraniums on window sills, and a yellow canary was singing in its cage, and we could hear the voices of children at play somewhere, in some sequestered courtyard, and our daughter was dead.

The hotel proprietor was a swarthy, big-chested old fellow with greased grey hair and a manicured moustache, a dead ringer for the film star Vittorio De Sica, if anyone now remembers him. He greeted us circumspectly, staying resolutely behind the protective barrier of the reception desk, looking at everything except us and humming to himself. He kept on nodding at everything we asked him, but the nods seemed more like shrugs, and he would tell us nothing. His fat wife, round and thick as a totem pole, had planted herself behind him with her hands implacably folded on her stomach, her Mussolini scowl fixed on the back of his head, willing him to caution. He was sorry, he could tell us nothing, he said, nothing. Cass had arrived two days ago, he said, and paid in advance. They had hardly seen her since she came, she had spent her days in the hills above the town, or walking on the beach. As he spoke he was fiddling with things on the desk, pens, cards, a sheaf of folded maps. I asked if anyone had been with her, and he shook his head—too quickly, I thought. I noticed his shoes—tassels, little gold buckles, Quirke would have been envious—and the fine silk of his too-white shirt. Quite the dandy. He led us up the narrow stairs, past a set of mildly indecent eighteenth-century prints in plastic frames, and applied a large, mock-antique key to the door of Cass's room and opened it for us. We hung back, Lydia and I, looking incompetently in. Big bed, washstand and pitcher, straight chair with a straw seat, a narrow window squinting down on the sunstruck harbour. There was, incongruously, a smell of suntan lotion. Cass's suitcase was open on the floor, still half unpacked. A dress, a pair of shorts, her remembered shoes, mute things clamouring to speak. "I can't," Lydia said, as listlessly as before, and turned aside. I looked at De Sica and he looked at his nails. His lumpy wife was still there at his shoulder. She would once have been as young as Cass, and as lissom too, most likely. I gazed full into her face, beseeching her silently to tell us what had happened here to our poor damaged daughter, our eclipsed light, that had driven her to death, but she just stood and stared back at me stonily and offered not a word.

We lodged there at the hotel that night, it seemed the simplest thing to do. Our room was eerily similar to the one Cass had been in, with the same washstand and chair, and the same window framing what seemed an identical view of the harbour. We ate dinner in the silent dining room, and then went down to the harbour and walked up and down the quayside for what seemed hours. It was quiet, there at the season's end. We held hands, for the first time since the days of the Hotel Halcyon. A gold and smoke-grey sunset sank out at sea like a slow catastrophe, and the warm night came on, and the lamps on the harbour glowed, and the bristling masts tilted, and a bat swooped and swerved soundlessly about us. In the room we lay sleepless side by side on the big high bed, like a pair of long-term hospital patients, listening to the faint far whisperings of the sea. Softly I sang the little song I used to sing for Cass, to make her laugh:

> *I've got tears in my ears*
> *From lying on my back,*
> *In my bed,*
> *While I cry,*
> *Over you.*

"What did that man say to you?" Lydia asked out of the darkness. "The one at the police station." She rose up on an elbow, making the mattress wobble, and peered at me. In the faint glow from the window the whites of her eyes glittered. "What was it, that he didn't want me to hear?"

"He told me her surprise," I said, "the one she told you not to tell me. You were right: I am amazed." She said nothing to that, only gave what might have been an angry sigh, and laid her head down again. "I suppose," I said, "we don't know who the father is?" I could see him, a lost one like herself, most probably, some pimply young savant haggard with ambition and the weight of useless knowledge agonisingly acquired; I wonder if he knew how close he had come to replicating himself. "Not that it matters, now."

In the morning there was no sea, just a pale gold glare stretching off to the non-horizon. Lydia stayed in bed, with her face turned away from me, saying nothing, although I knew she was not asleep; I crept down the stairs, feeling, I am not sure why, like a murderer leaving the scene of the crime. Perfect day, sun, sea-smell, all that. As I walked through the morning quiet I felt that I was walking in her footsteps; before, she had inhabited me, now I was inhabiting her. I went up to the old church standing on its crag at the far end of the harbour, tottering over the stones shined by the feet of generations of the devout, as if I were climbing to Golgotha. The church was built by the Templars on the site of a Roman shrine dedicated to Venus—yes, I had bought a guidebook. Here Cass performed her last act. In the porch, drifts of confetti were lodged in crevices between the flagstones. The interior was sparsely adorned. There was a Madonna, attributed to Gentileschi—the father, that is, not the notorious daughter—stuck away in a side chapel, a dark piece, badly lit and in need of cleaning, but displaying the master's luminous touch, all the same.

Candles burned on a black iron stand with a tin box for offerings slung beneath it, and a big pot of sickly smelling flowers stood on the flags before the bare altar. A priest appeared, and knew at once who I was. He was squat and brown and bald. He had not a word of English, and I not many of Italian, but he babbled away happily, making elaborate gestures with his hands and head. He steered me out through an arched doorway by the side of the altar, to a little stone bower that hung a hundred feet above rocks and foaming sea, where by tradition, so my tasty guidebook tells me, newly-weds come directly after the marriage ceremony, so that the bride may fling her bouquet as a sacrifice to the seething waters far below. A breeze was blowing upward along the rocks; I held my face out into its strong, iodine-smelling draught and shut my eyes. The Lord temper the wind to the shorn lamp, says the Psalmist, but I am here to tell you that the Psalmist is wrong. The priest was showing me the place where Cass must have scrambled up on to the stone parapet and launched herself out upon the salt-bruised air, he even demonstrated how she would have done it, miming her actions for me, nimble as a goat and smiling all the while and nodding, as if it were some bold foolhardy prank he was describing, the initiatory swallow dive performed by George Gordon himself, perhaps. I picked up a jagged piece of stone newly dislodged from the parapet, and feeling its sharp weight in my hand, I wept at last, plunging headlong helplessly into the suddenly hollow depths of myself, while the old priest stood by, patting me on the shoulder and murmuring what seemed a series of soft, mild reproaches.

So I began that day the painstaking trek back over our lives, I mean our lives when Cass was there, the years she was with us. I was searching for the pattern, the one I am searching for still, the set of clues laid out like the dots she used to join up with her crayon to make a picture of the beautiful fairy with wand and

wings. Was Lydia right when she accused me of somehow knowing what was to happen? I do not want to think so. For if I knew, if
the ghosts were a premonition that this was what was to come,
why did I not act? But then, I have always had the greatest difficulty distinguishing between action and acting. Besides, I was
looking the wrong way, I was looking into the past, and that was
not where those phantoms were from, at all. I used to daydream, in
those first weeks I spent alone in the house, that Cass would come
to live with me, that we would set up together some new version of
the old life I had misled here, that we would somehow redeem the
lost years. Was it out of these fantasies I conjured her? And did my
conjurations weaken her hold on the real life she might have had,
the life that now she will never live? The lives.

I have not begun to feel guilty, yet, not really; there will be
ample time for that.

That night, after my visit to the church, I had a strange and
strangely affecting dream, one that almost comforted me. I was in
the circus tent. Goodfellow was there, and Lily, and Lydia, and I
knew too that everyone in the audience, although I could not
properly see it, out there in the gloom, was known to me, or was a
relative of some kind. We were all gazing upward in rapt silence,
watching Cass, who was suspended motionless in midair, without
support, her arms outstretched, her calm face lit by a beam of
strong white soft light. As I watched, she started her descent
toward me, faster and faster, still impassive, still holding up her
arms as if in a blessing, but the nearer she drew, instead of growing larger in my sight, she steadily shrank, so that when at the end
I reached out to catch her she was hardly there at all, was hardly
more than a speck of light, that in a moment was extinguished.

I woke, clear-headed, the weariness of the past days all gone,
and rose and went and stood in the darkness by the window for a
long time, looking down on the deserted harbour, and the sea,

whose little, lapsing waves seemed something that was being sleepily spoken, over and over.

There was a storm on the day that we flew home. The plane unzipped the flooded runway and lifted with a howling whoosh. When we were over the mountains, Lydia, on her third gin, peered down at the flinty peaks and snow-streaked ravines and bleakly chuckled. "I wish we would crash," she said. I thought of our defaced daughter in her casket down in the baggage bay under our feet. What Goodfellow got hold of her, what Billy in the Bowl sank his teeth into her throat and sucked her blood?

It was strange, to be home, what used to be home, the funeral done with and life, in its heartless way, insisting on being lived. I was out, as often as I could be. Our house by the sea was no longer my home. An odd constraint had grown up between Lydia and me, a shyness, an embarrassment, almost, as if we had committed some misdemeanour together and each was shamed by the other's knowledge of what we had done. I spent long afternoons walking the streets of the city, favouring especially those neutral zones between the suburbs and the city proper, where the buddleia flourished, and abandoned cars sat rusting on their uppers in puddles of smashed glass, and the jagged windows of disused factories flashed with mysterious significance in the slanted autumn sunlight. Here gangs of urchins roamed freely, trotted after always by a grinning dog. Here the winos gathered, on patches of waste ground, to drink from their big brown bottles, and sing, and squabble, and cackle at me as I sidled past, sunk in my black coat. And here too I saw all manner of ghosts, people who could no longer be alive, people who were already old when I was young, figures from the past, from myth and legend. In those vacant streets I could not tell whether I was moving among the living or the dead. And I spoke to Cass, more freely, with more candour, than I ever could have when she was still here, though she never answered, never once, as she might have done. She might have told me why she chose to die on that sun-bleached coast. She might have told me who was the father of her child. She might have said if that was her suntan lotion I smelled that day in the hotel room. Would she have put on suntan lotion and then gone and jumped into the sea? These are the questions that occupy me.

I go through her papers, the scores of foolscap sheets she left behind her at the hotel. She would be proud of me, my scholarly application; I am as intent as any sizar under his lamp. Handwritten, largely illegible, they seemed a chaos, at first, all out of sequence, with no rhyme or reason to them that I could discern. Then, gradually, a pattern began to emerge, no, not a pattern, nothing so definite as a pattern—an aura, rather, a faint, flickering glow of almost-meaning. They seem to be in part a diary, though the things she records, the events and encounters, are fantastical in tone, impossibly coloured. Is it perhaps a story she was inventing, to amuse herself, or ward off the accumulating horrors in her head? There are certain recurrences, a name, or merely an initial, a place revisited again and again, a word repeatedly underlined. There are accounts of expulsions, deaths, extinctions, lost identities. Everything spins and swirls in the maelstrom of her imaginings. And at the core of it all there is an absence, an empty space where once there was something, or someone, who has removed himself. Though the pages are unnumbered, of course, I am convinced that some are missing: discarded, destroyed— or purloined? I feel for the gaps, the empty places, moving my mind like a blind man's fingers over the words, which still refuse to give up their secret. Am I going to have another ghost haunting me now, one I cannot even see, one impossible to recognise?

Then, at other times, I tell myself it is all in my fancy, that these are no more than the disjointed, desperate last vagaries of a dying mind. Yet I do not give up hope that one day these pages will speak to me, in that known voice, telling me all that I may or may not want to know.

I saw her, once more, a last time, I think it will be. I had gone down to the old house to collect my things. It was one of those smoked-glass autumn days, all sky and cloud and tawny distances. Quirke arrived while I was packing, and stood in the bedroom doorway in his blazer and his fish-grey slip-ons, leaning with one hand on the jamb, a thumb nervously working. After some huffing and throat-clearing he asked about Cass. "She got into difficulties," I said, "she got into difficulties, and drowned." He nodded, with a solemn frown. He seemed about to speak again, but changed his mind. I turned to him, expectantly, hopefully, even. Often with Quirke I had the feeling, and I had it again now, that he was about to impart some large and vital piece of information or instruction, some essential fact that is known to everyone, except me. He stands there, frowning, somewhat pop-eyed, amused a little despite himself, seeming to ponder the wisdom of disclosing to me at last the banal but all-important secret. Then the moment passes, and he gives himself a sort of mental shake, and is what he was before, just Quirke, and not the grave repository of momentous knowledge at all.

"When did your wife die?" I said.

He blinked. "My missus?"

I was stacking books in a cardboard box.

"Yes. I used to see a ghost here, I thought at one time it might be her."

He was shaking his head slowly, I fancied I could almost hear it turning on its cogs.

"My missus didn't die," he said, "who told you that? She ran off with a traveller."

"A . . . ?"

"Travelling salesman. Shoes." He gave a mournful, angry laugh. "The bitch."

He helped me to carry my bags and boxes of books downstairs. I told him I intended to give the house to the girl. "Not to you, mind," I said. "To Lily." He had stopped on the last step of the stair, and stood now, leaning forward with a heavy suitcase in each hand, his head on one side, looking at the floor. "There is only one condition," I said, "that she doesn't sell it. I want her to live here." I could see him deciding, with a sort of click, to believe I was in earnest. Already the light of anticipation was dawning in his eye; I suspect he was as much looking forward to drawing up the papers as he was to getting his hands, even if at one remove, on my property. He put down the bags as if all his troubles were in them, and straightened, unable to keep himself from grinning.

Yes, I shall give her the house. I hope that she will live here. I hope she will let me visit her, *la jeune châtelaine*. I have all kinds of wild ideas, mad projects. We might fix up the place between us, she and I. What is it the estate agents say?—major refurbishments. Why, we might even take in lodgers again! I shall ask her if I may keep my little room. I might write something about the town, a history, a topography, learn the place names at last. Yes, yes, all kinds of plans, there is time enough, and my! how slowly it goes. When I have got back the knack of driving we shall go for a jaunt around the country in search of that circus, have Goodfellow do his dance for us again, and this time hypnotise me, perhaps, and lay all my ghosts. Or I could take her with me back to that village clinging to its rocky hillside on that cerulean sea, and climb those cobbled streets again and grab De Sica by the throat and say that I will throttle him unless he tells me all he knows. Vain thoughts, vain fancies.

I walked into the kitchen. When I looked through the window, Cass was outside. She was standing on the rise beyond what once had been the vegetable garden, by the half-grown birch tree there. She was wearing an unbelted green dress that left her arms and her long calves bare. I noticed the echo between her glimmering skin and the silver-white bark of the tree. She had the child with her, though when I say it was the child I mean it was as always only the notion of a child, hardly even an image, a wavering transparency. Seeming to see me at the window she turned and started toward the house. In her green tunic and thonged sandals she might have been striding out of Arcady to meet me. As she advanced along the overgrown garden path the air pressed the stuff of her smock-dress against her, and I thought, not for the first time, how like one of Botticelli's girls she looked—even, like them, a little mannish. She came into the room and frowned and glanced about sharply, as if she had expected someone else to be here. One arm was lifted higher than her head, the hand open as if to catch some flung or flying thing out of the air. There was a brimming in her, an exalta-tion. Her eyes had a dazzlingly virescent shine. Her warm breath brushed my cheek, I swear it did. Remembered zephyr! How real she seemed, an incarnation sent ahead to greet me while the other she, the goddess of the birches, tarried outside, sheathing her arrows and unstringing her gilded bow. Cass! The glimmering brow, the aureole of russet hair, the fine-drawn nose with its saddle of apple-flecks, those grey-green eyes that are mine, the long pale pillar of neck. A pang went through me and I reached out a faltering hand to touch her, and I spoke her name, and she seemed to pause, and shiver, as if she had indeed heard me, and then at once she was gone, leaving only the glistening chord of her passing, that faded, and fell. Outside, in the garden, the bright day stood, a gold man, stilled in startlement. *Die Sonne, sie scheinet all-gemein* . . . I turned to the room again and there Lily was, leaning sideways on one leg and looking past me eagerly to the window, trying to see what I had seen, or perhaps not interested in me or my ghosts at all, perhaps just looking out into the world, the great world, waiting for her. Of Cass there was no sign, no sign at all. The living are too much for the dead. Lily was saying something. I could not hear her.

Blossom, speed thee well. The bud is in flower. Things can go wrong. My Marina, my Miranda, oh, my Perdita.

A Note on the Type

This book was set in Fournier, a typeface named for Pierre Simon Fournier *fils* (1712–1768), a celebrated French type designer. Coming from a family of typefounders, Fournier was an extraordinarily prolific designer of typefaces and of typographic ornaments. He was also the author of the important *Manuel typographique* (1764–1766), in which he attempted to work out a system that standardized type measurement in points—a system that is still in use internationally today. Fournier's type is considered transitional in that it drew its inspiration from the old style, yet was ingeniously innovational, providing for an elegant, legible appearance. In 1925 his type was revived by the Monotype Corporation of London.

Composed by
Stratford Publishing Services,
Brattleboro, Vermont

Printed and bound by
Quebecor Printing,
Martinsburg, West Virginia

Designed by
Soonyoung Kwon